Dutching the Book

By Ritch Gaiti

Dutching the Book

* * *

Published by

ISBN 978-0-9833837-2-7
www.SedonaEditions.com

Copyright 2011 by Ritch Gaiti

for Pop

-1-

Brooklyn, 1960

His arms raised to shield him from an inferno that grew fiercer at every moment, a single fireman moved cautiously forward down a smoke filled hallway. Around him, the fire roared, consuming everything in sight. He had come up empty in his task to find survivors; he didn't know whether to be thankful or pissed at the futility of his mission. It was all risk now; the best he could hope for is a break even. The odds were stacked the wrong way when the best you can get is break even. Time to get the hell out.

Under his mask, tears and mucous ran down his face as he struggled to hold his smoke-stung eyes open. Using the wall to guide him, he took deliberate steps, knowing that each one counted too much now. Above him, a loud crack exploded and a flaming beam shattered through the shredded ceiling. Reflexes took over and he sidestepped the full force of the impact as the beam knocked off his helmet and mask and slammed him to the floor. He rolled onto his stomach and brought his arms over his head, bracing for the next blow. His body grew rigid as he anticipated the weight of the building dropping onto on his back.

He waited. Through a crease in his sleeve, he looked up for the inevitable. It didn't come and he wasn't sticking around for it. He grasped his helmet and mask, quickly crawled into the temporary refuge offered by a doorway, and dropped to the floor, his only shot at air. His hands covered his mouth to filter out the smoke as he sucked in a breath between the fingers of his glove. Struggling to reseat his mask, he put his finger through a large crack in the plastic shield.

Shit.

It could not hold out the smoke—but it was still a buffer between him and everything else. He put it on, his gloved hand pressed tightly against the opening.

His back against the wall, he lowered his head and started forward. He straightened his smoke-filled mask, frequently exhaling hard to clear it. Wedging his hand tighter against the crack, he felt his way along the wall; his heavy helmet and coat dragged him down. The smoke briefly parted as he came to another doorway and looked in, hoping that what he was looking for wasn't there. Stopping to reorient, he caught his breath. The room was empty.

A familiar voice bellowed through the smoke: "Anyone in there?"

It was Bull.

He thought he was alone up there. Bull: the odds suddenly shifted. Ben looked in the room once more to be sure.

"No. Just memories."

No fuckin' time to be clever.

"Clear!" Bull shouted loudly through his mask, taking the lead down the hall in a low profile. If there was ever a time to follow him, this was it. Bull reached a partially opened doorway and carefully peered in.

"Going in," he disappeared into the smoke.

"Right behind you."

Both men cautiously rushed into the smoke-filled apartment. Suddenly, there was a loud blast, immediately followed by a crash, as the wall behind them broke apart and collapsed. He raised his arms as the buckling structure fell, burying him under a pile of burning debris. Flaming ruins covered him and Bull, separating them from each other and any retreat.

He took a breath and sucked in heat: no air, not even smoke, just heat. He breathed in again—and hell played in his throat and lungs.

Is this it?

He tried to wrest himself from the wreckage and find a path out. He couldn't move and couldn't see.

This is it . . .

He inhaled—nothing. He hadn't said goodbye to Kitty and the boys. He kissed her quickly this morning. Maybe she'll remember that; it'll have to do. If he knew it was his last, he would have done better.

This can't be it. Fuck.

The steady stream of black smoke enveloped the five-story brick apartment building and choked the street. Fire hugged the walls and steadily climbed the brick box as flames exploded through the windows, propelling burning debris and ash onto the gathering crowd below.

An inner wall—possibly a floor—crashed loudly, followed by another, louder and more definitive than the one before. The steel fire escapes, once a safe passage, had became molten traps, snaring several people forever in the fiery hell.

The fortress was giving way. A concrete eave split apart from the upper parapet that once adorned the structure. It fell, momentarily landing on a fire escape before ripping it from the infrastructure with a metallic scream. Both plummeted towards the ground, barraging the sidewalk with hot bricks and twisted metal. Fire and smoke consumed the building except in places where there was nothing left to devour.

Fire trucks from companies all over Brooklyn converged on the old dying building. One by one they methodically aligned to enter the battle—a battle in which the only possible victory was containment and that was still a long way off. There was no winning—the best outcome was a tie. Firemen jumped off the trucks and moved quickly through the intense heat. There was organized chaos as they rushed to open hydrants, spread hoses, and extend ladders.

Screams of terror melded with the wail of sirens. Panic, fear and helplessness gripped the neighborhood. People fled from their home that had suddenly become a destructive, consuming and killing monster. Horror had come to Brighton Beach.

Trapped, Ben held his mask, turned his head away from the flames and sucked in one more breath, probably his last. His eyes stung and his legs were pinned; even if he could move, he couldn't see or breathe.

Shit.

Unexpectedly, he was lifted, almost spiritually, over the burning mass. His arms hung at his side and his legs trailed behind as he floated through the cloud of smoke. All of a sudden there was no pain, no sensation. Fate had taken over; his bet was on the table and the dice were in the air.

He closed his eyes. At least there was no pain.

Bye, Kitty. Fuck.

His body transported through the wall of smoke and flame into a pocket of light and air. His legs, liberated from the encumbering debris, hung freely as he floated weightless through the haze. He closed his eyes and waited. He had no control now; fate had taken over.

Suddenly, his mask ripped off his face. He must be on the other side. He slowly opened his eyes anticipating he knew not what and he stared right into Bull's mug. Was Bull dead also? For an infinite moment, he tried to make sense of where he was and what had happened. He sucked in a lungful of smoke as Bull held him aloft by his collar. With almost uncanny strength, Bull had pulled him through the wall of fire.

"You ok?" He nodded, gasping for air. If they were going to get out, it had better be right now. Bull moved toward the light, dragging him along. They crashed through a window and onto a remaining fire escape, which dangled from the building. Their weight was all the structure could take; a loud screech of metal ripping away from metal penetrated the air as they were tossed into a cloud and whatever lay below.

The ground wasn't visible. But the unknown was far better than hell.

What floor were we on?

He bent his knees and braced for impact. This could be it. Again.

The ground came sooner than expected and his knees crunched into his chest, knocking out whatever wind remained within. He instinctively rolled forward while trying to suck life back into his lungs as he did. *Breathe, goddamn it.* A massive tire of the hook and ladder truck stopped him cold.

He lay flat on his back and just tried to breathe. A loud torturous wheeze escorted his first breath, as it filled his entire body. Air was never such a precious commodity; he would appreciate it more, along with Kitty, and the kids, and Bull, and anyplace that was not on fire. His eyes still closed, he ran a mental check of his body in search of pain; there was none except where the beam had slammed his helmet into his forehead. Can't get much luckier than that. Bull lay on his back right beside him, smiling. He looked up at the blackened sky: safe.

Hi, Kitty. I'm back.

They quietly caught their breath, dragged their gear, and sat well out of reach of the blaze. Their work was done. The building still burned, the flames reaching new heights. The top of the wall gave way and crashed to the ground where they landed moments earlier.

He shook as he absently touched his heavy rubber coat, as one would a loyal dog. The worn yellow letters declared its owner:

Ben Collesano

3837

Perhaps it was the relief of being out of danger that allowed him to be vulnerable. His hands trembled. He had felt fear before but never death. He shook and covered it up with a cough, hoping Bull would buy it. They sat in silence for about ten minutes as the structure disintegrated in front of them.

Bull searched for a cigarette and lit up. He held out the smokes for Ben who nodded them off. It was unusual to be in a fire with Bull even though they had been in the same company for over eight years. It was rare for Ben to be in a fire at all; he typically tried to work out assignments better suited to his skills.

"You ok?" Bull wiped his nose, smearing a black trail across his face.

"Fine." Ben took a deep breath—it felt good, real good: pure and cleansing. He breathed in again. "A guy could get hurt up there," he coughed.

Bull smiled.

"Didn't get my quota." Ben tried to lighten the moment.

"Quota?"

"Survivors. Didn't bring anyone out."

"I did." Bull could have smiled then but he was smart enough not to. He wasn't bragging or asking for thanks. He was just stating a fact, pure and simple, and feeling good about it. He excelled at this: he was built for it and he loved the rush. And if he was lucky enough to bring someone out, there was no better high. Bull would have been a great blocking fullback, but he was a warrior, not an athlete.

"Yeah. Thanks." Ben knew he didn't need to say it.

"No problem. You'd do the same."

"Hope I never get the chance."

The company captain approached from behind them.

"You boys ok?"

Both men gave him the thumbs-up. Conversation required too much energy.

"You're off; we're letting this one burn out. Company Three is taking control."

The guys nodded.

An exterior wall of the building crashed down and blanketed the area in a shower of ash, cinders and debris. Bull lit another cigarette with his unfinished butt as they just watched the final phase of destruction. They were done.

Ben coughed up some ash. He hated this part of the job.

"Check that out," the captain said.

Ben nodded and looked for the strength to get up. He put his hand on Bull's shoulder, grasping it a little more firmly than necessary.

Shitty day, but it could've been worse. Ben coughed and looked back at the building, which had been reduced to a pile of smoking rubble. He coughed again and spat black.

- 2 -

Brooklyn, 1938

Ben had something good and he knew it. The calculations were not so much to prove it but to enjoy the mastery of his find.

He didn't acknowledge Willie, a few feet away; silently watching and he ignored the meaningless banter of the hyperactive high schoolers anxious to begin the weekend. And he wasn't thinking, he had done that part already.

Fixed in his zone, Ben sat at his desk and searched for some room on a crammed notebook page. He reviewed and recalculated the same premise over and over. It wasn't an answer that he was searching for; he was simply rechecking his logic, as he had done a thousand times in the last few days.

"Whacha' doin'?"

Willie's question orbited somewhere above Ben's head and went unheard.

Ben was his own audience: listening to his own private presentation, running though the same logical sequences and basic arithmetic, while he was trying to punch holes in his analysis, his computations or his premises. It was airtight and he knew it but he recalculated repetitively to pick up the smallest of errors or some little nuance that he had overlooked. But it never surfaced.

Willie absently picked at a pockmark on his cheek and almost pulled the scab off, as he stood patiently over Ben, not minding that he didn't respond. Willie knew he would eventually, because Willie was one of the guys. Not athletic like Ben and Sandy, certainly not as smart or good looking, he often bragged that he was just south of ugly. He was one of the guys and that was good enough.

Willie watched as Ben concentrated; it must have been important or Ben would've answered. The bell would ring soon and he had nothing to do anyway. Maybe Ben didn't notice him.

"Ben, whacha' doin'?"

The words finally leaked through Ben's shield.

"Math," he muttered without looking up. It was the shortest accurate answer that would not break his concentration. It wasn't the time to explain: not now, not yet. "Math" would hold Willie for now.

Ben tried to punch holes in his premise one more time. He failed, successfully.

"Saturday?" Ben broke his silence, startling Willie, and the scab ripped off under his fingernail.

"What?"

"What are you doing on Saturday?"

"Gotta work."

Still focused, Ben raised his voice slightly. "Sandy, what are you doing Saturday?"

Sandy Kane was about the same height as Ben; but his broad swimmer's shoulders and closely cropped light brown hair made him appear older and more rugged. He sat on a school desk and held court with two young ladies.

"Whatever you want Benny." Sandy didn't break his eye-lock on the girls.

"Fight!" someone yelled and the pointless banter turned into coordinated chaos. The room suddenly tilted as most of the class packed up against the windows to watch the action below. At the window, Willie turned back to Ben who still sat at his desk.

"It's Bull."

Ben raised his head for the first time.

On the sidewalk in front of the school, Al "Bull" Goldman, a strong stocky boy, swung wildly at another taller, older boy. A second teen was draped around Bull's neck from behind trying to wrestle him down. Ignoring his passenger for the moment, Bull connected with his fist, landing it squarely on the bridge of his opponent's nose. Blood sprayed the snow.

The crowd grew as the fight brought out the most primal high school feelings.

"How many?" Ben needed to assess the situation.

"Only two," Willie looked again. "Make it three!" This time with urgency in his voice.

Willie followed Ben and Sandy through the door.

Bull's head exploded in pain behind his left ear. He staggered blindly as he saw only white. Experience taught him to stay on his feet and keep moving until he could regain his senses. He swung wildly, missing his new aggressor by several feet. He swung again. And again. And now he was angry.

Fighting was what Bull did. He didn't provoke fights but, given an opportunity, he would take the first shot and, usually, the last. He wasn't unintelligent but he found strength in his toughness. And when he was in his element, he was king; fighting was his element. Taking on multiple opponents was not unusual either because there were not too many guys that could take him on alone. He knew how to deal with that: take out one right away, and then it's man to man.

But today was different; he was blindsided, cold cocked. He didn't know how many guys he was fighting until they declared themselves from behind.

Bull reached back and grabbed the guy hanging on his neck. His eyesight was coming back and his legs were like cement footings stabilizing the rest of his body. Bull groped the guy's face and stuck a fistful of fingers into his eyes; the guy released momentarily and Bull grabbed him around the waist and swung him like a baseball bat, crashing him into his new adversary, the prick that blindsided him.

The heads of both of his opponents slammed together as face met face in a nauseating thud. They went down hard as a bright crimson seeped through the snow.

Ben and Sandy approached the melee as Willie trailed. The action had peaked as one of the attackers, sitting in a patch of red snow against the cast iron fence, tried to stop a steady stream of blood from his nose. Bull had the other two pinned to the ground and deliberately alternated hitting one then the other. He'd hit the one on the left with his right fist, the one on the right with his left fist. He punctuated his victory—left, right, left, right.

Sandy and Ben let him validate his conquest then pulled him off of his two victims. He was out of steam but not out of fight; he could have gone on.

"Bull, it's me, Sandy. It's over."

When he heard Sandy's voice, Bull stopped swinging; he knew it was over as well. No point. It wasn't a fight anymore. He slowly stood, declared his victory and turned his back to the action.

Willie stepped up and stood over the fallen attackers. He looked down at them lying in the red slush.

"Back off unless you want to see how many friends he has!" Willie declared with authority built on the knowledge that he had three friends right behind him to back him up.

The four boys walked down Ocean Parkway and turned onto Quentin Road. They walked two and two, as the sidewalks could not accommodate four across. They shifted positions as they unconsciously navigated the occasional break in the sidewalk caused by the tree root poking through.

"Shit," Bull stopped and looked down at his torn pants. "Mom's gonna kill me".

It would be strange to hear such a remark from such a big powerful young man: but the boys knew better. Bull, Al, or Allan, as his mother called him, was actually a gentle and caring mother's boy. His mom would be as shocked to see him fight, as his recent opponents would be to see him gently and meekly explain away his torn pants to her.

They allowed him his moment of regret.

"What was that about?" asked Sandy.

"What?" Bull muttered, still concerned about his pants.

"The fight, remember?"

Silence.

Sandy continued to probe. "Al?"

"They were talking about me."

"Oh, what did they say?"

"I don't know . . . didn't hear them."

"How do you now it was about you?"

"What else could it be about?" Al's retort suggested finality to the conversation.

Stymied at Al's lack of logic, Sandy and Ben caught each other's glances and broke up.

Willie shouted, "Al, the Bull, strikes again!"

The weekend began.

- 3 -

Ben scanned the crowd, somewhat surprised at the outing on this blustery day; it was still winter, but not for long. He zippered his jacket to the top and put his hands in the pockets. Jamaica Racetrack, known as the people's racetrack, was situated near the Jamaica train station in Queens just down the road from Aqueduct and Belmont. A beautiful arena built just after the turn of the century, it was the last of the pre-automation era. It had charm, elegance and people.

School and work kept Ben away from the track more than he liked. But when there, he focused on the horses and ignored the people. Today was different; today he studied the people.

"The horses are this way." Sandy nodded towards the track.

"Yeah," Ben eyed a cluster of people around a bookmaker, "but the action is this way."

People bet with any of several bookmakers, *books*, who wore all white and were strategically positioned on small platforms in the Clubhouse and Grandstand. Behind each book, a large slate board listed the horses and the odds for the next race, which were calculated manually. A payoff man handled the transactions, recording and collecting bets. One or more runners, ready to be dispatched, stood at arms length. The team handled multiple bets, payoffs and changing odds. It was a coordinated and efficient system that had evolved though eons of wagering.

In the Clubhouse, which catered to the upscale bettors, the book turned to his board and erased all the odds. Ben normally studied the odds; today he studied the book.

The trumpet's blare signaled that the horses were on the track, a reminder to bettors to get the bets in and the adrenalin up. But Ben was not looking at the program or the horses or the odds. Sandy watched Ben; he must have had a horse or a tip, or knew something that would make today special.

"Who do you like?" Sandy tried to pick up the pace.

Ben studied the book.

"Are we betting or watching?" Sandy asked.

"Watching."

"No betting?"

"Not today."

The book continued his routine as he read from a piece of paper and simultaneously handed the runner another slip of paper. The odds were changing. The runner took off and the book began to update all the recalculated odds based on the cumulative betting: the more bet on a horse, the lower the odds.

"Every time a big bet is made, the odds change," Ben eyes never left the book as he narrated the action softly, talking as much to himself as he was to Sandy; confirming what he was seeing and what he already knew. "And, the books send out the runner to synchronize all the other books so their odds are the same. Watch."

The runner navigated through the crowd and stopped at the next book about one hundred feet away.

"What just happened?" Ben asked rhetorically.

"The runner updated the book with the current odds—" Sandy impatience was beginning to overtake his curiosity. "What are we doing here? Are we going to bet or . . ?"

"How many books are there in the Grandstand?"

"Five or —"

"Six," interrupted Ben to move the process along. Ben enjoyed his analysis as he was unraveling it to Sandy. "There are six books in the track, and how long do you think it takes for the runner to get from the first book to the last?"

"A couple of—"

"Two and a half minutes and —"

"Got it."

Ben smiled. He knew he would get it; he always did.

Sandy continued: "the first and the last book have different odds for two and a half minutes." He realized that he just said something important but he wasn't sure what to do with it. "So?"

- 4 -

The Great Depression and winter had almost gone. Brooklyn stirred.

Ocean Parkway, a long majestic six-lane thoroughfare that ran from Prospect Park to Coney Island and the Atlantic Ocean, was the aorta of Brooklyn. Huge maple trees, normally flourishing on that special city air, now dormant and barren, lined both sides of the road. Behind them, endless walls of private homes and apartment buildings.

Ocean Parkway, the virtual dividing line between east and west, bisected the borough. Brooklynites had little sense of compass direction; if the streets weren't prefixed east or west, there would be no recognition of classic direction. There were no north/south streets; hence, north and south did not exist as it pertained to Brooklyn. In fact, South Brooklyn was actually in the northwest corner of the borough. Ocean Parkway, void of stores, but full of life, nested delicately between the mega-neighborhoods of Bensonhurst, Flatbush, and Coney Island, and served as their conduit, connection and unofficial border. In Brooklyn, these were neighborhoods. Anywhere else in the world, they would be small cities with their own language, culture, transportation, schools and hundred thousand people. And within, there were mini-neighborhoods—blocks filled with klatches of Jews, Italians, and Irish—a microcosm of the world.

Lincoln High School, surrounded by a tall cast iron fence, stood squarely at the south end of Ocean Parkway—just a few blocks from the ocean and Coney Island. On Avenue P, a few blocks away from the school, stood Chadosh's Candy Store where you bought cigs, the paper, button candy or a cup of coffee. Over the entrance hung a huge red Coca Cola sign against a green background that said *Stationary*, but none could be found within. Inside, a long Formica counter with six swivel stools paralleled four booths; the last one overflowed with stacks of Sunday News comics, which arrived on Thursday, waiting to be joined with the latest news and sports on Saturday night.

Everyone in the neighborhood stopped at Chadosh's.

Kitty Urbanski looked at her reflection in Chadosh's dirty window and made sure that everything sat just right—her blouse was freshly pressed and buttoned, her auburn hair cut short unstylishly stylish—it was as perfect as it could be. She unconsciously wet her fingers over her tongue and patted down a few strands of hair that were tussled by the late March winds. Just sixteen, she was pretty, not beautiful, but a unique enough to make guys look twice, maybe more. She checked her mouth, far from perfect with her overlapping teeth and full lips. Her nose, slightly disproportionate and asymmetrical, added to the perfectly imperfect face. Individually, her features were substandard—together, they formed a very striking package. Not that she saw herself quite that way—her self confidence never transcended to social situations. It was hard to believe that she was Willie's sister.

Two friends, Marilyn and Steph, checked their reflections one more time, just long enough outside of Chadosh's to be noticed inside.

"Let's go, we'll be late," Steph was anxious to move on.

"Need gum," Marilyn led the way inside—her tight pale yellow sweater emphasized her figure and Steph's loose blouse hid hers.

Ben and Sandy sat in the first booth facing the door. A few minutes earlier, Bull and Willie occupied those seats but when Ben and Sandy arrived, they shifted to the opposite seats deferring the prime positions to them, just like always. This was the implicit arrangement. If only two or three of them were there, then the open seats were up for grabs. But, if the seat's owner arrived, everyone shifted to restore the proper order of things. It was unspoken and understood—that's just the way it was. It was Saturday night and everyone was there and in their regular seat. Chadosh's was where you were before and after you went somewhere else. And if there was nowhere else to go, you just stayed.

"So?" Willie's eyes darted back and forth between Sandy and Ben.

"So, what?" Sandy played back.

"So, how'd you do?"

"Didn't play."

"What do you mean?"

"We didn't play; we just watched." Sandy teased.

"I don't . . ."

"We did homework." Ben cut in. "Next time we play." He needed their support, financial and otherwise. He didn't want to explain the details of his scheme, because he wanted to wait for the right time; they probably wouldn't get it anyway. It didn't matter; he told them just enough to get their interest, that they would probably make money, no guarantees, and closed the deal with: "Trust me."

The boys all nodded and muttered their assurances, as he knew they would.

"So, you're in?" He needed to hear it from each of them: no loose ends, assumptions, or fence sitting. You're in or you're out.

"In," Willie responded without totally understanding what he just agreed to but, if Ben was in, he was in.

"In." Al echoed.

Sandy remained silent throughout the entire conversation.

"Sandy?"

"What?"

"In?"

Sandy's look said: *are you kidding; Of course I'm in, why are you bothering to ask?* Ben knew Sandy was in but he waited for a response. They had had a different level of understanding and communication than the others. They could share thoughts in a glance. There was no need for words as they usually agreed on most issues and picked up on the same observations. But not now; the others were 'in', so he needed Sandy to declare himself to make it unambiguous and official. Sandy knew that as well.

"In like Flynn."

When Ben had a plan or an investment, he would always have backers, co-investors and partners. He needed to protect his downside and work with the power that only bigger numbers could bring. The team was critical to Ben—not only to carry out his plan and to supply enough funding to make it work—he needed to lead. Control was important—not authority, control. They had all followed

Ben before, usually to their benefit, but not on anything this big. But they didn't know that yet.

Ben raised his almost empty cup of cold coffee. Collectively they would be known as:

"The Syndicate," Ben toasted.

The boys raised their cups and in a single voice said: "The syndicate."

The Syndicate—the unit might exist for one bet or for a season or forever. It had no structure, other than Ben lead and they followed. The boys had an identity, a name, known only to them—the Syndicate; it added just the right amount of credibility, anonymity and mystery.

Willie and Al spun around as soon as they saw Sandy and Ben looking up. Kitty and her friends had just entered. The four boys just blatantly stared—a primal bravado stare that declared that they were the boys and they had the right and responsibility to just stare—if they were inclined.

"That Marilyn is sweet," Bull muttered and he turned back to Sandy, "you getting skin yet?" Sandy ignored him. Bull pursued, "meow?" Sandy just smiled as Marilyn looked back at him making sure he knew that she knew.

Al turned back to watch the girls leave, "Jeez, Willie, your sister is looking ripe, getting tits."

Willie grabbed Bull in a playful headlock and the Bull laughed it off as he let Willie have his mock victory.

Ben just watched—he had their buy-in—the Syndicate was out of the gate. He had accomplished what he needed to today.

The boys arrived just in time to see Terry throw up in Howard's mouth as they were making out on the sofa. Saturday night parties were always the most intense and everyone in the house had been going at it for hours. The smell of vomit cleared the living room; Al migrated to a crowd of guys while Willie meandered in search of a comfortable place to land. Sandy and Marilyn stood eye-to-eye in each other's personal space in the corner of the hallway—and slowly disappeared into a closet.

Ben went into the kitchen to find food and it didn't take long before several girls hovered around him. He was a catch, but he was never caught for too long.

Willie wandered until he found safe haven in Kitty, Steph and three other girls.

"Hi ladies," Willie tried to mask his discomfort with bravado. Like Kitty, but for different reasons, Willie never felt comfortable in social situations.

The girls muttered "hi" and some just muttered. Whatever conversation was going on before he arrived turned into an awkward silence—and Willie didn't know how to break it. They all stood there uncomfortably watching other cliques engaged in party chatter. One by one, the girls found an opening to seek out another conversation or the bathroom or anything else—and left Willie silently alone with Kitty and Steph.

Ben meanwhile engaged in meaningless flirtatious conversations, moving from girl to girl without appearing disinterested when he was just that. He was looking for someone.

It didn't take him long to find her.

"Hi."

"Hi," Kitty smiled politely.

Ben had never seen her at one of these parties; she had always been Willie's sis, out of range and out of consideration. Tonight she glowed and came into his field of view. Something drew him in.

He watched as she bantered with the girls, with a bit more grace that distanced her from the rest of them. She was one of them, younger, but somehow more elegant. He sensed that she could flow with the crowd or without them equally well. She was a girl's girl, almost a woman.

He searched for an opening.

At that moment, she turned to Steph, her eyes passing his, en route. "Ready?" Steph nodded. She turned to Willie, then Ben: "Night."

Ben instinctively reached to grab her arm but pulled back. "Stay a while," was all that he could muster.

Her eyes met his momentarily and she smiled warmly. "Have to feed my goldfish," she offered unapologetically.

Ben nodded and silently watched her move towards the door. She was polite, cordial and evasive. He waited for that inevitable glance back over her shoulder—a sign that she was interested and he should be as well: nothing more than a quick look back just to see if he was waiting for her look. It was just a sign, nothing more; but it would be the go-ahead, the all clear, and the green light.

It didn't come.

Ben and Willie stood alone in the empty living room as the pungent smell of vomit hung in the air.

- 5 -

This was it, Willie thought, *the big thing whatever it is.*

Ben looked around; it was just what he wanted: a crowded track because of the big race and the beautiful spring like weather. Willie, Al and Sandy stood by waiting for Ben's directions. They were dressed today as Ben suggested. Not just dressed, dressed up, big time dressed up: suits. Willie's suit, discreetly borrowed from his uncle, hung loosely and he rolled his cuffs up three times to keep from tripping. Soft felt brimmed hats topped the suits—players wore hats and today they were players.

People maneuvered in every direction and the murmur of a thousand conversations made it difficult to hear what Ben was saying. Right now, he was just scanning the crowd looking for—

"There he is," Ben covertly pointed to Caz Frankel, a dapper, well-dressed man of about forty. His wide moustache and bright white silk handkerchief in his suit pocket were his signatures as were the two men that followed closely behind. Caz Frankel was one of the best horseplayers and owners in the area. The crowd parted several feet before him as he walked through with authority.

"You guys got him?" Ben did not wait for their response and he looked Al directly in the eyes. "When you see Frankel or any of the owners or their clan . . ." Ben had carefully spent the better part of the morning educating the guys on who the key players were and the beards they often used to front for them. "When you see any of them get to the book, keep your eyes open. When the odds change on one of the favorites, that's when you signal Willie. Got it?"

He looked in Al's eyes and waited until he was satisfied that it registered. Al acknowledged and Ben turned to Willie. He spoke slowly and directly.

"Willie, this is the most important part. When you get the signal from Al, you pass it on to Sandy who will be down near the last book." Ben gave Willie the simplest role and magnified its importance to keep him focused. "If you're not one hundred percent sure of the signal, don't do anything. I'd rather miss a bet than make a bad one. And don't be too obvious." He looked at the group once more, checking to see if it registered clearly or if he had omitted anything. "Once you pass the signal, take a walk, take a piss or something. I don't want you guys to become too familiar. In a few races, you'll switch places."

"And you?" Al asked.

"I'll be by the last book," Ben explained. After going through this three times earlier, anyone else might have been a bit impatient—not Ben. He answered clearly without omitting a detail. The more they understood, the better. After all, he had run through this in his mind about a hundred times.

Al looked perplexed. Ben put his hand on Al's shoulder.

"One last time. When you see Frankel betting and the odds change, you signal Willie," Ben put his hand on Willie's shoulder. "And you, when you get the high sign from Al, you signal Sandy who will make the bet. I'll wait until the odds change, then I'll bet the other way."

Willie thought a moment, started to speak, but hesitated just to ensure that he had it right. He recapped: "so we are going to beat the runner to the last book and bet on the old odds." He thought a moment longer: "so the runner is the pony express and we're the telegraph."

Ben looked at Willie and squeezed his shoulder with a mixture of amazement and pride.

"You got it. And, after the runner gets there, I will lay the bet back to the book—at lower odds."

Ben saw that Al was beginning to get it but wasn't quite sure.

"I'll take you through it again, but now we work. Remember, we have a clock on us: only two and a half minutes to nail it." He considered going through it once more but passed. It wasn't that difficult to understand: but if it wasn't, how come no one has done it before? Unlikely that no one thought of it; maybe they know that the track would come down heavy on anyone messing with their business. Enough planning—time for action.

They waited two races until the situation played out. In the Clubhouse, Bull watched from a distance as Caz Frankel approached the book and handed the payoff man a stack of bills. The book turned to the slate boy who erased the odds on the *three horse* and replaced the six with a four. Caz's bet drove down the odds on the *three horse* from six-to-one to four-to-one—a significant change.

Al casually moved to his left and lifted his right hand with a thumbs-up signal. He then discreetly raised three fingers.

Willie, in the Grandstand about fifty feet away, saw Al's signal. He coolly picked up his program to partially obscure his next move from unwanted eyes and repeated the signal to Sandy who stood about one hundred feet away.

Sandy bet fifty dollars on the *three horse* with the last book and took a short walk.

The entire sequence took just under two minutes. The boys meandered and blended in the crowd. A few minutes later Ben stepped up to another book after the runner had come by and the odds had been updated.

"I want to lay odds against the *three horse*," Ben enunciated slowly so that there would be no confusion.

The book looked at the slate board: "you're laying four to one. How much?"

He handed him two hundred dollars: "laying two hundred."

The book, as always, played it back, "You're betting that the three loses," he looked at Ben for confirmation, "your two hundred against my fifty. It's a bet." The payoff man counted the money and handed him a slip confirming the transaction.

Ben thought through his scheme and played the transaction back just for the enjoyment of playing it back. It was the perfect bet—*be in a position where you can win but can't lose.*

We placed a fifty-dollar bet that the three horse would win at six-to-one: payoff three hundred. And we have a two hundred dollar bet that the three horse will lose: payoff fifty bucks. So, if the three horse wins, the Syndicate wins one hundred: the three hundred win payoff minus the two hundred lose bet we laid. If it loses, we break even: win fifty on the lose bet and lose fifty on the win bet.

Pure fucking genius.

The boys leaned on the rail and watched in silence as the horses entered the starting gate at the other end of the track. They knew they had accomplished something but there wasn't a universal understanding of what that was—at least not yet. Ben sensed the uneasiness as he stared out at the horses. He broke their silence.

"There was a small difference in the odds for a short time and we took advantage of it . . . and the books will eat it." He watched as the last horse was ushered into his position. "We can only win." He reassured himself and any of the guys that cared to listen.

The crowd din softened in anticipation of the start. Ben stared straight ahead—fearing that he would miss the first second or two of a two-minute race. Yet, his mind was still clearly focused on what they had just accomplished. Internally, he celebrated the victory of his strategy, not the outcome, the strategy.

"Guys," he broke his focus downfield, turned to them and punctuated the moment: "we just *dutched the book*."

Their tension grew as the boys pushed closer to the rail and waited for the race to start. Ben stood next to Willie; with his eyes still focused downfield at the starting gate, he casually inquired: "do you have goldfish?"

The horses broke interrupting Willie's quizzical look.

Everyone leaned forward for the best view—as if a few more inches would make a difference in seeing a race that was still a half-mile away. Ben watched but he was far away, thinking that they had already won. This race really didn't matter; he couldn't lose. He may not win, but he couldn't lose. He knew over time there would be many races that they would win now that he had proven the system. Now it was simply numbers and odds and chance—finally, they were on his side.

The volume cranked up as the horses rounded the head of the stretch. They appeared as a single well-coordinated organism undulating in rhythm: packed in solidly around the turn then spread out and contracted and expanded again as they battled for position.

The boys strained forward as if their combined energy could thrust the horse forward to a sure victory. They cheered as if everything were on it.

"C'mon three!" They shouted in ragged unison: "three, three!"

They didn't know what Ben had figured out; no matter who won this race, they had already won. This was just the beginning.

They had dutched the book.

- 6 -

Ben crossed the street just as Kitty left Chadosh's. He picked up his pace to intercept her without being too obvious. In the two years he had known her she was always Willie's kid sister—the almost nondescript fourteen-year-old hiding in the kitchen. But there's a huge difference between fourteen and sixteen, particularly for an eighteen-year-old boy. Something about the way she carried herself now: confident, straight posture, not stiff like a ballet dancer—and an air of resourcefulness, self-reliance and softness.

She lived most of her life in Williamsburg, Brooklyn, an Orthodox Jewish neighborhood; Coney Island was a welcome change. Her parents, although not Orthodox, were very religious and conservative, so they kept her very close to home. Before she was in high school and to some degree after, she was required to come home after school and help her mother with the household. That was her life: no socializing, no friends. She was sheltered, a little uncomfortable in social situations, but not naïve. She knew no better than to be the white sheep of the family.

Now a sophomore at Lincoln, she had a little more freedom, just a little. Making new friends didn't come easy—but friends weren't her priority. She worked in her father's pawnshop on Atlantic Avenue, downtown Brooklyn, almost every day except Saturday. She dreamt: school, a job, maybe a legal secretary, maybe, just maybe, a lawyer. But, one step at a time, she told herself; get through school.

Ben carefully converged, sided up to Kitty and silently matched her pace. Her lack of reaction made him unsure whether she knew he was there.

"Hi," he said gently, not wanting to startle her. It was if they had been walking silently together for hours and he was reawakening an interrupted conversation—the way only lovers and old friends would. Ben knew to play down that he had hardly spoken to her for the two years they had almost known each other.

A faint smile crossed the corner of her mouth as she kept walking at a casual pace—not as if she was trying to avoid or outrun him—but she wasn't slowing down for him either. Ben strolled alongside—he knew how to get the hard-to-get ones. They walked another half a block in silence. On one hand, it felt comfortable—Ben didn't feel pressured to make meaningless chatter; on the other, he was on a mission that required the right timing.

"You left quickly the other night." He uncomfortably tried to get some rhythm going.

She looked up at him quizzically.

"Something about rescuing a starving Goldfish." He reminded her.

"You didn't believe me?"

Ben quietly celebrated the breakthrough. Her eyes glistened and, at that moment, he didn't care whether she was telling the truth or not—as long as they were talking.

"Didn't want you to leave."

Once again, they walked in silence. It seemed as if this conversation was never going to take place.

"It was two." She said softly.

"Two?"

"Goldfish. Two goldfish."

"Oh."

A small smile broke through—the one he waited for—the all clear.

"How about . . ." He was never nervous about asking a girl out—never caring that much about the answer—until now. "Would you like to go to movie or something sometime?"

"I don't think so." Her smile indicated otherwise, "but thank you."

He was caught off guard. Most girls that he asked out, he went out with—particularly if they were smiling. Now, strangely off balance, the few seconds of silence lasted forever. There was something non-offensive about Kitty's refusal but it was rejection nevertheless.

"You sure?"

She nodded gently.

"Ok," he looked for a graceful exit when one was not possible. "Willie inside?"

"Inside?"

"Chadosh's . . ." Why was being next to her so easy and talking to her so difficult? "Is Willie inside—?"

"Yes." Her direct eye contact confused him further.

They reached the corner and Ben used the logical break. "Gotta go. Take care."

She smiled goodbye and, once again, he watched her walk away.

Al moved out of Ben's seat to his own, jostling Willie as he sat, back to the door. Ben stopped at the counter and picked up some stale coffee and joined the guys. Disturbed by his recent conversation, he jumped right to business. He took out one hundred dollars from his pocket and spread it neatly across the table and smiled. He let the guys take it in.

"We can split this up now . . ." Ben had an implicit deal with his partners; getting a little more than they did—his payback for his contribution. They all put up the stake and they all worked the scheme; but it was his plan, his knowledge of the game that made it work. They had no problem with Ben getting a little more. "Or keep it in the Syndicate to fund the operation."

It was clear what Ben wanted to do but he always put it in front of the guys; after all that's what made it a partnership, a Syndicate.

"Leave it in," Sandy said.

"In," echoed Willie, slamming his hand on the table for emphasis.

Al briefly hesitated; he needed the money more than the others, reluctantly concurred. "Good by me."

Ben held up the money. "Let's give these guys some company . . . then we'll pay some dividends," he said, enjoying the business speak.

"When are we going back?" said Willie.

Al jumped in. "Saturday," then looked at Ben to make sure he wasn't overstepping.

"We have to be careful. This can be very good but—" Ben started to explain.

"Careful?" Al interrupted, "we can't lose. All we have to do is win. We can bet every race and we'll win some of them and never—."

"If we don't get caught," Sandy cut Al off.

"Sandy's right, we have to be careful," Ben regained control. "We'll go back next Saturday, but we have to make some changes."

- 7 -

The daily conversations in Chadosh's had migrated from tits to horses. But too much of a good thing was not good, particularly in this case. It reached a point where Ben had to de-motivate the boys. He knew that the only risk they had was getting caught; some folks might not appreciate their skimming a little bit of the track's profits.

They kept going back: not always on Saturday, sometimes on a holiday or whenever there was a big race, but only when the track was crowded. Ben knew that they had to camouflage the operation any way they could. It was easy money but he had to be smart to keep it going. They would bet close to post time when the book was a little more harried. Each time out they varied the pattern—changed the books; rotated their positions and roles and even let Willie make the bets from time to time. Anything to keep from being uncovered. They limited their bets to one or two each time out; several times, they stayed away for a few weeks. Once Ben even grew a beard for two weeks and went to the track. He shaved it later, as it hid his dimples.

Sometimes instead of laying off the *lose* bet on the book, he'd find another bettor in the crowd that liked the same horse and bet against him—Ben would become the track, the book. It was the same payoff to the Syndicate and it kept the operation alive a lot longer—but it was a little harder to pull off in the two and a half minutes. He did not realize how important this nuance would be down the road.

He also realized that, even though they couldn't lose, every bet is a risk and it must count. He became very selective about which horses to bet on and he started handicapping seriously, studied the horses and bet on horses that he thought had a shot. If it were in someone else's hands, they would be in there betting every day and probably raking in the cash—for a short time. But it wasn't in someone else's hands, it was in Ben's hands and he managed the downside very well. He kept everything in check.

And every once in a while, when the boys started talking about the track, he'd talk about tits.

Kitty was history. In the few months since their initial conversation, Ben had run into her twice. Once in the hallway at school, which was unusual since they had different schedules—Ben was a senior and seniors were rarely in school at this time of the year. And now, at Chadosh's.

Kitty sat in their booth with Steph as Ben arrived with Sandy. After a short and polite greeting, Ben and Sandy slid into the second booth—Ben sitting back to back with Kitty. He couldn't figure her out and assumed that she just wasn't ready to date, or wasn't ready to date him, and probably never would be. It didn't matter, he would have made the effort if he felt that there was some chance, but somehow he didn't. She wasn't playing hard-to-get; she was impossible-to-get. She had only crossed his mind occasionally in the last couple of months. Each time, he replayed their short conversations, trying to detect a clue as to what went wrong. It was unresolved at best and a failure at worst. Either way, it gnawed at him. He tried to block thinking about it again, failing at that as well.

Brought up on challenges, Ben was very close to his mom, a handsome Jewish woman whose parents came from Poland when she was a teen. Her father was a rabbi in Coney Island. She took ill when Ben was nine and he took care of her before and after school. He slept in her room many nights during her last days. She died five months later and he took it badly, withdrawing for several months. Ben's father, Calogero, an aristocratic Italian Catholic from a small town near Siracusa, Sicily, remarried two years later to an Italian woman, Domenica.

Caught between religions, Ben's early Jewish heritage evaporated over time and he developed his own beliefs. This was unusual for the time and place. He believed in God, he told himself, but did not have the religious training or culture to underpin his thought process. Ben became a very independent thinker and often used logic and common sense. Others had faith in God; he had faith in himself.

He worked almost every day since he was eleven: stocked in grocery stores, swept barbershops and even occasional stints behind the counter at Chadosh's. There was little money and therefore he valued it more than most—not for itself but for what it could get. As he entered high school, his parents did a little better; his stepmother, a seamstress, and his father, a printer, brought in enough money for the family to be comfortable. He quit Chadosh's when he signed up for football and baseball in his sophomore year. A natural athlete, he started for both; in his junior year he became an *all-city* baseball player and played both offense and defense in football. In his senior year, he went for an interception, made it, and took out the opposing coach and ripped a tendon. He sat out senior baseball.

Ben could almost smell Kitty as she sat inches behind him. Seeing her again awakened some unresolved feelings. The thought of reconnecting quickly subsided when he realized he could get shot down again—he stayed cool. He had some business to discuss with Sandy, but he was hesitant when other people were around. Business is business. He put it off until later. No business; no tits; so they talked sports.

Maybe one more try . . . just to be friendly.

He turned around, casual-like, just to say: *Hey, haven't seen you around in a . . .*

The words never left his mouth. When he turned, Kitty and Steph were half way to the front door. Just then, Kitty stopped, turned back, walked deliberately towards the booth and stood over them. She smiled another polite smile; she was more desirable than he remembered.

"Hi kid sister." Ben immediately regretted his choice of words.

She didn't even respond with a smile as she bent down, whispered in Sandy's ear, nodded goodbye to both of them, and left.

Ben didn't know whether to be insulted, rejected, or just confused. This time, Ben did not watch her leave—he watched Sandy watch her leave. She had just gone from hard-to-get to off-the-card—it was time to scratch her forever. The door swung shut.

Ben held back for as long as he could.

"Well?"

"Well what?"

"What did she say?"

Sandy, a little confused, said, "She said to tell you that her goldfish died."

Ben could not hold back the smile that was erupting from within, so he didn't.

- 8 -

Coney Island was like the big toe of Brooklyn. It jutted out from the bottom and was the gateway to the Atlantic Ocean. In spite of its name, the fact that it was an island was lost on Brooklynites, being connected to the mainland by so many roads and bridges that it was totally integrated into Brooklyn. Surf Avenue divided Coney Island laterally into two—the living half and the fun half.

Only the residents knew the living half of Coney Island: a quiet, primarily Jewish neighborhood, populated by street after street of mid income, turn of the century, two-story houses and several small apartment buildings. Kitty lived in one of these houses, a pretty white one, not far from the corner. This was a friendly neighborhood where people sat out on their porches or gathered by the local barbershop and just talked. At the very tip of the toe was Sea Gate, a private residential community inhabited by a few well-off people.

However, when most people thought of Coney Island, they thought of the fun half, with its mile long deep beach providing a huge hot playground for thousands of people. A long and wide boardwalk that rose about twenty feet over the sand framed the beach and provided a natural barrier between the end of civilization and the beginning of nature. During the day, the boardwalk was a major pedestrian highway providing access to the beach and the fresh salt air. At night, people idly strolled above while a quieter form of passionate activity took place under the boardwalk in the soft cool sand.

Adjacent to the boardwalk was a mile of amusement rides, carnival games, tattoo parlors, fortunetellers, hot dog and corn vendors and Brooklyn's biggest entertainment center. Luna Park was a mega theme park hosting hundreds of unique and thrilling rides and amusements. When you wanted to escape and have fun in Brooklyn, you went to Coney Island—for a day out, a night out, a family venture or a date.

Ben and Kitty walked laughing as the 250,000 lights of Luna Park illuminated the clear night sky. It was a perfect night of rides and games and just laughing together. This was different, she was different: intelligent and witty. She was able to handle his teasing and parry with him without flinching.

She was no longer Willie's kid sister; she was fresh and new and special. He must be careful and delicate with this one.

The boardwalk was crowded and the couple walked near the railing on the beach side, against the flow of people. Kitty carefully held a bag with a small fishbowl and a goldfish. They walked side-by-side, close, but not touching.

"Thank you," Kitty looked at the goldfish. "I think I'll call him Rover."

"Rover?"

"Not a good name for a fish?"

"For a boy fish maybe—she's a girl."

Kitty laughed and Ben glowed inside with a feeling that grew from his abdomen and took over his body. She hesitated a moment and then said, "I have a confession."

Ben waited for her next words, anticipating the worst: the end of a beautiful, magical night.

"My goldfish didn't die."

"He ran away?" Ben quipped, relieved.

"No," she laughed and Ben glowed, "I didn't really have a . . . you knew?"

"I didn't want to think of you as a liar, so you have one now."

She smiled. This was a side of him that she hadn't seen before. He was always Willie's friend: older, popular, very handsome, and way out of reach. He never really talked to her and she felt somewhat intimidated by him, but not tonight. Tonight she felt comfortable and safe.

"It's Kay." She broke a silence that neither knew existed.

"What is?"

"My name. My real name, Kay."

"Where did Kitty come from?"

"Third grade play. I played a kitten, called . . ."

"Kitty."

"It stuck."

"I'll call you Kitty."

"Everyone does."

They continued walking. This time the silence was his ally—he was with her and felt no pressure to prove himself or win her over.

"A question," Ben said.

"Yes?"

"Why didn't you —?"

"Why didn't I respond to you at the party, or in the street, or in—?"

"Yes."

"Because you could have had any girl in the room. You had to know that I was different, not just Willie's kid sister."

They stopped walking and he just looked at her. "That was it?"

"And, I was afraid."

"Afraid?"

"Of you."

"And now?"

"Now I don't remember what I was afraid of . . . now that I told you, did I blow it?"

"Just the opposite," Ben smiled and they began walking again.

"Any girl in the room?" Ben said, and Kitty gave him a sharp elbow in the ribs that let him know that she had her limits.

They walked from one end of the boardwalk to the other and then turned around and walked back. Time did not exist as they talked about everything. Each conversation revealed a boundary that, when they were through, yielded a three dimensional personal sculpture. They continued to explore and felt safe enough to admit dreams and weaknesses as well.

"I just don't want to struggle through life," Ben shared.

"Money isn't everything," Kitty reached into her pocket and came up with a Tootsie Pop. "Tootsie Pop?"

"It's not about money, it's—"

"It's cherry." Kitty interrupted Ben as she held the Tootsie Pop in his face.

"No thanks."

"Cherry's the best."

"I know." Ben continued. "Look, when I have a family, I don't want them to want anything. Life doesn't have to be hard you know. I just don't want to be trapped in nowhere land. Everyone around here is a cop or a mailman or a barber. It's more about being somebody, to be respected, to be on top, the best—"

"Nothing wrong with wanting money," Kitty teased, feeling secure.

"Look," he felt frustrated that she didn't get it. "I need to get up in the morning and look forward to the day and go to sleep at night feeling like I've moved the peanut a little further."

"So it's about peanuts?"

Ben finally realized that she had been playing with him.

"No, it's about money."

"And how do you plan to get it?"

Ben started walking backwards in front of her. "Easy, you just follow the directions on the box." He teased as he raised one finger. They continued walking face to face. "Step one: know where you're going." A second finger joined the first. "Step two: keep doing things that will get you there."

Kitty playfully grabbed Ben's raised fingers and he grabbed her and pulled her into a deep and strong embrace. The warmth of her body seeped into his, contrasting the cool night air. A new energy grew and all the walls were down. Their playfulness turned into passion, their unfamiliarity into comfort, and their independence into unity.

They kissed the kiss that had been building for hours, days and months. They formed a single silhouette in the middle of the boardwalk as the surrounding lights cast their shadows in every direction—infinitely radiating outward and then pointing back at them. They became the hub of a spoked wheel. They became the center of the universe.

They stared and looked directly into each other's eyes, seeing, for the first time, the person each embraced, and sharing recognition that their relationship had just jumped a thousand levels. This was new territory for both of them. They walked down the center of the boardwalk arm in arm, inseparable. They were as much part of the night as the smell of the salt air, the sound of the waves that gently met the shoreline, and the magnificent luminescence of Luna Park.

A new entity had been created, an organism that did not exist before: an alliance, a partnership, an understanding and a trust.

After a few minutes of incredibly beautiful silence . . .

"I'll take that Tootsie Pop now." He said, his voice barely above a whisper as he looked at her head lying comfortably on his shoulder as they walked.

"I ate it."

They walked.

- 9 -

The summer blew by.

"Benny, What're we up?" Al was antsy.

It was the last day of racing at Jamaica. The boys, except Ben, sat in the first booth at Chadosh's—he sat in the second booth studying *The Racing Form* and the *Daily Mirror* in preparation for the day's events. He studied the charts, the horses' past performances, trying to figure what made one horse better than the other. What was the key factor? He kept careful notes, not trusting his memory or instinct, at least not yet.

"Seventeen sixty." He answered Al for the third time this morning.

"After—?"

"After everything." It was a net number.

The boys had gone to Robert Hall in July and picked out new suits, ties and hats—the Syndicate picked up the tab. Willie quietly returned his uncle's suit into his closet, after having it cleaned and pressed. But no matter how much he cleaned it, he could not patch the cigarette burn in the front pocket. He decided to own up to the damage and confess to his uncle about borrowing and ruining the suit, but thought better of it.

The new suits were an investment Ben had suggested—he knew that if he distributed the money first, paying for new clothes would not be their top priority, so instead it was a business expense. They had also distributed profits several times during the summer—after ensuring that there was enough in the pot to handle any dry spells. With the boy's agreement, he had put some of the funds in a side pool for just plain old betting—without dutching the book. It turned out to be profitable speculation.

Ben pulled out three hundred to stake next season's operation—no sense everyone digging into their pockets if they didn't have to. He would clear this with the guys when they cut up the money tonight. He also took today's investment off the top—that way, if they didn't win today, seventeen sixty was still the number, pure guaranteed profit. If they did win, much more.

One thousand, seven hundred, sixty bucks. Not bad.

He had wanted to go to NYU in the fall to study engineering, but he didn't have the money to be fully matriculated so he decided to go part time. Every day that he had the chance, he went to the track. Between work and Kitty, not as often as he liked. When he couldn't go, he still handicapped the races and made mock bets to track his progress. He spent every spare moment honing his skills—studying the horses, their past performances, the jockeys and the odds incessantly.

Since graduation, the boys didn't get together as a group as often because they all had jobs—Al pushed racks in the garment center and Willie pumped gas. Ben and Sandy were lifeguards on Coney Island. Sandy and Marilyn saw each other often, but not exclusively, at least not for Sandy.

The lifeguard jobs got in the way of their weekends and holidays at the track. Often, only two or three would go, crimping their scheme. Occasionally, Ben considered bringing someone else in to fill in, but it was too risky. As it turned out, their forced layoff actually kept them inconspicuous and less at risk. Somehow, they made it work. The Syndicate still had a good run, with no major problems, and Ben had really perfected his handicapping.

The boys knew better than to disturb Ben while he was figuring out the day: however long it took, it took. Handicapping horses had become a skill, an art and a passion. He wouldn't rush it because the process was everything: getting there was as important as being where you're going. Soon Ben would put the papers together, down his coffee, and stand up. They would join him, as usual, and be off to the track.

It was almost eleven. They had caught up on the events of the last week or so; it was too early to talk about tits; and they had run out of small talk. They waited quietly.

"Let's go," Al impatiently muttered under his breath. "Don't want to sit here all day looking at your mug."

"Could be worse," Willie said, "we could be in class doing nothing instead of here doing nothing."

"Since when did you go to class?"

"More than you."

"Only because you spent five years there."

"Fuck you, Bull-shitter," Willie snapped.

"Fuck you, and your mother, and your girlfriend, Ora."

Willie finally had become a man with a prostitute who he met through Al. Each Friday she came into the shop where Al worked and the guys would take turns going into the dark basement with her for a blowjob—hence her nickname. Every once in a while, they were allowed to invite a friend for Friday. Al invited Willie and he renewed his manhood almost every week that summer.

"Willie," Sandy tried to quell the ensuing action, "didn't know you had a girl. Bring her around."

"Yeah," Al chimed in. "I'm sure this place has a basement."

"Oh no? Estelle is down there with him now."

The older brothers of a guy he had a little problem with had jumped Al; they beat him up pretty badly. Al wore a cut nose and a blue welt over his right eye for two weeks. For some reason, this became a badge of honor and brought out a new vulnerable side to Al's personality. When people called him "Bull," he would politely correct them: "It's Al." And Al found that the girls liked him better as Al—particularly Estelle, who became Al's summer companion.

"Fuck you, Willie." Al slammed his open hand down on the table and sent his coffee cup flying to the floor; cold coffee sprayed their suit pants. He reached across the table and grabbed Willie's neck and crashed his head back against the booth. Sandy tried to wedge his body between them. Al stayed in his zone, choking the shit out of Willie.

Willie's face turned red as he struggled under Al's grip. His eyes bulged as if they were too big for his head. He clawed at Al futilely. Sandy tried to loosen it but Al was too strong. This was not one of their playful fights.

Just then, Ben stood.

"You guys ready? Last day out." Ben said, as if nothing was taking place. "Al, let go of Willie—if you kill him, it'll be a pain in the ass to make our bets."

The inertia of the moment stopped and shifted direction as everyone started to laugh. Al laughed so hard he forgot to let go of Willie's neck.

"Hey," Willie's struggled to breathe, laugh, and speak. "If you kill me . . ." he gasped, " . . . I want my share to go to Ora."

They laughed again: it was the end of the summer and they all sensed that their lives were to change once again.

Sandy went to get something to clean up the mess at the table as Al and Willie walked out of Chadosh's with their arms draped over each other's shoulders—best of friends.

Ben sat in that second booth and put his paperwork together—the same booth where he and Kitty had begun. The booth brought back that moment and how she looked so desirable, how she whispered into Sandy's ear and how he felt when he heard about her dead goldfish. It was a good summer—so much had changed.

She worked in her father's pawnshop every day except Saturday. Ben would see her almost every night, sometimes just sitting on Kitty's porch and talking. Other times they would walk the boardwalk and get lost in the cool sand beneath. They were exclusive—there was no other thought. It was a great summer, nothing could go wrong.

- 10 -

Clouds obliterated the sky above *Jamaica Race Track* and rain threatened as the crowds packed the stands for the last day of the racing season. Just one more outing before the horses moved to a warmer climate and the bettors moved indoors to more sedate activities.

Today was the day to press up the bets. There was nothing to lose now; they had made a nice profit on the summer so they could risk a bit of it and still be way ahead if they lost. Ben was proud of their play—not only the strategy, which worked as well as he had hoped—but the way they had played it, not greedy, not overdoing it. They had played it smart.

And now, dutch the book for one big score and make a killing to keep them warm through the winter. It made sense; the track wasn't onto them. It was the last day of the outing and the risk was low. Besides, they were playing for small stakes relative to the track's handle—it wouldn't be missed.

They had nothing going in this race or the next, so everyone scattered to maintain the group's anonymity. They had a little time to kill. Ben leaned against the railing and watched the horses warm up on the track. He looked for nothing specific, but perhaps he would see something that indicated the condition of the horses: a nervous energy, a hitch in their stride or some undetectable behavior. Anything that would give him insight into the horse's performance in the upcoming race. He knew enough to be observant—past performance and statistics are history; now is now.

He looked up; dark clouds covered most of the sky and the only natural light was off in the distance, like a light seeping from beneath a door. Clouds rolled upon clouds and the darkest hovered directly above, looming, as if it were about to drop right out of the sky and land right on him. Caught between a heavy sinking sky and an immovable earth, he felt pressed.

He checked the horses once again. Rain would change his picks. He had some mudders selected, but they were not his top choices. When conditions change, change with them. He checked upwards once again—not time to decide yet, maybe soon.

Sandy stood next to him and faced the other way, his back to the track. He lit up a Lucky and tracked a good-looking girl until she disappeared into the crowd.

"Look at that," Sandy spotted another. When he did not get a reaction, he turned to Ben, still fixated on the track. "You really like the ponies, don't you?"

"Huh?"

"The horses. You really like them."

"Nope," Ben answered; he looked at the horses but his mind was somewhere else.

Sandy just looked at him inquisitively.

Ben continued: "Do you know what you want to do? Next . . . I mean, with your life?"

"Not a clue."

"I do." He looked at Sandy. "This. I can do this. Really do it." Ben turned around and faced the stands. "See that?" He nodded to the Clubhouse and the Owner's Boxes. Caz

Frankel stood with his binoculars looking over his domain. "That's where I want to be, and the horses are my ticket to sitting up there." He spoke with uncommon passion and a depth that Sandy had not heard before. "I want to be the best in—"

Suddenly, his view was obscured. They were startled erect as two large hulks dwarfed them. One, a huge man, wore a suit two sizes too small but larger than Ben's; his companion was bigger. They just stood and stared, as if to warn them of some impending doom—a doom that only they could control and inflict.

Ben recognized the first guy, Zito, a local heavy who hung around the track. Never met him, never been this close. He had never seen Zito's pal before.

Zito looked at Sandy, "take a hike."

At first, Ben thought they wanted their spot at the rail, but it became clear that they wanted far more. Ben and Sandy were not fighters but they could handle themselves if warranted. Ordinarily, they would talk themselves out of unnecessary situations; if they couldn't, they didn't back down. They had come out on top of several tough situations over the years, but this was different. These guys were a different class of animal. Ben and Sandy were clearly overmatched.

Where the fuck is Bull?

The second guy sidled up to Ben to block any chance of escape—the rail held him on one side and the two gorillas blocked all other routes. They didn't seem to be interested in Sandy.

Zito looked at him and repeated emphatically, "Go!"

Sandy took a couple of steps backwards and just stood there.

54

The two thugs flanked Ben.

"Let's take a walk."

Shit!

They sandwiched Ben helplessly between them as they put their arms under his and lifted him off the ground. The human monoliths began to move further away from the stands, Ben with them. Sandy was about to bull-rush the duo, but Ben looked him off; they were no match, there will be another opportunity to get out of this.

Sandy bolted for the Grandstand for help and, in the distance, Ben saw Caz Frankel's white handkerchief and knew he was watching the action. Did he engineer this? He didn't think Caz knew he existed.

Didn't matter; there could be only one thing these guys wanted. They escorted him to the paddock area, far from the crowd, and threw him against the stable wall.

"Pal, your action is costing some people money." Zito was very businesslike. "And we would appreciate it very much if you don't come back."

You could've told me that at the rail.

"Ok. You made your point." Ben looked him straight in the eye—he needed to know that Ben meant it. This was going to end only one way—time to try anything. "We're done."

"You sure?"

"I'm sure. We're done. We're out of business—as of now. You'll never see me again."

"Now, I know you're done today, but what about next week?"

"Track's closed next week," his partner reminded him.

"Yeah, I forgot. I guess we don't have a problem then, do we?" Zito pressed.

Ben just looked at him.

Zito wanted an answer: "Do we?"

"No problem." Ben realized that no answer was good enough—this was just torturous foreplay. These guys were going to beat the shit out of him. He anticipated the escalation.

"You're not going to forget, are you?"

"No. I said you'll never see me again." Ben checked any avenues of escape, finding none. He tensed—he wasn't going down alone.

"Good." Zito looked around, picked up a blacksmith's hammer and fondled it. His tone became more threatening. "And I'm going to add some insurance."

Ben thought that this was the end of his perfect summer, his handicapping, Kitty, his life. There's only down from here. He coiled and looked for an opening, any opening. Maybe he could land a lucky shot and make a break.

Willie sprung around the corner. Breathing heavily, he didn't stop when he saw the two mammoths hover over Ben, threatening. He jumped between Ben and Zito. It didn't matter to Willie that they towered over him.

"Back off, unless you want to see how many friends he has!" Willie's fists clenched at his side. It must have been an instinctive flash of courage, pure love for his friend, and knowledge that Bull and Sandy were right behind him that gave Willie the courage to stand his ground.

Zito smiled at this ugly little joke.

"Willie," Ben reached for his shoulder to shove him aside but he was grabbed from behind.

In the distance, Sandy's voice was barely audible, "Ben . . . Willie."

Fuck!

Willie's face held unreasonably strong as he realized that the cavalry was far behind. *Fuck!*

Zito grabbed Willie's right arm while the other thug slammed Ben to the ground and pinned him down. Willie struggled as Zito's meaty hands wrapped around Willie's fist and isolated his index finger.

"This is just what I wanted, a memento of this fine moment."

"No!" Willie wasn't defending Ben now; he was pleading for his own life.

Zito dragged Willie and held his hand and outstretched finger on the anvil. He placed two hundred and fifty pounds of knee on his arm to steady it.

"From now on you'll have to pick your nose with your left hand," he grinned at his cleverness.

Willie, his nose and mouth oozing, struggled to get free. He looked back at Ben futilely hoping for a miracle to make this go away.

"Benny...." he trembled.

Al and Sandy turned the corner and ran towards the group but they were too far away. Ben swung at the thug holding Willie, connecting, but doing little damage. A fist slammed into Ben's forehead with enough force to drive his face into the ground. Blood and dirt seeped through his nose. He rose to his knees but was met with a shoe to his head.

Zito raised the hammer and savored the moment; enjoying Willie's terror.

"Hey, pal." Zito looked over at Ben lying face down in the dirt as he cocked the hammer high above Willie's hand. "Remember this."

The prick brought the hammer down hard on Willie's finger smashing right through to the anvil leaving a bloody mess of flesh and bone that bore no resemblance to a human part. Willie looked down at the bloody pulp and realized that it was no longer part of him. He opened his mouth and screamed; nothing came out.

Willie tried to catch his breath and pass out to avoid the pain but he couldn't. Finally, enough air had re-entered his lungs and the screeching sound of a trapped and wounded animal echoed through the stable area.

Al and Sandy approached and were horrified at the sight of Willie lying on the ground in a bloody mess. The thugs turned to walk away.

Zito looked at Ben; his face covered with bloody mud, and said, "Remember."

Ben crawled over to Willie and hugged him to comfort him.

"It should've been me. I'll never forget this." Ben saw the damage close up and shielded the mangled mess from Willie's view. It should have been him; but for a moment, he was glad it wasn't. He grabbed Willie's hand—a piece of shredded skin dangled where his finger used to be—and pressed down to stop the bleeding. "It's not bad, it'll be ok."

Frantically, Ben tried to gather the pieces of bloody flesh and bone from the soupy red mess on the anvil but nothing was big enough to grab.

He pulled Willie's head into his chest and held on.

"Jesus, Willie."

- 11 -

The Syndicate was dead.

A financial success with a bad ending. A good part of their winnings went to pay Willie's hospital bills, which went on for several months. Ben was going to pay for it himself until Sandy stepped up and Al followed: it was a "business expense."

Willie's missing finger became his badge of courage. He'd joke about it, embellishing slightly, and including every detail except for the betting scheme—Ben had cautioned him about sticking to the interesting part of the day. When Willie retold his experience, he would look to Ben, who would add: "only a real friend would do what he did . . ." followed by, "a crazy friend with guts." It got laughs—but Willie knew that Ben meant it.

The summer had a few highlights. He had Kitty. The strategy worked and they turned it into a money machine—finishing up a little over a thousand and down one finger. He was proud of his plan and the way the guys really came through—it was a *can't-lose* scheme, until it lost.

It was a good summer with a real bad ending, making it the worst summer of his life.

It had been almost two years since that day—Ben's last day at the track. Their lives, once so intertwined and convergent, had now split. Without the Syndicate or school to bind them, they saw each other less, sometimes going a month or two without reconnecting as a group. Each had taken a more conventional route until World War II got in the way.

It was a reunion of sorts.

Sandy had started college and dropped out to join the Marines. He was shipping out soon and the boys met for a rare beer to see him off. They hung at the bar and each, except Sandy, took turns buying rounds.

Willie playfully dusted off Sandy's uniform.

"Maybe this'll help you with the ladies."

"Good idea," Sandy mocked, "never thought of that."

Upbeat as usual—you couldn't tell that he was going to war.

Ben wasn't—he had gone to NYU for two years, funded in part by the prior summer's venture. Then Ben tried to enlist but was rejected when pulmonary problems were uncovered during his physical: 4F. Ben quit school and joined the New York Fire Department along with Al. Ben looked at Sandy; wishing it were him in the uniform.

They stood at the bar for a couple of hours then put Al in a booth so they wouldn't have to prop him up. It wasn't long before they joined him; they sat in their regular positions, same as Chadosh's. One old story sparked another, and that triggered another, anything that would conjure up a safe and fun memory, anything to take their minds off today. Most of the recollections centered on Willie and Al—their stories were always the most entertaining. Their friendships rekindled; reminding them that they were still close friends—just not as frequently.

The future hardly entered the conversation as they recycled the past, prolonging the inevitable. This would be the last time that they would be together for a long time, maybe forever.

"So," Willie asked for the third time, less coherently than earlier, "when you gonna marry my sister?"

"Not now" Ben said uncomfortably.

"How 'bout you?" Willie asked Sandy.

"Benny's got first dibs."

"Huh?"

"I mean, if she dumps him, I'm in."

"No. I mean, when you gonna marry what's-her-name?"

"Who?"

"The one you used to skunk under the boardwalk."

"Oh, Marilyn." Sandy had not seen Marilyn for over a year, ran into her in Macys about six months ago, screwed her in the dressing room, and hadn't seen her since. "Haven't seen her since Lincoln. Besides, you might have heard . . . I'm going away."

"Oh yeah. Where?"

"Don't know. Won't tell us until we're there."

"Guam. I bet they send you to Guam."

"Maybe. What season is it in Guam now?"

"Wartime."

The reality of the circumstance took hold as they staggered out of the bar. The street was cold, dark and wet, a perfect fall night, a perfect night for saying goodbye. Until recently, they had never been apart for more than a few days in the last six years. Tonight was a reminder of how close they had been.

Al jumped in and out of consciousness—he hugged Sandy, ordered another round from no one in particular, and lost his legs. He lay down in the street with the curb for a pillow. A childlike smile crept onto his face as his nose ran and drool seeped through the corner of his mouth. The boys stood over him.

"He looks so peaceful," Sandy observed, "who would believe he eats Buicks?"

"I think we should leave him there," Ben said. "Who's in?"

"In," Willie declared with his thumb raised skyward, reminiscent of their Syndicate buy-in.

"In," Sandy declared likewise.

Ben's thumb joined the others, finalizing the vote. They stood over him a few moments longer waiting to see if he would react. Nothing.

Ben bent down and lifted Al's shoulders, then looked up at the others.

"Can't do this myself."

Al was dead weight as the guys each grabbed an appendage and dragged him across the street to Willie's car. They tried to lift him into the car several times but could not manage his bulk.

Finally, Willie bent down and whispered into Al's ear.

Al rolled over and slowly got to his knees and crawled into the back seat of the car—and slid to the floor.

Ben and Sandy shared astonished looks.

"What did you say to him?" Sandy asked.

"Just told him Estelle was in the back seat of the car."

After a year of going steady, Al had proposed to Estelle. She dumped him the next day. Devastated, Al withdrew for many weeks. Some months later, they got together again, he proposed again, and she dumped him again.

Ben and Sandy looked at Willie incredulously.

"Ok." Willie admitted: "Told him his mom was looking for him and there'd be no dinner if he didn't get his ass home."

Willie hugged Sandy and brushed off his uniform admiringly. He held up his right hand with most of his index finger missing and said, "You know I'd be there with you but I can't reach the trigger."

"Bullshit," Sandy said, "If you can pump gas, you can pull a trigger."

"I pump lefty."

Their laughter was the last release of the night. Ben managed a smile as he stared at Willie's finger—this conversation brought up too many negatives.

Willie shook Sandy's hand and quickly turned, got into his car and drove off without looking back.

The street was quiet as Ben and Sandy watched them leave.

"Walk you home, Lieutenant?" Ben said.

"Unless I get a better offer."

They walked in silence for several minutes.

"Be careful over there," Ben said, breaking the stillness of the night and the sanctity of the moment.

"You know me better than that." Sandy's voice did not have its earlier buoyancy. "What are you going to do?"

"Fight fires. Ride it out for now, I guess." Ben turned towards Sandy—he had to be sure he understood. "You know I wanted in."

"I know."

"Can't figure it: they bounced me...and the FD takes me." Ben attempted to kick a can in stride and just topped it, sending it sideways and out of reach for a second shot. He sidestepped and instinctively swung his leg at the can and it took off in a high arc, and landed on the other side of the street. They silently admired the shot as if it were a winning field goal, and then resumed their pace. "I can't figure it. I don't want to be a fireman. I'll do it, but I wanted to . . ." Ben stopped short. "Sorry, my shit is nothing compared to what you're about to do. Be careful."

"Hey, I'll be out of uniform before you."

"Just come back."

"Yeah."

At the corner, they shook hands and hugged. This was not the time for leaving things unsaid or unclear, but words were unnecessary—they nodded goodbye.

Ben stood on the corner and watched Sandy walk down the street. He held the image of the moment as long as he could and wondered if this were the last time he would ever see him.

- 12 -

Brooklyn, 1960

Ben was the only one left in the shower; he let the water engulf his body. A few firemen were still in the locker and most had long gone. The grime and soot had dug deep under his skin and he didn't want to bring any part of today home with him. He trembled and breathed deeply to shake it off.

A cough brought up more black, an ugly reminder of this morning's fire and what was almost his last memory. One more deep breath and a pain seared across the inside of his chest as if he still breathed the heat. Ben shook his head as if it would rid him of any recall of almost being burnt to death. When it came right down to it, he was prepared to die, just not that way: not with so much notice, not with so much pain.

He shuddered and spat black again. It circled the drain; each revolution drew it nearer to oblivion until it disappeared into the vortex. If not for chance and Bull, that would have been him disappearing into the vortex.

He turned his face head on into the stream, closed his eyes and let the water wash the day away. The only thing that existed was the cool, clean water. In a little while he'd be home with Kitty and the boys.

Home for Hook & Ladder Company 921 was a firehouse on Voorhees Avenue just off the Belt Parkway in Sheepshead Bay. The firehouse was a majestic place. More than just a garage to house the trucks and men, it was home to a family of men that spent more time together than they did with their real families. They did everything together: cooked, ate, slept, played, cleaned, and fought fires.

The men relied on each other and on their tools. The trucks, a powerful mass of shiny red and chrome muscle, were old but in great condition. The long Hook & Ladder truck was deceptively high to allow the second driver the visibility to steer the massively long frame through the narrow city streets. It was a magnificent creature, reminiscent of some prehistoric dinosaur, particularly when fully extended in battle. The pump truck stood next to its senior brother and provided the weapons of engagement: the hoses and water supply. The trucks all carried men and were always ready for battle.

In spite of being an old building, the firehouse was extremely clean and orderly. When it was time for action, lives depended on efficiency and structure and regimen. The men's gear, the helmets, boots and heavy coats, were lined up and hung in neat rows—at the ready. Coffee brewed continuously in the large kitchen that served over twenty men three or more meals every day.

In the small backyard, when the men were not out on a call, abbreviated games of softball, slap ball or handball prevailed. The men slept on cots on the second floor, which had a four-foot hole with the polished brass fire pole rising up the middle for rapid access to a middle of the night emergency.

It was a job of highs and lows, with little middle ground. The only thing consistent about the job was the inconsistency. Most of the time, they waited—hoping that what they waited for didn't happen—filling their time by maintaining equipment or competing in some way. On some days, they rose to action two or three times, on others, not at all. The majority were minor: a small kitchen fire; an electrical fire in a private house; a store front; a car crash; or the dreaded false alarm. Even the small stuff presented danger as the trucks sped through the streets, the men hanging on to a single handle, never sure if they would make the turn or a car would miss-time a light. Too many of them had died fighting false alarms. Occasionally, like today, the engagements were huge. It was always grueling; it was always dangerous.

The firehouse was a place of great camaraderie: their clubhouse, their fort, and their home for twelve to eighteen hours a day. The men worked several shifts, back to back, which allowed several consecutive days off. They alternated between their two families.

The duties varied. In addition to fire fighting, men may be assigned special assignments such as building inspection; fire control and containment; and, Ben's job, policing. He made sure the fire zones and fire hydrants were clear of cars and wrote summonses—it was boring but it kept him away from fires. It was a choice assignment for most of the men. They would have been surprised if they saw him in the shower today, shaken. But they didn't see that side of him. Ben never showed all he had—good or bad, there was always something in reserve.

Ben slowly got dressed in the empty locker room.
"You Ok?" The Captain surprised him.

"Ok."

"You sure? Not used to being out there."

"Part of the job."

"Bad luck."

"Don't believe in luck." Ben offered, wishing he hadn't.

"It could've been a pile of burning leaves."

"But it wasn't."

"Yeah. Well, if Stansky doesn't break his arm playing softball, you're writing tickets today. See? Bad luck."

"No." Ben couldn't resist. "If Bull isn't there to pull me out, that's bad luck. But he was, so it isn't."

The Captain smiled.

"Like I said," Ben muffled a cough, "part of the job."

"Yeah. Check that . . ."

"I will. Thanks Cap."

The conversation was almost as bad as this morning's fire. But Cap was right; it's just the draw. Ben could have been writing some schmuck a ticket for parking by a hydrant. In spite of it, he felt better about doing something that made a difference—as long as he was still around to know that he did it—and it doesn't happen again for a long time, make that forever.

He pushed the last button through on his blue shirt as he headed down the staircase. A loud argument from the next room interrupted his exit. He looked in through the doorway and saw Al in a shouting match with another fireman. The words would burn out; he went downstairs to wait for Al.

He sat on a ledge next to the firehouse and let the sun bake his face. It felt good; he loved to be tan and stole every solar moment that he could. He could take this kind of heat all day long. He closed his eyes and absorbed the energy.

Finally.

"Ready?" Al broke Ben's solace.

"What was that all about?" Ben asked, not really wanting to get into it.

"What?"

"Upstairs."

"About twenty bucks, forget it," Al's agitation showed through.

If Al didn't want to talk, that was fine with him. The less he knew, the better. "Drop me off at Willie's, have to pick up my car."

- 13 -

Willie's gas station stood on the corner of Avenue P and East 5th Street, just off of Ocean Parkway. It was a good spot without much competition nearby. Willie sat in the office reading the Daily News—a typical pose on a typical day.

Willie finished the Jumble, a simple word puzzle, in about fifteen minutes. A good start to the day. Earlier he had run through the Gulfstream entries. Picked six horses in three races—crossed them out and picked another six and then went back to his first choices. He didn't bet on any of them. He'd check the results tonight and if any of the first six came in, he'd think he was a genius; first for picking them, then for following his instinct and not going with the second six. If any of the second six came in, he'd think he was a genius for being smart enough to avoid his instinct, which was usually wrong.

I should be down in Florida.

That was just his warm-up. Next, he doped out the races at Aqueduct. He checked the *best bets* of every tout and tried to figure some angle, something that would give him that little edge—something no one else figured. He had circled every horse in every race and his notes in the margin of the newspaper were, by this time, unreadable.

There's gotta be an angle.

The grease under his fingernails tasted rank as he unconsciously but vigorously chewed them down until they appeared as a small gray dots framed in sludge at the end of nine of his nine and a half fingers. This was his life—this and gambling.

Today was a slow day, just like all the rest.

Life had broken right for Willie. He had dropped some hair and put on some pounds; his teeth were still crooked and he was still short. He was a handsome ugly. He never wanted or expected much, and he didn't get it. He actually did better than most expected, but he didn't see it that way. He had a small, attached house and his own business with his own name over the door—he and the bank, that is.

He always figured, *there's gotta be an angle. There's gotta be a shortcut* so that he could leapfrog to the next level, sell the station, sit on his porch, read the Daily News, do the Jumble and figure the races.

He married Rowan, an ex-hooker who was known as Jackie, and he was lucky to get her. He was one of her regulars and on one of his visits, they just talked. On the next visit, she let him ride on the cuff for her standard services. From the beginning, a unique relationship had developed. Each of them finding something valued in the other—something that no one had penetrated before. When Jackie dropped out of the life, he became just a friend. Befriending women did not come easy to Willie but he felt that he knew her in a special way. More importantly, she knew him and accepted him in spite of him.

She saw the light and found God and Willie at the same time. In the beginning, she would be in church every day, now only on Sundays. As far as Willie was concerned, she could go to church ninety times a week as long as he didn't have to go and she was home when he got there. She was a good wife; she stayed home, took care of their two teenage girls and lost whatever meager looks she had, but she was exactly what Willie needed. Everyone who knew her would be in disbelief if they knew how she used to earn her living. Willie appreciated her. He never told her that, but he did.

The annunciator bell rang and interrupted Willie's void. He was alone today and knew that he had to service the customers. He knew them all: what they did for a living, whether they took high test or regular and who was cheating with whom. His weekly three-minute conversations were the only form of interaction he had with people, other than the track or the guys.

He slowly lifted his head and jumped up when he saw Al's '56 Dodge. The glare in the car window made it difficult to see inside but he recognized two familiar silhouettes. He started to greet them, stopping first to straighten his greasy attendant overalls with a worn *Willie* nametag and *Willie's Service Station* logo. He walked slowly trying not to appear too anxious or needy.

"Gentlemen," Willie said, with a mock authority, proprietor and king of Willie's Service Station.

"I see business is good," Ben teased as he jumped out of the passenger seat.

"Not bad . . . doesn't matter. I spend more than I make anyhow."

"Car ready?" Ben inquired.

"Ready."

Al put his car in drive. "You Ok Benny? I gotta go."

Ben turned to him. "Ok, thanks for . . ." Al's car pulled out.

. . . the lift and saving my life.

Willie and Ben watched as Al's car swerved onto Avenue P, narrowly missing an ice cream truck.

"What's with him?" asked Willie.

"Tough day."

Willie nodded knowingly, and then focused on the business at hand. "I had to rig the shocks. You'll need new ones next—"

"That'll be next time. What's the damage?" Ben took out cash.

"On the house," Willie felt good to say that.

"Willie . . ."

"No, I mean it. It's on the house."

"Thanks." Ben put his hand back in his pocket but didn't release the cash from his grip.

"But I could use a hundred if you got it."

"Again? I thought business was good."

"I have to pay down some stuff."

"Not to Charlie?"

"No."

"Then who?"

"What's the diff?"

"The diff is you want to borrow money from me to pay someone and I want to know who."

"Charlie."

"Thought so. He's not a good guy to owe."

"Yeah. But I'm almost square." Willie offered as consolation.

"Are you?" Ben handed him fifty dollars.

"No."

The annunciator rang as a customer pulled in. Willie used the opportunity to break away.

"Thanks Benny."

"Take it slower, no more of that crazy shit."

- 14 -

Al took a deep breath before he opened the door to his apartment. He had been in the fire department for eighteen years; it was a good life, kept him away from home just enough.

A coupla more years and I'll retire, maybe buy a boat or something. Maybe a small house in Staten Island, near a marina. Maybe Long Island, nah, I hate Long Island. Maybe Florida. Maybe winter there and summer here.

He walked in slowly.

I'm not gonna get into it with her tonight.

He tried to rally every sensibility he had. Today was already rough enough. In spite of how he looked to Ben and the guys, it was rough. Being the fearless valiant *Bull* was a high standard to maintain, too high. But now he couldn't seem to back down from being *the* guy in *the* situation. And he was goddamn lucky to pull Ben out of that mess, he was just trying to find his way through the hellhole when he inadvertently grabbed Ben's coat. Lucky. Lucky for Ben.

Now there's a different hellhole to deal with.

Al had met Paula when she waited on him in Cookies, a large 24-hour restaurant on Avenue M. She was working graveyard as Al and another guy came in after a night of cards and beer. He had lost and was pissed. He wasn't in the mood for flirting but she was, and needed the tips.

It didn't take her long to mention that she was a working actress and had been in a small play and was up for a radio commercial. It didn't take Al long to mention that he knew a guy that was in theater and it went from there. Al forgot about losing at cards.

They went out a few times and she continually pressed him for his theatrical contact. It was in a moment of passion and truth that Al confessed that the only one he knew in theater was an usher.

"You lying bastard. Well, I've never been in a play." Paula laughed.

Her laughter was a great relief: he joined her but he mistook her laugh for fun.

"In fact," she went on, "I never even been *to* a play. How could you lie to me, you big piece of meat?"

He tried to calm her and put his hands on her shoulders and she recoiled and shouted: "Don't touch me with those meat hooks." She became more incensed at his betrayal and shouted, "You fuck like a fuckin' toad."

Then she swung wildly, just missing his nose, and followed with two bell-ringing shots to each ear sending Al backwards onto her sofa, shocked. She then threw his clothes out into the hall and, when he went to retrieve them, she locked him out.

They were both too lazy to end the relationship, so they got married. She quit working to focus on her acting and, after two months of hell, she moved out and they got divorced. Al was relieved but missed her. One night, he went back to Cookies, graveyard shift, and she was there. They talked for a long time, moved in together and got remarried the next week.

They divorced a second time, ten years later, when Al didn't come home for two days after a one-day fishing trip. She was so angry that she trashed the apartment and took all of his clothes and stuffed them down the incinerator chute.

He insisted that he told her it was a two-day trip and she heard him wrong. He waved the receipt from *Emerald's Joy*, the boat he was on, and displayed his ripped pants where one of the guys hooked him in the crotch. "Nearly hooked my dick. Scared the livin' shit outa me."

He even picked up the phone and offered to call Lou or Stacks, the guys he was with.

It didn't matter. She didn't really care what the truth was—she really thrived on being angry with Al. It was one of the few joys she had because marrying him prevented her from becoming an actress, her dream.

She would have really been angry if she knew that it really was a one-day trip and Al had gotten drunk and shacked up with a woman that used to hang around the firehouse.

Al had dated a few women after Paula, but none of them understood him the way she did. A year ago, he ran into her again at Cookies, graveyard shift. They went out to breakfast and talked. They had matured; they confessed, come to a new understanding and really missed each other. They remarried. They did not fight anymore. They just didn't talk.

Al stalled in the foyer and straightened a painting of fruit on a wall that used to be stucco but had been painted over so many times that it was almost smooth. He lingered over the painting, attempting to get it just right, perfectly aligned. After enough time, he walked into the living room where Paula sat on the sofa watching a soap. Ritz Crackers decorated the sofa and table and floor. He draped his jacket over a chair and it fell straight to the floor.

"Hi," Al said unemotionally.

Tone was very important to them now. It was their only method of communicating.

Without turning or acknowledging Al's presence in any way, Paula said, "Don't expect me to pick that up for you."

He picked up his jacket and neatly hung it.

"How was your day?" Al marshaled every constraint he could.

"Same as yesterday and the day before and the day before that," Paula said resentfully.

Al bit down hard.

"What's for dinner?"

"I ate," she broke apart another Ritz.

"I had a tough one today, a four alarmer in Brighton Beach. It, I . . ." The impact of the day began to get to Al who found himself unusually vulnerable. " . . . I nearly got killed," he sighed.

"Shhh, I'm watching."

"I said I nearly got killed."

"But you didn't, did you? If you did, you'd be quiet so I could watch my program. But you're standing here, so you didn't. So shush."

That's it. Fighting is one thing but this nothing shit is nothing.

"I'm going out," Al walked into the foyer where he noticed the fruit painting was again hanging crooked. He carefully removed it, put his fist through it, and re-hung it, ensuring that it was, once again, perfectly straight. The door slammed behind him.

Paula yelled after him: "Next time, don't bother me unless you're really dead."

- 15 -

Kitty was in the kitchen when Ben slid through the back door, still unsettled from the day. When he saw her washing dishes he snapped back into the present. She still had her shape and that certain cuteness that separated her from just being pretty. After all these years, she still did it for him. He felt grounded.

They'd gotten married after seeing each other for three years, followed by a yearlong engagement. After high school she worked in her father's pawnshop, where she picked up a lot about business, until he died a year later. She went on to secretarial school and excelled in the several jobs that she had afterwards. Her first job was with a flower and watch importer, which she left after she came back from a business trip to Stockholm with her boss and six other men. Ben had found out who was on the trip and had a fit in spite of her insistence that it was strictly business. Her second job was with a small jewelry manufacturer. She was the boss' secretary, did some of the books and some sales. She stayed out later than normal one night, one a.m., when the office celebrated delivering a huge client—she left two weeks later. They had tried to raise a family but were detoured by two miscarriages. They stopped trying for a while.

Ben stared at her butt as she fiddled in the sink. He didn't realize how long he had been standing there when she said, "Could use a drier."

He smiled. *Yeah, she still did it for him.*

"Hungry? Some chicken in the fridge."

Ben kissed her neck, which she returned without turning around. He put his arm around her waist and held on for just a second. Her warmth penetrated; her energy recharged him.

"Everything Ok?" She asked.

"Yep. Where's that chicken?" He opened the fridge and took out a plate of food, examined it, sat and ate.

"Where are the boys?"

"Upstairs," she turned around to face him and noticed the red abrasion on his forehead. It had swelled a little since the building nearly took his head off.

"What happened to you?"

Ben had forgotten it was there—he was trying to forget the day entirely.

"Was in a burner today," Ben said matter of factly.

"You were in a fire?" she removed her washing gloves and stood behind him. She stroked his head, "You Ok?"

This was what he needed, his head resting comfortably on her breasts; he felt safe again. Ben looked up at her and swung her around to his lap—as they had done hundreds of times before.

"You Ok?" She repeated.

"Fine now. Good thing Al was there," he coughed, "just worn out."

"You sure?"

He ran his hand slowly up the familiar curve of her back.

She pulled his head into her breast again and he brought her even closer. Kitty could feel him tremble; something he didn't want her to see and she knew it. She held tight. This was his first moment of comfort all day and his emotions leaked through. Instinctively, his hand slowly climbed her waist. Her breasts were still firm and full; his hand very slowly crept under her housedress and gently cupped the underside of her breast. She never wore a bra when she was home—a soft spot, for both of them.

"Still love me?" Kitty faltered.

Ben's hand slowly explored her breasts. His answer was in his touch.

Sunday, family day, Ben stood in the middle of the driveway, which was just large enough to have his local Yankee game. Kitty watched from their small stoop.

"Bottom of the ninth, two out," Ben stood on the makeshift pitcher's mound and announced in his best Mel Allen voice. "Yanks are in trouble, down by one and . . . Mantle is at the plate."

Scooter, seven years old and missing a front tooth, hung on to the drainpipe, which served as first base. Rick, nine and lanky, was up at bat with a taped stickball bat hanging on his shoulder. He studied the pitcher and stepped up to the plate, which was chalked onto the driveway. Rick checked the bat, stepped out of the batter's box and studied the pitcher. He took a couple of half swings and stepped back in, bat cocked.

Ben squeezed the spaldeen, stared down the batter and checked first base.

"Hey, you forgot me," Scooter shouted as he took a lead off the drainpipe.

"Hey Koufax, got a minute?" Willie yelled, as his car pulled up with him leaning out the window. Kitty waved and walked towards the car. Ben kept his eye on the business at hand, not wanting to lose his concentration on the crucial game.

"And on first base," Ben continued his soliloquy, "the shortest of shortstops, speedy Phil, the Scooter, Rizzuto." Again, Ben checked the batter and first and went into a long windup.

"And the pitch, an overball knuckle slider curve fastball gonna breeze by the Mick." He exaggerated the windup, reared backed and threw.

Rick swung away eyes closed and connected with a line drive that seared passed Ben towards the street. Willie dove to the car floor as the ball slammed into his rear window. The boys rounded the bases screaming and celebrating the Yankees' victory.

"Shoulda thrown a changeup," Ben lamented. "Nice hit, champ," He watched Rick triumphantly round the garbage can cover which served as second base. He continued his romp towards home plate with his hands held high overhead. Ben unknowingly smiled.

As quickly as he showed up, Willie pulled out. Ben joined Kitty as they both watched the car fade down the street.

"What was that?"

"Money," said Kitty.

"You didn't give him any?"

"Twenty."

"That all?"

"He wanted fifty. He's been strange."

"Business is a little tight."

"I don't know. Rowan said that he came home the other night almost doubled up. He wouldn't tell her what was wrong. Went right to bed. She's worried about him. Me too."

"He's Ok," Ben lied. "You know Willie."

- 16 -

Smoke and beer filled the air in Sandy's basement as Al walked in the door. The players around the card table were too interested in their cards to look up. The Tuesday night regulars: Pacey Diamond, a bookie's bookie; Doc Brodsky, a retired Doctor of nobody knew what; Willie; Al; Ben; and Sandy. They always tried to get a seventh for a better game, bigger pots and fresh money.

"Look who decided to show," Willie looked at his hole cards for the fifth time.

"Don't, just don't," Al scowled. "Where's the beer?"

"Right where it always is," Sandy said. "Willie, you in?"

Willie called the bet, "Jacks up."

The players dropped their cards to the table and Willie raked in the chips and added to his growing stacks.

"Let's lighten up guys, looks like everyone's having a bad week, except me of course." Willie couldn't hold back the smile. "Sandy had to put on a tie. Ben was in a fire," Willie went on. "And Al is Al."

"You were in a fire, Benny?" Doc questioned.

"No big deal."

"No big deal?" Al said, as he took out cash. "He was almost killed. He fought the flames, broke down the doors, rescued the maiden . . ."

Everyone laughed, missing Al's sarcasm.

"Ben's a hero," he added. "I think this was your first fire, right, Benny?"

Ben smiled to hide his annoyance. "Not my first."

"He's been in the fire department for eighteen fuckin' years and they forget to invite him to the fires." Al was on a roll.

"I don't think they forgot," Willie added naively. "Ben's got an angle."

Al ignored Willie. "Oh shit, I forgot about the Coney Island fire you were in."

"They heard it, let's play," Ben said.

"Let's hear it," Doc was losing and needed a break.

Ben really didn't want to get into this.

"Yeah, let loose, Ben." Pacey Diamond meekly echoed as he held the cards hostage.

"OK, deal." Ben took a moment to get into the mood. "I was in the department two years, on special fire hydrant duty. I finish early . . ." Ben got louder for emphasis "actually about five hours early."

Al regretted starting this.

"And I park next to the beach. Luckily," Ben added sarcastically, "I had my bathing suit on under my uniform. So I'm lying on the beach sunning myself and had this babe doing a headstand on my chest and I look back," Ben bent his head backwards, "and see the sky is filled with smoke." Ben jumped out of his chair and enacted the scene. "Jesus! Coney Island is on fire! Luna Park was burning down."

The guys were filled with a mix of hilarity and awe.

"Smoke is everywhere." Ben became more animated. "So I run back to my car and put on my uniform and drive to the fire to cover my ass. I was looking for someone in my company, anyone, so they could see me there. Just then a captain from another company puts me on a hose line. And here I am, one minute with a broad on the beach, the next, playing footsy with a fire . . . a guy could get hurt that way."

Doc choked on his cigar, Pacey Diamond emitted loud intermittent snorts and Willie inhaled beer into his nose. Even Al broke into a smile.

"And there I was hanging on the some hose," Ben demonstrated as he recounted, "and trying to scratch my crotch 'cause I still had sand in my shorts!"

"My hero, let's play cards," Al said impatiently as he sat.

"One dollar," Sandy bet.

"Gotta make a call." Ben folded his cards and walked to the phone by the bar.

"Get the price on the Yankee game," Sandy said.

"Ben likes the Yanks?" Doc inquired.

"Ben could care less about the Yanks or any other team." Sandy said. "He likes value."

"Huh?"

"Figures the odds are better when you bet against a local team."

"He's always got something going, doesn't he?" Doc was somewhat in awe.

"Not really," Sandy said, "a little football and baseball, that's it." But no horses, and no Syndicate.

"He does good."

"Good enough. Down card Doc," Sandy kept the action moving. "Don't let him fool you. That Luna Park thing, he was in it big time and nearly got killed. He was trapped too deep inside and nearly bought it—lucky to get out. He worked it out so he could stay away from fires since then. It was that or quit; and he'd rather do something he hated than quit it."

"How does he—?" Doc didn't have to finish the question.

"Anticipates, always looks for the edge. Just knows where he's going."

"Well, wherever he's going, I'm going," Willie chimed in. "I'll never strike gold in the gas station."

Sandy grabbed Willie's hand and looked at his fingernails.

"Well, it looks like you struck oil."

Willie laughed the loudest—he was winning.

"Two dollars," Willie bet confidently.

"Four," Al jumped in.

Pacey Diamond dropped and Sandy called the bet.

"Call," Willie opened his cards victoriously. "Trip nines."

"No good," Al looked to Sandy, "And what about you counselor?"

"Flush."

Al slammed his cards down. "Shit, you just pulled that, didn't you?"

Sandy tried not to provoke Al. "Yeah just got lucky," knowing that he had the flush since the sixth card.

Al reluctantly pulled out more cash.

"Filling your tank again, Al?" Willie needled.

"Fuck you, Willie."

"Easy guys, just a game, who deals?"

"Fuck you too, Al," Willie retorted.

Suddenly Al reached across the table, raised his fist and brought it down hard on Willie's hand crushing it on the table. Willie recoiled in surprise and pain.

"I'm not in the mood."

- 17 -

The fire bell rang somewhere deep in Ben's dream and it somehow became the phone as he crossed the line into consciousness. He swung out of bed quickly and answered it without turning on the light—challenging himself to guess the time as he always did. *Three twenty-one.*

"Hello." He whispered, checking the clock as he listened: *three twenty-two, not bad for the middle of the night.*

"On my way." He muttered and hung up.

Kitty mumbled: "What?"

"Nothing, go to sleep."

Ben washed his face and dressed downstairs and made a call.

Willie stared at the single streetlight that reflected off the floor of his gas station, which was covered in black oil. Reluctantly, he surveyed his entire premises—the oil blanketed every inch of concrete as it slowly expanded its breadth and seeped down the driveway and into the street.

Just beneath the gas pumps, two fifty-gallon oil drums lay on their side as if to declare their part in the mess. Willie walked directly to them, ignoring the oil that crept into his shoes and overalls. He stood above them and stared at the culprits and deliberately rolled them to their proper place along the station's wall. He righted them and turned them around so he wouldn't have to see the gaping holes that had been gouged into the sides. After ensuring that the drums were carefully aligned, as they should be, he turned back and stared at the damage.

The even glow of the streetlight was interrupted by small dancing flares of red lights that gradually grew larger and more pronounced. A fire engine quietly glided to a stop alongside the station.

Two firemen surveyed the mess and, without a word, manned a hose. The water blasted the mounds of oil and sprayed a glistening coat over the building. The oil maneuvered to one side but it had nowhere to go and just built into a solid oily muck and slowly slid back into place.

Ben approached from behind the fire truck and acknowledged the firemen. They talked briefly for a few moments and then resumed the cleaning.

Ben walked the perimeter of the station and carefully avoided the tar pit. Willie was quiet as he approached. They studied the firemen as they wrestled with the flowing oil and water.

After a few moments, Ben broke the vigil: "One of your lube jobs run over?" Bad timing, he thought.

"Nah, probably a valve or busted pump."

"Yeah."

"It happens."

Ben nodded.

The fireman approached. "Can't do no more. The drains can't handle it; we're just adding to the mess. How about we pass by tomorrow and give it one more shot?"

"That'd be great." Willie reached into his pocket and came up empty. He looked to Ben and spoke softly: "Got some cash?"

"Just say thanks. They don't want your money."

Willie put his arm on the firemen's shoulder. "Thanks, a lot. Really appreciate it. Come by for a fill up or a lube or something on the station." He nodded and left.

They stood together and just stared at the waste. The gleaming red flares in the oil became smaller, and then disappeared, as the fire truck pulled away—leaving the reflection of the single streetlight undulating on the ground. Willie took out a cigarette and match—he thought better of it and put the match away. The cigarette hung from his lips, unlit. He looked up at the sign just over the doorway:

Willie's Service Station.

It was covered in sludge, along with the windows and most of the building.

"Eight years," Willie finally said, "eight fuckin' years."

"You were due for a paint job anyway."

Willie nodded.

"In a couple of weeks, it'll be like brand new."

"Better than new." Willie mustered. "Fuckin' luck."

They didn't say it, but they both knew what had happened.

Willie circled the premises several times to inspect the damage as Ben stared at the primordial gunk that used to be a gas station. There was something ironic about it turning to an oily sludge pit.

Willie stood at the far end and looked up at the sign, which hung slightly askew; he turned his back to Ben and wiped the swell in his eyes.

- 18 -

It occurred to Ben to stay out of it and let Willie work this out by himself, but he knew he wouldn't. He turned his '58 Buick Century onto MacDonald Avenue and rode under the elevated tracks. The car bounced as he straddled the long abandoned trolley tracks under the El. He should have gone the other way and given the shocks a break. But he didn't go the other way—he went this way and endured the bounce.

The screech of metal on metal from a train passing overhead meshed with the clatter of rough road. It was tough to stay focused. He knew what he wanted to get done; he had to do it and get out.

His eyes scanned right. He knew where it was, passed it a hundred times, but never went in. Before it was just a nondescript sign hanging over a common building with a bunch of anonymous people inside. It was a blur in his memory, hardly scratching the surface. That was about to change.

He pulled over, got out of the car and walked in.

The Gravesend Bar was filled with the local late afternoon crowd: two guys at the bar and the bartender. The other guys Ben knew by reputation: the big guy had to be Beefy Leonard and, of course, Charlie.

Charlie usually showed up late afternoons and late evenings, after the heavy betting was in. He didn't take book himself; he had guys for that. He just facilitated the cash flow and, like other businessmen, managed the operation, applying resources wherever necessary.

Baseball was a light season—particularly during the week—when only the heaviest gamblers bet regularly. It picked up a bit on weekends or during the Pennant and Series. Most waited for football, which drew a little more action. The horses, however, were a steady source of revenue no matter what the season. In the summer, the action was heavy from guys who couldn't make it to the track. Even when the horses went south to Hialeah and Gulfstream for the winter, they drew constant action. In fact, his handle was larger during the off-season because he didn't have to compete with the local tracks.

Charles Anthony Imperiale knew that to stay on top of his little world, a franchise that covered parts of Brighton Beach and Coney Island, he needed to be on top of every deal, every transaction. He couldn't let anyone put him over—bad for business. He had worked his way up through all the shortcuts: booze, broads, recycled cars and even owned the entire Brooklyn hubcap market.

That was before he was impaled on the rear fin of a Caddy and ruptured his spleen: an unfortunate accident that occurred as he fell from a moving car. Now he preferred to stay in the background and count the money. He loved money.

Ben had never been in the Gravesend and never met Charlie but he walked directly to him as he was taking an off-hour count at a back table. Beefy Leonard, whose looks resembled a homely Neanderthal, watched closely from the bar, ready to move if necessary. Charlie looked up.

"I'm Ben Collesano, we never met personally but we do a little business together from time—"

"A little football, a little baseball, I know."

Charlie's white hair and thick glasses made him look older than his fifty years and less intimidating than his reputation. Ben knew about the strength of power—if people think you have it, then you do. Right now, Charlie did.

"How's the wife . . . and kids?" Charlie asked.

Ben was uncomfortable dealing face to face with Charlie, preferring relatively anonymous phone transactions with his lieutenants, as small as they might be. Right to business, chitchat later, or better yet, not at all.

"Willie Urbanski's tab, I want to settle up. How much?"

"Are you sure?" Charlie was suspicious.

"I'm sure. How much?"

Charlie played with his weight: "And I was just thinking how nice it would be to own a gas station." Charlie quickly looked up Willie's tab on a small sheet of paper that magically appeared in his hand. It was an unnecessary step because he knew the number. He knew all the numbers.

"Let's see. Willie has had a string of bad luck lately."

"How much?"

"You know, he probably shouldn't be betting at all. Of course, as long as he does, I am happy that he chose to do business with me." Charlie stalled. "Of course, that implies that he pays when he loses."

"How much?"

"Nineteen thousand two hundred," Charlie was suddenly very businesslike.

"What?" Ben blurted as he was caught off guard. *Goddamn, Willie.*

"Ben, a word. You're smart. You do good business, clean. You lose, you pay. You win, you collect. Your friend is not so smart. A few more customers like him and I retire early. You want to cover for him, ok by me. I don't care where the money comes from. He'll owe you plenty."

"That's my problem."

"Nineteen thousand two hundred and still counting. Still want to settle?"

Ben hesitated but he didn't want to look indecisive. He didn't want Charlie to back him down either. He counted some bills.

"Here's twenty five hundred." Ben put them on the table without letting go. "But . . . you take no more of Willie's action. Nothing."

Charlie stared at Ben and did not look at the money.

Ben let go of the cash and said: "I'll stand up for the rest."

They stared at each other and reached an implicit understanding.

Charlie smiled, nodded and slowly picked up the money.

"How're you going to do that Ben?"

Ben ignored his shocks as he again bounced over the trolley tracks. Maybe he should have backed off and let Willie suffer the consequences. That would have been a very expensive lesson. That's what he would have done if he didn't care about the guy. *Goddamn, Willie.*

Anyway, too late, he was in—just another installment on his lifelong debt to Willie that he never could repay, no matter what. Willie didn't see it that way, but Ben did, and that was that. The car hit a pothole hard.

Goddamn.

He turned off of MacDonald Avenue and rolled the window down to let the sun bake directly on his arm. The salt air smelled like Brighton Beach. He took a deep breath, it felt good. He was tired. Strange day: first early at Willie's, then downtown for a physical and now Charlie.

And he had no clue how to answer Charlie's question.

- 19 -

Sandy Kane sat in his conference room flanked by two clients—business partners looking for a divorce. He absently looked out the window while they each recounted their own version of the history, throwing sarcastic barbs whenever the opportunity allowed. It had been raining for two weeks since Willie's station became a tar pit and now the sun was finally breaking through. The rain didn't help the cleanup and, when Willie added detergent, it became a black bubble bath and covered the sidewalk for half a block. Sandy advised Willie to file an insurance claim. He didn't and Sandy didn't push it.

Sandy turned back to *Frick and Frack*. The soon-to-be-ex-partners were suddenly quiet, each avoiding each other's gaze. "He goes or I go," they both said but they couldn't agree on whom, or more importantly, how much.

Sandy figured that he spent more time splitting people up than putting them together, not much value in that, he thought, unless you are getting paid and they are better off apart. Normally, he would see if there was an opportunity for reconciliation; sometimes people just need a mediator and a coach. Then they vent for a while and ultimately kiss and make up.

Sandy was pissed today and he was getting bored with these guys. He had waited until they dumped everything they had individually built up. Now, they both had shot their load; time to end it.

"Let me suggest a path," Sandy said in his best conciliatory and fatherly tone. "Forget about who's buying or selling. Let's decide on a price first: a number you both can live with. Then, we'll flip a coin to see who stays and who goes."

There was something elegantly simple about the solution, one that Sandy had used several times before, and *Frick and Frack* were on board. The rest was mechanical.

Sandy walked back to his office feeling satisfied. He limped slightly; his war injury got aggravated when he sat a little too long. He was awarded a Purple Heart in the Philippines for taking shrapnel in both buttocks and served the rest of his tour standing behind a desk.

With Wasserman, of Wasserman and Kane, semi-retired, Sandy ran the show which was primarily small business dealings, real estate, parking lots, some union contracts and an occasional divorce as an accommodation to a client. Not a big show, but his show nevertheless.

Eileen, his secretary, was on the phone. Sandy glanced at the inviting opening in her blouse where it should have been buttoned and took a not-so-subtle whiff as he passed. He wouldn't go beyond that with her, he thought, *too young, twenty-two, an old twenty-two, but twenty-two.*

Sandy turned into his office; Ben stood there in his fireman's uniform.

"Beer?"

The afternoon bar crowd was light as Ben listened intently. The muffled sounds of a baseball game came from the small TV over the bar.

"Al and Paula are over," Sandy confided. "He came home one night, all warm and cuddly, wanted a truce." He looked around to make sure that their conversation was private. "Tried to renew the feelings they had when they got married . . . any of the times," Sandy paused then proceeded in a dramatic whisper. "It was a beautiful night and they're in bed . . . he gets up and looks out the window and tells her to get out of bed and look at the moon."

"The moon?"

"The moon."

"Al? My Al? Bull?"

"This is his side of it remember." Sandy tried to hold back the laugh but the grin on his face gave him away. "So she looks up at him, all romantic and loving," Sandy widened his eyes and blinked romantically, "and she says . . . she says, for him to take the moon and the stars and, if he could work it out, a coupla planets and shove them all up his ass."

Ben's beer splattered on his pants. Sandy somehow continued the roll.

"So he loses it and goes apeshit. He proceeds to destroy every piece of furniture in the apartment. It took the police twenty minutes to find her . . . stuffed in a closet. Anyway, they're over."

"That's why he hasn't been around. He alright?"

"Fine. He's staying with his mom."

"Good."

"The moon?"

"The moon."

They let the Al situation digest as they sat in silence.

"And you?" Sandy said. "You just happen to be in the neighborhood?"

"Was downtown filling out some papers. I'm quitting the department."

"Quitting?"

"Well, they're retiring me. They want me to take a medical discharge. Out in eighteen years instead of forever. Besides I'm not cut out to write tickets or be on the line again. And,' Ben hesitated, "I'd never make it out of another burner. Used up all my chances. Anyway, I don't have a choice; they want me to take it now."

"Now?"

"I have a month. It'll get me out at a little more than half pay."

"Then what? You couldn't live on twice pay."

"It's worse than that." Ben signaled for another round. Usually one beer was enough but today wasn't usual. Sandy waited for Ben to complete his thought. "Willie. I stepped up to Willie's paper to Charlie."

"What? Why did you . . .?"

The look on Ben's face answered Sandy's question.

"How much?"

"Nineteen thousand, some change."

"What? How the fuck did he—"

"Doesn't matter, he did. And they were pressing. That's how come the oil bath at the station."

The bartender brought over two fresh bottles.

"The oil leak?" Sandy asked.

Ben nodded: "not a leak. At least, not an accident."

"Fuck. That's why Willie didn't jump on it."

"What do you mean?"

"I wanted him to file an insurance claim or something to cover some of the costs but he didn't want to talk about it. Now I understand. How did I miss that? Shit. And you stepped up for his nut?"

"I would've done it for you too. And you, me."

Sandy nodded. "What about you? What're you going to do?"

"I didn't pick the timing. I'm starting over again at forty—from deep in a hole." Ben went on. His tone changed to one of admiration: "Look, you go to work, people pay for your advice and they respect you. All I have is a lot of years behind me and nothing to show for it. Even if I stayed with the department, I'd just be treading water. I'm going to leave some good friends behind but the path I was on was just getting narrower. I always knew I'd have to face this day—just thought I'd have more time to plan for it. If I have any chance at anything, I've got to take the shot now."

"What are you going to do?"

"The only thing I can."

Sandy knew what he meant and what the upshot was. They sat silently.

"Does Kitty know?" Sandy asked.

Ben had been avoiding that inevitable question. But he couldn't duck it now—it was the next hurdle between now and the future.

The lights of Luna Park glowed against the overcast sky as Kitty and Ben walked the boardwalk in drizzle.

"Do you know how many times we've been here?" Kitty asked.

"Twenty three."

"Really?"

"Yep, twenty seven times."

"You don't know."

"I could be right." Ben stalled for the right moment. "Quit your job and let's get married."

Surprised, Kitty asked, "Why?"

"Because we love each other and—"

"No, why should I quit my job?"

"Too much travel and—"

"We've been through this . . . going to Stockholm with Mr. Sacker was just—"

"And six other guys."

"And six other guys. But that was . . ." Ben could have completed the sentence. This was a replay of a conversation that would head in the same direction as it had many times before. They continued to walk in silence as the rain picked up. This was not the comfortable silence of two friends; this was different—this silence was loud and uncomfortable. Ben sensed the distance between them and he felt uncharacteristically insecure. He glanced over at Kitty to get a reading when she stopped and turned toward him. "Ok." She slowly brought her head up and met his eyes. "Ok."

"Ok?"

"Ok. Let's get married . . . after all; I have to do something after I quit my job."

Ben embraced her like she had been totally lost for an instant and just as quickly found again. Her smile was only outdone by his. They kissed and all the anxiety of the last few moments had evaporated. They became one, once again.

"Your father? Should I ask him?"

"What?"

Ben raised his voice to be heard against the rain. *"Your father? Should I ask him?"*

"I already asked him for you."

"You did? And, what did he say?"

"Who?" She played with him. It was her moment.

"Your father."

"He said that you're a good man," she spoke softly and her words seem to meld with the raindrops, *"and when you're ready to provide for a family properly you should marry me."* She looked into his eyes. *"Are you ready?"*

"Your father didn't say that."

"He would have." Kitty had a painless way of being direct.

"You want me to stop playing the horses, don't you?"

"Yes. Will you?" Kitty's voice trembled as if the answer would have significant consequences. *"Will you?"* She repeated, even less secure than before.

He knew that that was more than just a question. It was her perfect moment. She had carved out a perfect package: the job and the marriage in exchange for the horses. He knew that if she was ever going to get him to stop, this was the right time and the right reason—for both of them.

The raindrops splashed off the boardwalk and sparkled with the billion lights of Luna Park. They walked arm in arm and followed a luminescent path that seemed to lead them just where they were going—knowing that everything had just changed; that everything had just begun.

Ben hadn't been to the track since that night.

- 20 -

Ben sat shotgun and studied *The Racing Form* as Sandy's Olds wove through the rainy evening traffic on the Deegan. The tires shushed over the wet road and the wipers pulsed to a sleepy rhythm as he tried to focus—trying to reorient himself to an ancient language. But everything was new now. He momentarily rested his eyes.

Suddenly, he was thrown right and slammed against the door as the car swerved. It skidded left; out of the center lane, then smoothly right again, back to its original position. It was as if the move was intentional—as if it never happened. Everyone was awake now; no one spoke.

Ben glanced towards Willie who clenched the steering wheel with both hands and peered intently through the rain-swept windshield. In the rear, Al absently watched the water track over the window and Sandy settled back in to his half sleep. It was like Chadosh's—only different.

Willie carefully checked the rear view mirror and abruptly tried to change lanes again.

"Signal." Al's deep voice broke the silence.

"Did." Willie replied.

"No fuckin' way." Al backed off and stared out the window. Al felt sorry for Willie ever since Willie's station became a big oil slick. He declared a truce, an amnesty, no more bickering.

"If I signaled, I wouldn't have had time to make the maneuver."

"What maneuver? You changed lanes—it's not a fuckin' maneuver. You wouldn't know a maneuver from shinola. You shoulda signaled." His tone became more condescending: "Maneuver."

"I'll signal twice next time."

"Putz." Fuck the amnesty.

Willie let it drop—Al could be a prick sometimes. He looked in the rearview and caught Sandy momentarily awake.

"As much as I like driving your car," Willie engaged Sandy, "it's time for a new one."

"Your piece of shit is older than this," Sandy responded without opening his eyes. A confident smile crossed his face. "After tonight, new cars for everybody." He resumed his half sleep and focused on slowly unbuttoning Eileen's blouse.

Slowly, button by button: his hand just grazed her soft twenty-two year old breasts. She breathed heavily. He undid one button, then another—his fingers lightly touching her soft skin. He could feel her warm breath now as he became conscious of his own. This is what he promised himself would never happen—and it never would. Maybe this is why it excited him so much. She was untouchable. But he was touching her now. He felt himself get hard. His hand slid across her skin and methodically reached under her—

"Just kidding boychik," Willie's voice once again shattered the quiet. "Besides, I like your wreck. I mean, I like to repair it every month, it'll put my kids through high school."

"Can you drive this heap any faster?" Al's sarcasm couldn't camouflage his jitters. "Where the fuck are we?"

"You drive sometime." Willie checked the mirror once more—he had succeeded in waking up the car.

"Benny," Al leaned forward and put his hand on Ben's shoulder and broke his concentration, "how good is this?"

"It's good."

"You sure?"

"You want a guarantee?" Ben snapped back, realizing that he really didn't know how good it was. *It's a tip—sometimes they work, sometimes not.* Twenty years ago, it would've been different—he would've known how good it was. But then, twenty years ago, he knew how good he was. Ben turned back to Al: "It's good, we got a shot."

"I was just thinking . . . if this works . . ." Al contemplated.

"The Syndicate!" Willie blurted out. "Just like the old days at Jamaica. The Syndicate is back. I can't wait; I haven't made a bet in weeks."

"Getting religion?" Al teased.

"Just took a break."

Ben knew that it was time to get off this subject. "Take the next exit, it's quicker."

Willie caught his own smile in the rear view mirror. He abruptly changed lanes and narrowly missed another car that had the same idea. The Olds fishtailed, swerved back and somehow, once again, righted itself into the lane.

"Jesus Christ, Willie!" Al jumped.

"Sorry."

"No fuckin' signal that time."

Putz.

"We've got time," Ben said calmly as he put *The Racing Form* aside and watched the road.

"You really want me to get rid of this car, don't you?" Sandy joked. "Tell you what, give me a thousand and free gas for a year and it's yours."

"I told you, I appreciate your repeat business."

"I hope you guys know what you're doing?" Al added.

"You want out now, just say so," Sandy countered.

"No."

"You sure?"

"I'm sure."

"Willie?" Sandy polled.

"I want a state."

"What?"

"I want a state. Nothing big, you know, like Rhode Island."

Everyone laughed, even Al. The release was timely.

"Benny, what's the count?" Sandy had a way of bringing everyone back to the mission.

"All in, about a thousand."

"A couple of months pay." Willie chimed in.

If you're working. The thought bounced inside of Ben's head as he tried not to think about Kitty. He was unsuccessful. She wouldn't be happy about his being here, doing what he was about to do; but she wasn't dealing with Willie's crap, and she wasn't supporting the family, and she wasn't about to be out of a job. A promise is a promise; that was a long time ago. Now is now.

The distant glow in the night sky refocused Ben on the matters of the moment. An anxiety slowly grew—it was familiar and there was something strangely secure about the uncertainty of the outcome. His skills were ancient, rusty. This was new territory—but new territory in an old way. His stomach tightened.

Yonkers Raceway looked like a huge luminescent snow globe that hovered just alongside the highway. The drizzle and fog caught the millions of candlepower coming from the track below and created an aura of excitement and anticipation. Even in a rain storm in the middle of the week Yonkers Raceway drew a crowd.

- 21 -

The fourth race had just gone off when they stepped into the grandstand. The four men stood there taking it in—almost unsure of what to do next. Ben knew they were counting on him; *he* was counting on him, which made him the least sure of them all. This was the *trots*. The horses were standardbreds, not thoroughbreds like Jamaica, which had closed the year earlier. The horses had sulkies and drivers as opposed to jockeys. The handicapping was different and everyone knew that they were fixed. Ben had no advantage here—it wasn't his game.

Instead of studying the horses, he had spent the week studying the betting—the mechanics, the numbers and the payoffs. Everything changed since Jamaica, everything. It was totally automated and there were no flaws in the system; there were no books to *dutch*. He'd have to find something else, an edge.

For the next few races, each of the guys went his own way and just bet: casual, dumb, civilian betting. In the fifth race, Willie bet on two horses, a tip from a customer, and on another horse, Laurel, which reminded him of his daughter, Laura. Laurel won, paying $11.40. He was ecstatic and down only sixty bucks. Al just bet the three and the eight in each race because those were Paula's favorite numbers. Sandy was still thinking of Eileen and couldn't concentrate so he went to the men's room and masturbated. His head clear, he went on to bet the sixth and the seventh races and lost both. Ben didn't bet; he just watched the action: the betting, the races and the players. The machine started in motion just after the seventh race.

It was the second half of the Twin Double, a new betting phenomenon designed for huge payoffs to attract more people to the track. Ben and Sandy conferred and slowly approached three men standing by the Cashier's window.

Al walked up to Willie who watched the transaction from a distance.

"How good is this tip?" Al asked.

"Hold on. I want to see this."

"What's going on?"

They watched Ben and the strangers talk: one then the other. They were negotiating.

"Ok, you're in my league now." Willie tutored with a rare display of authority. "The Twin Double is a four-race parley—you win the first two races you can bet the next two. Win all four and you're in pig heaven, a gazillionaire."

"And if you only win three?"

"You go home with the rest of the losers."

They stood and watched the action until Al asked: "So?"

"So?"

"So . . . what're they doing?"

"I think they're buying tickets from some guys who won the first two races."

"Got it."

Willie did not have to see Al's face to know that he didn't get it.

Ben and Sandy exchanged money and tickets with the three guys and shook hands. Ben walked to the Seller's window.

"What's going on?"

"Dunno."

Sandy rejoined and updated the group.

"Ben just bought tickets from guys that are still alive. They walked away with a big profit and we have tickets to parlay into the last two races."

"What's the—" Al started.

"One of the first two horses was a long shot, which means that the payoff will be big." Sandy turned to look for Ben who was returning. "And, it's even better if you've got a lock on the last race."

Ben joined them.

"Done. We have the three, five, six and eight in the eighth race and wheeled them into the three in the ninth."

As the men walked to their seats, Willie continued to educate Al. "If any of the four horses wins in this race, then we're alive for the last race with Ben's tip."

Al had enough. "Yeah, yeah." He liked him better stupid.

The men sat just as the track announcer blared: "They're off!"

"Root for the three," Sandy yelled, "or the five, six or eight."

"C'mon six," Willie yelled. "My favorite number," he said to Al as if he cared.

The crowd moved slowly to the rail and the horses rounded the track in single file for the first lap. As the second lap began, the intensity of the crowd picked up. Willie and Al stood on their feet, Sandy joined them.

Ben sat. This was too familiar—a rush of memories traversed his body from every direction. His adrenalin pumped and there was electricity tingling through his body. It was as if every cell that was asleep for so long awakened to the sound of the crowd and the tension of the moment.

The horses came around the final turn with the six in front. In the stretch, his lead increased and no one was going to catch him.

"Six, six, six!" Willie yelled as he slapped Al with his program. "My favorite number, I told you."

Everyone stood as the horse crossed the finish line. Al hugged Willie who stood on his seat. Sandy and Ben smiled professionally and gave each other the Jamaica thumbs-up.

"One down, one to go," Willie announced.

"Who do we like here?" Al said, feeling the electricity.

"Only one, the three," Ben said.

"Are you saving?" Sandy asked Ben.

"Now is as good a time as any."

Ben and Sandy got up and walked to the Seller's windows.

Al didn't want Willie to start again but—

"A save." Willie jumped in. "He's just hedging his bet—our bet. Betting another horse just in case."

"I thought his tip was good, a lock."

"You never know."

Willie and Al sat silently facing the track and watched the horses warm up for the next race.

The horses were beginning to get ushered into the starting gate when Ben and Sandy returned with two clean cut, stocky guys in their thirties.

"Guys, meet Carl and Tommy, they're our new partners," Ben explained. "They have a twin ticket on the *five* horse and we have the *three*. We've got twenty percent of their action and they've got twenty percent of ours."

The men shook hands and wished each other luck.

"Did you see the price?" Willie screeched. "The *three* pays thirty six thousand, thirty six thousand!" He looked at the tote board in the center of the track. "The *five* pays twelve thousand. C'mon *three*."

Willie realized that he had new partners and continued: "C'mon *five*... but mostly *three*."

Everybody was ecstatic and joined Willie's rooting.

Willie plopped down next to Al. "Ok. We get twenty percent of their twelve grand, if the five wins. But if the three wins, we gotta give them twenty percent of our thirty six grand which comes to . . ."

"Seventy two hundred beanos. I got it."

Ben sat back. This is exactly where he wanted to be. They had a sure thing and, just in case, an insurance bet. He kept his optimism in check because he knew: *you never know*. There was still another race to win.

"I want to hold the tickets," Willie demanded.

"We'll hold them together," Carl said suspiciously and diplomatically.

Ben handed the tickets to Willie who put them together with Carl's tickets and both men held an end, imprisoning Al who sat between them.

"Gotta take a leak," Al said.

Neither man was letting go of the tickets. Al tried to slide under this human bridge but was too big. Willie and Carl hung on. Al stood on his seat and climbed over the back, cursing as he left. Ben and Sandy observed this scene incredulously and couldn't hold back the laugh. Why hold it back now? They were in great shape.

"And, they're off!" blared over the speakers.

Willie and Carl jumped to their feet like they were attached at the hip. Al returned as the horses lined the rail and at the end of the first lap, the *three* was in third place, the *five* dead last. Everyone was on his feet now.

"C'mon *three* and *five*," Willie yelled, "but mostly *three*."

The roar started earlier than normal; there was still half a race to go. Al bellowed, "*three*, you mother fucker, *three!*"

Ben and Sandy reserved their cheering for the stretch run.

"This is the big one Benny," Sandy said. "Let's bring it home."

"Bigger than you know," Ben confessed. "I put the house on this."

Sandy stopped watching the race and just looked at Ben.

"I took out a second mortgage—" Ben did not make eye contact.

Sandy continued looking at Ben waiting for him to finish.

Ben turned to Sandy: "With Charlie." Ben's look told Sandy that he had no choice.

The crowd noise intensified and they both strained to see the horses enter the final eighth mile. There was only one thing they could do now; they yelled, "C'mon *three, three, three!*"

The *seven* was in front with the *one* and the *five* packed closely behind. The *three* came out of the turn wide and was furiously trying to advance on the leader but had extra ground to cover.

There was an amnesty for everything in this spiritual moment. Willie and Al held hands. Al even missed Paula and promised that, should they ever get together again, it would be for forever. Willie told God he wanted to collect on what he owed him because half of Rowan's visits to church were actually his and, as a bonus, he promised to give up smoking and stop biting his nails. It seemed to help because at the sixteenth pole, the three started to advance on the pack. The *three* was in third position with a hundred yards to go. Everything was riding on this.

"C'mon, c'mon." Ben thought he was whispering but he was as loud as everyone else. "Three! Three!"

The crowd was so loud it almost could not be heard. The men were screaming at the top of their range. Willie stood on the seat and jumped up and down.

Three, three, three!

Inches separated the *three* from the leader and those inches were disappearing fast. Ben gripped the program tightly. *He was moving but was there enough track left for him to close?*

The driver cracked the whip high over the horse's head.

Three, three, three!

The horses matched strides—in rhythm. The driver lifted the whip showed it to the horse; suddenly, the *three* horse lunged forward and instinctively stretched for the invisible line.

The *three* wins at the wire!

Willie jumped on Ben's back. Carl, Tommy and Al hugged.

Ben threw his arms in the air in a rare display of raw emotion and let out a yell, "We did it!"

They did it. At that moment they were the happiest men on the planet. Ben fell into his seat, shaken and relieved. Every emotion that he had stored up the last few weeks crisscrossed through his body. He shivered.

It worked, Jesus Christ, it worked.

- 22 -

The rest was simple: collect the money, divvy it up and go home. The crowd dispersed and the six men stood nervously outside the Cashier's window. They were animated, happy and edgy. Nothing could go wrong now because they were winners. Collect and go. Sandy walked over to a uniformed Pinkerton guard, a black man, about fifty. He handed the guard the winning tickets and the guard walked to the Cashier's window.

"What's goin' on?" Carl wanted to know.

"We're getting a ten percenter to cash our tickets to avoid Uncle Sam." Ben explained as he watched the guard go inside. "He pays the taxes and we give him ten percent. Capice?"

Carl nodded, but was still suspicious. "Out of whose end?"

"Out of everybody's end. It comes off the top."

Carl thought about it and nodded. He looked around and checked out Willie who stood behind him.

Willie anxiously lit a cigarette. *Who are these guys?* He checked out Tommy who was looking at Al circling the group like a sheep dog.

Al caught Tommy's eye and didn't release until he did. He then looked at Carl and saw a gun holstered in Carl's belt. Al caught Ben's eye who caught the gun also. *Shit.*

Ben looked at Sandy who eyed an attractive girl passing behind Carl. Ben and Sandy connected and Sandy picked up on the gun as well. They all looked at Tommy and Carl who were looking for the Pinkerton with the cash.

Willie looked at his watch. "Been gone a long time."

"Yeah," Sandy agreed. "Be right back."

"Where's he going?" Carl asked.

"Dunno."

The men continued checking out everything as their euphoria abruptly changed into paranoia. Sandy returned.

"Got it covered," Sandy said, "I hired another Pinkerton to watch the first."

"We got us a posse," Willie joked.

No one was laughing; there was a higher priority now. Sandy pulled Ben aside while the men focused on the Cashier's door.

"These guys ok?" Ben asked.

"I hope so. I think they're cops from upstate."

"You sure?"

"No."

"Oh. Be right back," Ben headed towards the Men's room.

"Where's he going?" Tommy asked suspiciously.

"Man's gotta pee," Willie said.

Carl and Tommy looked at each other to see if the other thought that this was ok. They looked at the Cashier's door and at Willie and Sandy. Sandy focused on the Cashier's door.

Ben stood in front of the mirror and stared straight ahead but didn't see anything; his mind was somewhere else. He took a breath and a chill ran through his body and welled in his eyes. He thought about the hole he put himself in by stepping up for Willie and putting up his house—definitely out of character. It was an unnecessary risk. But that's history—with their cuts, they're just about off the hook.

Much too close.

He exhaled and a thousand pounds of pressure dissipated from his head. An image of Kitty flashed and he imagined her reaction if she had found out about everything. He splashed enough water on his face to clear him of everything except getting the money and cleaning his slate. One more sigh of relief to acknowledge that he had just dodged two major bullets. Then he put it to bed.

Everyone stood, eyes fixed on the Cashier's door, as Ben rejoined the group.

"Not out yet?" He looked at Sandy, "Get somebody else to—"

Sandy anticipated the request and was on his way. He approached another Pinkerton guard and after a brief discussion, the guard walked to the Cashier's door, which opened as he got there. The first Pinkerton motioned Sandy inside. Sandy motioned to Willie who walked briskly into the door with Sandy.

Carl checked out Ben as Tommy strained to follow Al who continued to slowly circle the group. Ben glanced at Carl's gun and focused on the door. It was quiet. The floor was almost empty except for the guys, a few cleaning people and several men who lingered—nowhere better to go. They waited in the quiet which had its own way of adding pressure to the moment.

The door opened.

Willie beamed as he exited followed by Sandy and the three Pinkertons close behind. Willie's pockets bulged, unmistakably filled with cash. He did not hold back his smile as he approached the group but then, seeing Ben, he must have realized that he should be more discreet and turned it off. The group huddled around Willie, forming a human cordon as they walked towards the exit.

The six men walked unnaturally close in a tight group down a long empty hallway, then down a ramp. They were serious and even more suspicious, now that they had the money. Three cheerful and laughing Pinkertons followed closely behind.

Sandy edged Al aside. "Go ahead with the Pinkies and get us a room." He looked towards his new partners, "and when we're there, keep your eyes on Frick and Frack."

He then turned to his new partners: "We'll meet you at the motel."

"We'll go together," Carl asserted.

"We'll go together."

The rain had stopped by the time Sandy's Olds pulled into the motel parking lot. The headlights beamed onto Al standing at the open motel room door as if he were the grand host welcoming very special guests. Next to him stood the three Pinkies enjoying a private joke or just happy to be off work and collecting a little extra cash. Al clapped to welcome the entourage.

Ben and Willie popped out of the front seat and Sandy, wedged between beefy Carl and Tommy, crawled out last. They walked briskly into the room. Sandy, last in the room, closed and locked the door behind him.

Suddenly, money filled the air. Willie took a stack of bills from each pocket, tossed them up as they separated into smaller floaters. Bills rained down as Willie took the rest of the money and dumped it on the bed. Sandy kept one eye on the money and the other one his new partners. The men enjoyed the brief celebration in the small room. After all, this was what it was all about—the payoff.

"OK, let's cut this up quickly and get out of here," Ben gathered the money and, in full view, put it into neat bundles once again—he started to divvy it. "We'll pay the Pinkies first, then we'll split the rest." He looked to the group for agreement, which came immediately.

"Here's the count we owe you." He isolated a stack of bills. "Thirty six hundred for cashing the ticket," he said to the first Pinky.

"And you guys," He looked to the other Pinkies for affirmation, "get one fifty each for keeping us company. And, because you were such good company, we're going to make it an even two hundred each."

The Pinkies, cheerful and laughing a moment ago, were not now. Pinky three, a large black man, looked at Ben, "Not enough."

"Not enough?" Sandy jumped in, "we agreed to one fifty and we're giving you two, plus the ten percent. Want do you want?"

"All of it," Pinky three said as he unbuttoned his holster and brought his gun to his side. He cocked it menacingly.

The other Pinkies stood behind him and casually brought out their weapons.

Fuck!

Carl and Tommy froze.

"Guys, be smart," Sandy put on his best negotiating hat. He was focused on preventing the situation from sliding further downhill as much as keeping the money. "You've got four thousand here without a problem. Why fuck it up?"

"I'll tell you what," Ben reached for anything, "we'll double your cut to eight thousand for the three of you. No questions asked. Clean, still friends. Eight thousand and you walk away with a clean conscience."

"The money," Pinky three was adamant as he pointed to the money, "one way or the other."

Willie looked at Ben.

Ben was trapped. *Make the smart bet.*

Carl and Tommy, confused, looked at each other and the money.

Ben handed him the money.

"Be smart gentlemen," Pinky three said as he made for the door. "It was never in your pocket so it's not coming out of your pocket. Cut your losses right here."

The door closed.

Al stood next to the door just as the posse closed it behind them. He looked back towards Ben and the guys. He tensed and started to coil as if to explode; his hand grabbed the doorknob. Ben had seen that look before—usually right before some kind of mayhem. But right now, that look could only take this spiral further down.

Ben grabbed his arm and wedged his leg against the door. He knew he could not hold him back if Bull really wanted after them. *Don't do anything stupid Bull.*

"Cool down." He whispered, knowing that the sound of his voice would do more for Al than his words. "We'll get it back."

Al looked at Ben again.

"Fuck!"

Ben put his hand on top of Al's on the doorknob and gently removed it.

"Al, there'll be another time."

Al's face displayed an anguish that Ben hadn't seen before. He backed down, defeated.

Ben turned to Carl, "You guys do something. You're cops, do something."

"Cops? We're not cops. We're security guards."

"What?"

". . . at Sears."

"You have guns," Willie jumped in. "Use them."

"Not loaded—too dangerous."

Shit.

Suddenly, the door flew open and Al ran out as if he were going to tackle the car and shake it until the posse and the money fell at his feet.

Ben and the rest followed him out.

The car was gone—with the posse and the winnings.

Shit!

"Goddamn it, call the police," Willie yelled to no one in particular. "We know where to find these guys."

Ben looked at Sandy, then Willie. "Can't do it."

"Why not? Throw their asses in jail. Beat the living crap outa them."

"Wouldn't do any good." Sandy explained. "They cashed the ticket."

"I know."

"No, *they* cashed the ticket—not us. Legally, it's theirs."

"But . . . you're a lawyer, do something."

"Legally, we're fucked," Sandy added.

Carl woke up from his trance and approached Ben with a new bravado. "Well, you do something. We have a deal—a piece of ours for a piece of yours. Your nag won. You owe us twenty percent, that's over seven grand."

"Actually, after their cut, it's sixty four hundred," Ben corrected him as he looked down the empty Yonkers street. "And it just left with the posse."

- 23 -

Ben's house, a modest two-story white frame structure, was a little above his means. He liked it that way. Money, is to enjoy, not put aside—live one level above where you are so you have something to aspire to and, more importantly, to be able to show that you belonged.

He took the stairs deliberately, two at a time, careful not to awaken anyone. The rain had started again and the constant drumming against the windows was a reminder of the night that had just passed. He stopped by his sons' room and peered in through the open door: unconscious of time, he just stood there. He never had the feeling that he had let them down—until now.

He kissed them on the forehead and slowly pulled the blankets over their shoulders to protect them from the cold rainy night—a night that had suddenly turned on them. He closed the door gently and walked into the bedroom. Kitty should be asleep.

She was. She lay there softly, safely. Kitty was a rock—she always knew what she wanted: never wavered, never hesitated. And she would do anything to protect what was hers. Yet, she shared freely—as long as it was her choice. A wisp of hair lay across her face.

He leaned over her and put her hair back into its position, careful not to wake her. Her warmth emanated from the bed and he wanted to crawl in with her and hold her close and escape in some indefinable cocoon. He wanted to tell her that everything would work out; and not to worry because he never let her down before and he wouldn't this time. He has it figured out, just needed a little time, some breathing room. He wanted to tell her all of that and more but now was not a good time. As if there was a good time.

He touched her shoulder lightly to connect and the wisp of hair dropped over her face again. He left it there.

As he took off his shirt, he stood by the window and watched as the rain slanted through the aura of the streetlight. It was an early fall shower that made the leaves glisten as they made their final lazy trip to the street below. It had been a long time since he stared at the rain. How could something so simple, so common, could be so beautiful? He pictured young boys running through leaves piled high on the edges of the street. There was nothing on their minds except the leaves; for them, there was only that pile of leaves until the next one. For an instant he forgot where he was; a smile emerged.

But not for long.

Goddamn it. I was out.

He did everything right, everything. All of his problems had been swept away—his and Willie's—in one brilliant move. Then they reappeared.

Fuck!

The night had fatigued him. The bed was inviting but once he lay down, he would be one step closer to waking up. It was a tough night.

Tomorrow will be tougher.

A handful of Cheerios flew through the air as Rick sat innocently reading his Action comic. They landed on Scooter, the dinette table and the floor.

"Hey."

Rick didn't look up. This was the best part: the test to see how long he could keep from laughing. He bit the inside of his cheek as he continued reading.

Scooter decided to let it lie and went back to Batman.

Rick slyly scooped a bigger batch of Cheerios and let them fly. Again he sat innocently oblivious as the game continued. Each time, Rick was more brazen, until Scooter spun around just as he let go with the Cheerio assault.

Retaliation came in the form of a spoonful of milk in Rick's face: a bold move, considering that his older brother dominated him and was always the victorious in the inevitable fight. They fought the way brothers fought—no real damage, just a clash that would usually wind up with laughter and occasional crying. They wouldn't be so happy if they heard the conversation Ben and Kitty were having on the other side of the screen door.

The smell of rain still permeated the air. A shaft of sunlight brightened the small lawn bordered by some rose beds and a peach tree that Ben's father had planted the year before he died. It was flanked on two sides by garage walls and on the other by a stockade fence. This was the family's oasis—their private enclave. The last roses of the season hung limply from their stems as the rain and the prior night's chill too had beaten them down as well. Wet leaves littered the lawn.

Kitty turned away from Ben, trembling. He reached out and put his hand on her shoulder to comfort her; she stepped forward to disengage. The few feet between them were insignificant to the gap that had just grown.

If you have a bad run, clean it up and move on. Ben had wiped the slate clean and told Kitty everything—the job, Charlie, the house, and the horses. He didn't know which would be the hardest part. As it unfolded, each confession was worse than the one before. He told her about everything—everything except Willie; for some reason he didn't tell her about Willie.

"The track?"

Ben nodded.

"The track, Ben. The track?"

There was nothing more to say. No defense was good enough—not for her and, suddenly, not even for him. He explained everything once, twice, until it began to sound implausible—and some of it was. He didn't define his debt to Charlie or how it occurred. It was just a big number, big enough so that everything was on the line. It happened, he was sorry and he would figure a way out of it; that's the bottom line, the details were irrelevant. Then he started to doubt his actions and his motivation. Was that his only way out? There were other choices—just not good ones. Sometimes all you have are bad choices—and no matter what you do, the best you can hope for is that the wind is blowing your way.

The distance grew.

His confession stopped but she had stopped listening long before. It was just a bad turn. He didn't have to mention the twenty years of good turns—that was history; that was expected; that was the past. He did what he did and they are where they are.

You can't change the past.

He stepped behind her and put his hands on her shoulders—hoping that she would sink back into him and they would reach the point where they could figure this out together. It was all on the table.

"It will be Ok." He whispered. "Everything will work . . ."

She turned to him and dropped her head in his chest.

"I'm pregnant."

She stood in the yard long after Ben had tried his best to explain, apologize and comfort. She heard little of what she said after his initial confession. The rest was details, explanation, rationalization—none of that mattered. He did what he did and we are where we are.

It wasn't the job, or the house, or even the horses; it was all of it. Everything she had, or thought she had, and everything she had believed in, suddenly didn't exist. Suddenly it was all in front of her again; the future was uncertain. But not like when she was back in her father's house starting her life and the future held beautiful unknowns, beautiful adventure and a partner that she trusted more than she trusted herself. Suddenly, it was dark and onerous and she had two kids and one on the way and a house that probably wouldn't be theirs anymore.

She had been let down and her foundation was shattered.

She cried for the rest of that day and hadn't cried since. That was the last time they had that conversation or any part of it—there wasn't any follow up, questions, further confessions, explanations or support. Nothing.

Their interaction was limited to events of the day and kid stuff. They were civil but their relationship clearly regressed; emptiness and formality permeated. She was violated and betrayed and uncharacteristically unstable.

And the one question asked Ben had still not been answered.

"What now, Ben? What now?"

- 24 -

"Why did we get the Pinkies?" Willie lifted his beer and emptied the bottle. "We didn't need the Pinkies." Goodies Tavern reeked like a beer-filled ashtray: a welcoming smell to the regulars, a home away from home, a respite, a shelter, a no-hassle escape. No job, wife, no nothing. Bitch when you want and talk however the fuck you wanted to talk. The guys were guys and even the few ladies who showed could handle the guys being guys. The Yankees were on the small black and white TV over the bar.

Sandy, Al and Willie hovered over their beer at a table in the center of the room performing a post mortem on the preceding night's events. They went through what happened, what they thought happened, what should've happened, and what didn't happen—like going home with a ton of money.

They took a hit—they had the money, counted the money, split the money, and even spent some of it—but they didn't. They talked about it until there was a scab over it and they couldn't feel it anymore. There was nothing new to add to this conversation as they had been through every aspect of the events several times. They almost beat it to death—so they would never have to talk or think about it again—although they knew they would.

"Still didn't need the Pinkies." Willie went on. "There were four of us; besides we had Bull. Bull is like four guys; we woulda had eight guys. Eight guys; we didn't need the Pinkies."

"Seven." Al countered.

"Huh?"

"Seven of us; you said eight. You counted me five times. I should be only four."

"So?"

"So, if I'm four, then Sandy and Ben and you putzo makes seven, not eight, seven."

"Ok. So we woulda had seven guys—still shoulda never had gotten the Pinkies—didn't need them."

Al nodded—not necessarily in agreement—more to punctuate that the conversation had been worn down and had, once again, ended. Willie nodded. Sandy nodded absently—almost robotically—he hadn't been part of this exchange. They lifted their beers. Al looked over at the Yankee game—anything to shift gears.

"How much?" Willie asked.

"How much what?" Al said reluctantly, without taking his eyes off the small TV over the bar.

"How much was our take. I mean the split. How much didn't I win?"

"Who the fuck cares?"

"Well, we didn't need the goddamn Pinkies." Willie repeated.

"You said that already." Al didn't take his eyes off the game.

"So, I'm saying it again."

Al didn't respond.

"Actually, we did need them." Sandy's response startled Willie; he hadn't said anything for the past half hour.

"Yeah, I guess." Willie thought about it. "You sure?"

"We needed them to cash the ticket so we wouldn't have to pay taxes on the money we didn't get. And we needed them for insurance that someone, like the upstate Frick and Frack cops from Sears, wouldn't get some stupid ideas about the money that we don't have."

"Yeah. Forgot about them."

"Well, it's over," Al, sensing that Sandy had put the nail in it, went for closure. "And we almost won. Who needs another beer? Tomorrow's another . . ."

"We *did* win. Benny did real good." Willie added. "But . . ."

"But it's history." Sandy was exasperated. He made brief eye contact with Al who rolled his eyes back. "Let's move on."

"It was a good play," Willie signaled for another round, "We just got burnt."

"We didn't get burnt," Al punctuated, "we got fucked."

"Yeah."

They sat silently for a moment.

"What I can't figure," Sandy wondered, "Was those Pinkies. I totally misread them."

"How could you know?" The veins in Al's neck started to bulge pumping blood into his reddened face. "When is this fuckin' conversation going to end? I've been at funerals that were parties compared to you guys. You couldn't know. It just happened; let's forget it. It happened; it never happened. Who the fuck cares? We got fucked or burnt up the ass—it doesn't fuckin' matter. For all we know the four horse could've stepped on its dick and finished next Thursday. Who the fuck cares? It's done."

"It was the three horse." Willie corrected.

"What?"

"You said the four horse; it was the three horse."

Al's eyes defocused and widened; his face flushed as he straightened up and his choke hold on the bottle tightened. He clenched as his body tensed.

Willie had seen that look before—usually just before someone lay on the ground in a limp heap. He braced. But then, just as abruptly, Al slumped back in his chair, uncharacteristically defeated. He looked towards the corner of the bar. "What's Benny doing? What's taking him so long?"

Sandy glanced back over his shoulder. Ben stood by the phone beyond the bar, not talking, not listening, nothing.

Ben held the phone in his hand with the cord stretched to the end of its tether as if he was protecting it from receiving any more calls and himself from making any. He was far off, yet focused. He didn't expect a good conversation, and he didn't get one. Now, his mind was a void—somewhere between his business with Charlie and the wedge that had formed between he and Kitty. Problems as different as they could be—yet not unrelated.

He never had a real plan but, if he had, this wasn't part of it. He hit rough spots before—but he had always seen a way out. No matter how tough things got, he always landed right side up. Maybe it was optimism, maybe good fortune or maybe he was just good enough to figure it out. It didn't matter. He got out. More importantly, he knew that he would—that was what kept him going.

But now had been set back and set back again. Maybe this time there was no magic bullet, maybe there was no way out of the box he crawled into. This was bad and getting worse; the direction was down and the pace was picking up. Maybe this time, there was no out.

He was unaware of Sandy behind him.

"You Ok?"

Sandy's voice didn't register.

He touched Ben's shoulder. "Benny, you Ok?"

Ben nodded as if they had been in fluid conversation.

"Have to see Charlie." He absently hung the phone.

Sandy's look prompted more.

"Tried to pull Willie out of a hole and I wind up putting myself in one." This time Ben's voice was a little more exasperated.

"Want some company?" Sandy offered as they walked back to the table.

"Huh?"

"To see Charlie. I'll go with you."

"No, I'll go tomorrow. I'm calling it a night, maybe the kids are still up."

Ben picked up his untouched bottle and took a small swallow. "Taking off. Speak to you tomorrow," he said to no one in particular.

They watched him leave. There was a certain resignation in the air.

"He took a big hit. It's one thing to be wrong and lose, but when you send it in and you're right . . ." Sandy's voice resonated his frustration, " . . . you're right and you win! And then lose!"

"We all lost." Al added.

"Yeah. But that was his seed. That was . . ." Sandy realized that they didn't know that Ben had stepped up for Willie and his house was on the line. They only knew they won then they lost—a singular event which would be a distant memory next week—and a story of a bad beat months from now. Down the road, they'll recall the deals Ben and Sandy made to parlay into the big payoff and the horse coming from behind and crossing the finish line and they will raise their bottles and toast to the night they won, then lost. But right now, they didn't know shit and Sandy was not going to be the one to tell them. Ben's business is Ben's business. If he wanted anyone to know, he'd tell them. "Let's move on, last night was last `night. There'll be plenty of other shots."

He raised his bottle; the others followed. They clinked three empty bottles to define the official end of this caper.

He looked around and spotted an almost good-looking woman at the bar. They made eye contact immediately.

"Al, isn't that one of your ex wives?"

Al and Willie swung around to view the target. Al took the bait.

"Not yet, but she has potential." Al got up, brushed down his sweat-marked shirt, downed the last drops out of the bottle and headed for the bar. "Excuse me gentlemen. Going to get another round."

"He means his next ex," Willie said when Al was safely out of earshot.

"He's so easy," Sandy looked Willie. "You Ok?"

"Me? Couldn't be better."

"Good." Sandy looked at his watch, "Willie, my friend. Goodnight. I have something to do."

He stood and walked passed Al at the bar, "night Al."

Al nodded without losing focus on his prey, whose eyes tracked Sandy out the door, through the front window, into the rain, into the street and into his car. He gently pawed her shoulder and regained her attention as he maneuvered his stool to block any thought of a getaway—his leg strategically perched on the crossbar of her stool.

She reminded him of Paula—maybe her hair or smile or the way she exhaled the cigarette smoke off to the side so she wouldn't blow it in his face. Paula was always considerate in that way.

His hand found her knee while his eyes locked on hers. She was about to be his prisoner; he just needed her validation. His hand worked up to her thigh while he continued penetrating what remained of her mind. She smiled politely.

Too bad about the track and what happened. Easy come, easy go. Maybe that was callous—maybe he should have felt worse about everything. It's not as if the guys lost everything—it was only money—money that they didn't have before and don't have now. They got a little less than they started the night with—a normal night at the track. It's not as if they don't have wives and families. They have plenty.

Maybe he should feel worse, maybe not. Tonight he felt good. Maybe tomorrow or next week they'll forget about it.

"Ow!"

"Sorry," Al said as he released his grip on her thigh.

"That hurt," she said as she rubbed her leg a little too dramatically.

"I said sorry." He signaled for another round and, without dismounting the stool, bent down and gently kissed her thigh.

"All better," she picked his head up and grabbed her pack of cigarettes off the bar, "want?"

Validation; he had her.

Willie, alone at the table, looked up for the Yankee game to keep him company but some Senator Kennedy jabbering about something or other had replaced it. He grabbed Ben's almost full beer and downed it slowly. He absently stared at the TV not able to discern what the talk was about but he was pretty sure that he wouldn't understand it if he heard it. And if he understood it, he probably wouldn't give a shit. But if he looked liked that guy on TV he would've understood it: but he wouldn't be pumping gas, that's for sure. Maybe own a chain of stations—all over Brooklyn. But he'd still be married to Rowan. She's the best. Glad he found her.

Too early to go home.

He retrieved a crumbled Jumble and pencil stub from his pocket then methodically hand ironed the creased piece of paper. The first word came easy. He smiled inwardly at his small victory. Solving puzzles was his thing—he could do them better than anyone. The best in the biz: Ben and the ponies, Willie and the Jumble.

Last night was the night—almost. The three horse rounded the head of the stretch—four lengths back, maybe five He knew it would win, knew it; he even said to Ben or what's-his-name next to him, 'the three's a lock.' He knew it. He should've put some extra cash down on the three—on the side, not much, just a little bonus money—maybe buy Rowan something nice. Maybe parlay it into a bigger payoff.

Sandy counted on him to carry the money down that long corridor and to the motel—Willie at the center of the convoy; the guys all around him. Surrounded him in the car also. He had to stuff some of it in his BVDs because his pockets were too small—almost fell out while they were walking. The guys didn't know that and he wasn't going to tell them that because then someone else would've carried some of it. It was his job. Period. Too bad he didn't keep it there when those pricks showed. He would've split it with the guys and been a hero. Of course, he'd clean it first or exchange it for some bills from the station. Or maybe, just tell them that he had it stashed in another pocket just in case the Pinkies weren't straight up.

Yeah, what if, after it was all over and those schmucks left and they were sitting in Goodies like tonight, he reached into his shorts and pulled out a couple of thousand and dropped it on the table. The guys would've gone apeshit and they would've wanted him to keep a big piece but he would insist that the regular split is the way to go—Benny would get the lion's share. After all, he put the whole thing together.

Yeah, they trusted him. Could've been Sandy or Al with the moola but it was him. He should've held a couple of thousand in his shorts.

Must've been tough on Ben losing like that. I mean winning and losing. It was a tough night . . . a good night.

He took another long swig from the bottle.

Shoulda never got those Pinkies.

He looked at the second clue on the Jumble but it didn't register. Absently, he picked up the bottle and stared at his distorted reflection to keep him company. A large smile emerged.

Jesus H Christ!

He replayed his thought just so he could hear it.

"The Syndicate is back."

- 25 -

The rain stopped briefly and the firehouse was empty save for the dispatcher and a couple of guys asleep upstairs on their bunks. The rest of the crew hung out back soaking some energy from the sun and some long overdue activity, other than fires. A dozen deep blue shirts were scattered along a fence. Jutting out from the main building, a concrete apron extended from the building and ended in a short stone wall—the perfect boundary for a makeshift handball court. It was early fall and there was still plenty of handball left before they had to retreat indoors for cards.

The rhythmic sounds of a small black ball hitting a wall and careening onto the ground repeatedly echoed through the enclosed yard.

Ping. The ball slammed the wall and cut sharply out of bounds, just out of Ben's reach.

"C'mon Ben, get off your ass," Al chided. "This guy's nothing."

Ben unconsciously grabbed his undershirt and wiped the sweat from his forehead. The cheering was good: pumps the adrenalin. This was just what Ben needed: to sweat and pound the crap of a little black ball. His hand hurt so much that it felt good. But he could do without Al hassling him, jumping on every point.

Several men lay in the sun, just relaxing; others watched the game. Al sat on a broken concrete wall and watched

Ben combat Louis Realmuto, a good athlete, perhaps as good as Ben, maybe better. This was a tough match—the first two games went to the two-takes-it and they split them. After the second game, the crowd and the wagering got more intense.

"You gave that away, you had him." Al heckled.

Ben didn't look up. During the second game when Ben was behind, Al got into it with one of the other guys. And, when Ben eventually lost, he accused Ben of dumping. Ben ignored him and Al apologized.

Game three was a battle. Neither player had been up by more than two points at any time and the lead changed constantly.

"Two takes it," Ben breathed heavily.

Louis served and Ben returned a killer to the left corner. Still even: Ben's serve.

He put the serve low and unreachable but Louis got to it and returned it to his backside, Ben lunged and missed. Both players searched for breath and tried to camouflage it from the other. Louis served quickly; to keep Ben off guard, and put a killer passed Ben.

"Jesus, Ben, you're sleeping," Al yelled.

"Point game," Louis gasped.

Ben nodded. Sweat covered his body as he planted his feet, prepared to take the serve. He breathed through his nose, so his mouth wouldn't dry out, as he was taught in high school football.

Louis served short. Ben ran it down and hit it cross-court. Louis backhanded it low, to the opposite side. Ben rallied, fully extended, and reached it off balance—he returned it high but he was out of position. Louis put it away.

The battle was done. Both men, exhausted, stood for a minute. They caught their breath and shook hands.

"Nice game." Ben gasped as he grabbed Louis arm, an indication that he meant it.

"Yeah, thanks."

As Ben walked off the court, he heard Louis' victory cry behind him: "Next?"

Al stepped in front of Ben. "You cost me."

Ben ignored him as he continued to towel himself. He started for the firehouse door.

"You shoulda beat him."

"Well, I didn't." Ben turned. "Since when are you betting on this shit?"

"Just for laughs. But you should've won," Al goaded further. "And what are you doing here? I thought you graduated."

"What's with you lately?" Ben was annoyed but controlled. But this wasn't the place; he turned to go inside.

"What's with me?" Al exploded, drawing everyone's attention. Ben continued to walk and Al followed him inside ranting: "What's with *you*? You too good for us? You're outa here . . . you won't have to write tickets while we run hose lines anymore. You won't have to fight a burner and cry in the shower again."

Ben quickly turned and pressed his body against Al's larger frame throwing Al off balance. Al backpedaled. Using his legs for leverage and his anger for strength, Ben leaned in and pinned him to the wall. Al's faced wreaked of surprise—Ben had never moved at him before.

"Look, I don't know what your problem is," Ben said in a strong undertone, his forearm pressed firmly against Al's neck, "but you're adding to it right now. If you want to talk about something, talk." Ben pressed harder. "But don't get in my face in front of the company. Now, what's the problem, Bull? What's the fuckin' problem? What's the problem?"

Al's face dropped in defeat as he didn't try to move Ben off of him. He just remained pinned to the wall—staring vacantly into Ben's eyes. Ben gradually eased up. They stared at each other, knowing that the next move would be critical to their friendship. They had known each other—been friends—for better than twenty-five years. Never had a fight: never close. Al stared.

Ben dropped his arm and turned to walk away.

"Benny, wait."

Ben stopped.

"Look . . . "Al stammered. "Having a bad day, bad year . . . bad life. Sorry."

"Ok, forget it."

"I mean it, I'm sorry."

"I know."

"Paula and me are over."

"I heard, sorry."

"I'm not, plenty of fish in the sea."

"You've been down this road with her before."

"Yeah. Same fuckin' road."

"You want to talk?" Ben placed his hand on Al's shoulder in a gesture that said he understood.

"Just did."

Ben stared for a moment. "Remember who your friends are."

Al nodded without making make eye contact. They stood facing each other; neither with anything to say, neither wanting to leave.

"Gotta go," Ben said as he tapped the back of Al's head in light reprimand, the way his third grade teacher did to him.

Al nodded again, apologetically.

"You Ok?"

Al nodded again; a small smile emerged.

"Ok."

As Ben headed upstairs, he glanced back. Al stood isolated in the center of the firehouse—somewhat lost. Predicting Al's course was easy; he'll come out of it, divorce Paula, and marry her again next year. The guy keeps going down the same road and expects it to wind up in a different place each time.

Ben didn't remember dropping his sweaty clothes; he just sat naked in front of his locker staring inside his head. A shower would feel real good, but he hesitated—putting off the inevitable. The shift would be over soon.

He had his own problems to deal with.

- 26 -

SLAM.

Murph's fat Irish hand rocked Sandy's desk. The vibration shook Sandy but he didn't flinch; it was just Murph's style. After all these years in law, Sandy knew how to deal with people—as powerful as he was, Murph was just another client.

SLAM.

Unfortunately, he slammed the desk so often that everything carried the same weight. Sandy didn't show his displeasure; he just nonchalantly stared at Murph's meaty hand turning red as it pummeled the desk—the same desk he had since he started in the law business. Fuck the desk; this is a client, a big one: slam away.

"It's simple, the parking lots are free," Murph slammed. "The restaurants are free," SLAM. "Even the haircuts are free." SLAM, SLAM, SLAM.

His head throbbed but Sandy never took his eyes off of Murph. He hoped that his silence would be interpreted as thoughtful contemplation and attentiveness: a bit of lawyerly consideration of Murph's slamming proposal. It was.

Sandy wrote something on his pad. Let Murph blow off his steam so he could take this conversation to the next step. Murph paced. Murph sat, winded.

Now, this was it; he's done.

Sandy stood slowly, walked around his desk and circled Murph—his chair buckling under his three hundred plus slamming pounds. The legs started caving inward. *After this contract, new furniture.*

"And," Murph looked up at Sandy and blurted, as if with his last breath, "we get three percent!" SLAM.

This was it, he's done.

"Ok, back to reality." Sandy knew that Murph respected tough direct talk. "Let me go in with an offer that they can chew on, not throw up on." A little street talk always added credibility with certain clients. "If . . . you come in too high and unreasonable, then they'll dig in their heels and it'll be Christmas Eve and we'll still be negotiating and you still won't get what you want. And you'll be paying me a ton of fees."

Murph turned and nodded at his son, "You with this?"

Little Murph, who was anything but little, stretched across two cushions on the sofa: "Yeah."

"Sit up. Pay attention." Big Murph's grin was part boss, part father, part teacher. It meant that he was in control; that he would allow Sandy to continue; and to pay attention and learn something you little prick. He looked up at Sandy hovering over him. "What are you proposing?"

Sandy stepped back, sat on the desk and looked down at Murph. He paused for emphasis—sometimes silence and anticipation are your best weapons.

"Ok. Take the forty hour work week." Sandy spoke deliberately, briefly stopping after each point. "Overtime after forty, not forty-five. And no free rides, they cost too much over time." He looked at junior and waited for his acknowledgement, someday he might be dealing directly with him. He looked back at Murph, "and they put nothing in your pocket."

Murph considered it, looked at Little Murph and back at Sandy.

Sandy had him.

"And," Sandy sat on the desk, arms crossed, signaling that he was secure in what he recommended—what he was saying was a fact, not just his opinion. He lowered his tone as if he were reporting an event in history: "Management contributes to the union's retirement plan . . . with stock. It costs them nothing out of pocket and we'd have a better chance of getting it. Long run, you make out better—much better."

Murph checked with junior.

"What about our three percent?" Junior finally spoke.

Feeling that he was in the stretch run of this conversation, Sandy walked around his desk and slowly sat in his chair. He looked at junior as if he had asked the most brilliant question of the day. "That's the retirement plan contribution. I don't think they'll go for three, but we can start there—probably come in around one, one and a half. Think about it—all in, a pretty good deal if we can pull it off and it's relatively painless for them. Win win. Think about it for a couple of days."

Sandy wrote something on a piece of paper: to give Murph time to digest everything.

SLAM! Sandy's desk shook. He didn't expect that one.

"I like this guy," senior said to junior, what do you think?" Junior nodded rhetorically. He turned back to Sandy. "I like the way you think, no bullshit. I don't need two days. You do it."

"Good. You know they'll reject the first few rounds no matter what we come in with."

"I only care about the last round."

Murph laughed; Sandy joined him; they shook across the desk. SLAM.

"Now, maybe I can do something for you." Murph hefted out of the chair, walked around the desk and leaned over Sandy. Murph looked towards junior who hoisted himself off of the sofa and exited the office. Murph's direct eye contact signified that this was important information. He had a different look on his face—more determined—less combative. It was his show now. Sandy's curiosity overtook his apprehension. He sensed that he needed to seriously consider what was about to come. He waited.

Murph leaned in close and captured Sandy's ear. They were alone in the room but Murph still felt it necessary to talk low as he stared directly into Sandy's eyes.

The conversation only lasted a few seconds but Sandy didn't remember the words; or how Murph started out; or if he asked him how he knew; or if he reacted to him at all.

He didn't remember if he said that it was bullshit and that Murph didn't know what the fuck he was talking about. He didn't remember any conversation—just Murph saying something and him listening—that was that. And now he had information that he didn't have before.

He didn't even remember seeing the Murphs leave or what he did for the hour or so afterwards. He didn't remember anything about the exchange except the one thing he didn't want to remember. He wished that he knew no more than he did an hour ago. But he didn't.

Unconsciously, he pulled out his pack of Luckies, popped a butt out and lit it. He took a drag and let it burn out in the ashtray alongside the others. His face flushed and the nausea swelled inside as he sat at his desk.

The intercom buzzed.

He didn't answer it.

Ben took the long way to the Gravesend—to save the shocks; but he knew he was just stalling. He pulled up and just sat for a minute. The next few weeks would depend upon the next few minutes.

The car door flew open and he jumped out like he was back running track. He walked in briskly, passed Beefy Leonard who didn't see him, passed the jukebox which played Bobby Darin's *Beyond the Sea* and directly to Charlie. He sat without waiting for the invitation.

"Sit."

Charlie studied him: part of his power ritual.

"I heard you were quitting the department."

"How did you . . .?"

Charlie smiled. *Another part of his ritual.*

"I'm thinking about it."

"I know a lot of guys in the department; a couple of chiefs. You're not like them Ben. Never figured you to be a fireman."

"You figured wrong."

"Not for long." Charlie smiled to punctuate his retort.

"Why am I here?"

"You like to get right to the point. No chit chat."

"We're doing business—I gotta settle up with you, I know that and I will. Down the road, we'll chit chat."

"I heard about your problem the other night."

"What problem?"

"Don't insult me Ben. I know what I know. Now you know it."

Ben nodded. "You almost got paid off."

"*Almost* doesn't pay the rent. This is not going to affect our business, is it?" Charlie continued.

"I need some time."

"Are you sure? I wouldn't want to take your house; it's a bit small for me."

Ben held back. He had no cards anyway.

"I'm good for it."

"Business is business. And you're overextended, very overextended."

"You know you'll get paid."

"You see," Charlie stood, took a few meaningless steps and turned back to Ben, "I don't know just that. If I knew that, we wouldn't be having this little talk and I wouldn't be worried about you. What I do know is that you owe me a lot of cash plus the vig and you have no means to get it. Your Buick isn't even worth two."

He probably even knew about the bad shocks.

"You'll get paid."

"I know. I wouldn't want your missus living on the street."

Ben stood and stared Charlie down. He then turned and walked towards the door.

"I wasn't finished, Ben."

"I am." Ben kept walking.

"I expect to hear from you shortly, Ben."

Ben kept walking: "You'll get paid." He walked through the door.

"I always do."

- 27 -

The tone in Sandy's office was a little more upbeat than a morgue. Ben lay on the sofa slowly tossing a handball in the air trying to come close to, but not hit, the ceiling. Sandy rolled paper into balls and shot baskets across the room. Both were unsuccessful. The day started badly for both of them and went downhill from there.

"I don't know how I'm going to pay the guy." The ball grazed the ceiling leaving a black mark—next to several other black marks. Ben caught it nonchalantly.

"I can come up with part of it, but not close what you need."

"I know, thanks. I don't want your money. I just need a play."

"I know, let me think."

"I fucked up," Ben said as he slammed the handball into the ceiling cracking a tile. "Sorry."

"Don't sweat it. You were in the middle of fucking up."

"Huh? Oh yeah, I fucked up. I just wanted to start over and now I'm trying to figure out how to keep my house. Kitty's not too happy."

"She know you bailed Willie?"

"No. Let's keep it that way." He lofted another ball and caught it without looking. "She's pregnant."

That woke Sandy up. "No shit?"

"No shit."

"Congrats."

"Timing sucks."

"It'll change."

"Yeah, all of a sudden I'm deep in a hole and I'm going down instead of up. And I'm not sure there's enough time to fix it. Last week I had a job and . . . if I don't come up with some cash soon, I may not have a house . . . and everything that goes with it."

"You been here before."

"No, not here. Not at these stakes." Ben looked around at the office. "You did it right . . . cushy practice, name on the door, big tits out front." Ben looked over his shoulder to see if Eileen was in earshot. She was, but did not react to comment—at least she didn't show it.

"Wasn't that easy, and the income is sometimes less than the outgo."

"At least you're a lawyer."

Two more balls fell far short of the ceiling.

"I didn't pass the bar," Sandy confessed.

The handball bounced off the ceiling and hit Ben square in the forehead.

"What?"

"I didn't pass the bar."

"How could you be—?"

"The Army. I had a good war record, two purple hearts. Ok, one, but two injuries. They went to bat for me—the Army and Wasserman. They waived the bar exam."

"Holy shit."

"Back then they did a lot for GIs. You could bend the rules if you had enough weight."

"Holy shit. Here I am, jealous of you, Mister professional, big shit, barrister. You're just an ordinary Joe. I mean, you were always an ordinary Joe, but you were an ordinary Joe lawyer." Ben laughed.

"Still am."

"Yeah, but you took a short cut."

"What's wrong with short cuts?"

"Nothing. I love them but I didn't think you . . ." his laughter broke his reality—it felt good. "Holy shit."

The laughter got contagious and pretty soon it filled the morose office. It felt real good.

Eileen looked into the opened door. "You folks need anything?"

Ben sat up, looked at Sandy, then at her. She was more striking than Ben remembered. Every time he had been here before, she was involved with something or other—or he was. Never really took a good look before. He made up for it now. No wonder Sandy liked to come to work.

"No, thanks, kiddo." Sandy nodded. "We're good. Close the door. Thanks."

She complied.

"Why did you do that?"

"What?" Sandy asked.

"Send her away. She wanted to play also."

"Nope. She's a doll but very straight."

"She feel that way?"

"Huh?"

"She looked you up and down."

"Off limits." Sandy said.

"C'mon. You getting moral on me?"

"Just practical. Too close to home. And she's too young."

"Which is it?"

"Both, asshole." He winged a paper ball at Ben who caught it and threw it right back at him catching him in the chest. "Holy shit." Sandy stood up.

Ben sat up. "What?"

"Pacey Diamond. I almost forgot." Sandy's excitement level began to rise.

"What about him?"

"He's got a tip."

"Everybody's got a tip."

"Not like this. He was running money between two books and picked something up. Some inside money—on a long shot. I can't believe I forgot."

"He ever give you anything before?"

"A few times."

"They work out?"

"Some."

He needed a tip—but he needed a good tip. No room for speculation. "Where?"

"Tonight at Monticello. Up for a ride?"

"Shit. I should go home. How good is it?"

"We'll know when we know."

"That's my line." Ben deliberated. "I should go home."

Then he thought about that hole he had to fill.

- 28 -

Sandy's Olds sped off the Thruway onto Route 17, the path of the annual summer migration of thousands of Jews to the Catskills, their bungalows, Grossinger's, and Monticello Raceway.

Everyone was in position except Al, who had other plans.

"Heard that Al is becoming single-o again," Willie said to break the monotony of the drive.

Ben hoped that Sandy would pick up the conversation so he could continue his sleep. Sandy hoped Ben would. Neither did.

"Shoulda changed the date on the check," Willie tried again. This time he just waited for a response.

"What check?" Sandy broke first.

"My wedding gift . . . when they got married." He said as if Sandy should know exactly what check he was talking about. "I postdated it."

"What?"

"I postdated the check. They've been married so many times that I gave him a postdated check—figured when they break up again I could stop it."

That did it. Ben was up.

Ben looked at Willie. He wasn't the sharpest guy in the car, or maybe on Route 17 and maybe in the entire state, but he had this unique way of looking at things. Ben always figured that he didn't understand a lot of the complexities so they didn't get in his way, which let him to see things clearer, although a bit more tilted, than the average guy. They started to laugh and Willie picked up momentum.

"I just didn't date it out far enough." He got the reaction that he wanted as everyone were fully engaged, laughing. Willie rolled on. "His old girlfriends showed up at the last wedding. Maybe a coupla new ex-wives too. He'll probably get married again inside of six months. Odds on, it's Paula."

The car was fully awake. It was good timing; they just pulled into Monticello Raceway.

Ben studied the track and the crowd: mostly mid-week summer vacationers. For the next three races they made casual uninformed bets—the kind the rest of the crowd was making. It wasn't serious money and neither of them really paid much attention to the racing form except Willie who played exactas on every horse that had letters that were in his kids' names and lost.

Ben didn't pay much attention to the horses—this was not like the flats where his handicapping was a real asset. This was the trots where he looked for different angles: people and odds and tips. Tonight he had a tip—it had better be good. It was mechanical from here; buy some tickets for the second half of the Twin Double, bet on Sandy's tip and wheel it into a bunch of horses in the last race.

This was easy—no major decisions—either it happens or it doesn't. This was much easier than his conversation with Kitty earlier tonight.

Kitty occupied herself with household crap, trying not to think about what was important. She felt heavy as the boys finished dinner and she cleared the dishes: not pregnancy heavy, but pressure chamber heavy. This was not a good time to be pregnant, but it wasn't planned and she couldn't second-guess herself, no matter how much she wanted to. And she knew the job wasn't Ben's fault, just bad timing with everything else; it was just the *everything else* that was fucking things up. And, the worst of it was, she didn't know what was happening, or why. And she had no control. She had control over the dishes and that's where she focused.

"Hi guys." Ben startled her.

The boys left their seats and jumped him.

"How're you guys doing?"

"They're doing fine," Kitty offered with icing.

"Sorry I'm late, had to take care of something."

Kitty's look told him that this lousy day wasn't over.

"Why don't you guys get into your pj's and I'll come up in a few minutes."

Scooter didn't let go of Ben.

"Hey," Ben hugged him. "What's up?"

"He's having a bad day," Kitty turned away from her dishes, "had a small accident in school."

"Accident?" Ben kneeled and examined Scooter's face. "You ok?"

"Not that kind, the other kind."

Ben looked at Kitty inquisitively.

She nodded towards Scooter's crotch.

"Oh." Ben talked directly to Scooter. "Hey, do you know when I was a delivery boy for a drug store, I had an accident."

Scooter's head was buried on Ben's chest.

"I had a lot of deliveries, too many, and I had to go; really go—really, really go. And, when I was making my last delivery," Ben said in his best storytelling tone, "I couldn't hold it . . . peed right in my pants right in front of a lady. Told her it was a water balloon in my pocket."

Scooter wiped his eyes and broke into a smile. He looked incredulously at Ben, then Kitty, then Rick. The smiles quickly turned to laughter.

"Did she believe you?" Scooter asked.

"Would you?"

And, for a moment, they forgot everything and laughter filled the kitchen.

"Upstairs, now."

The boys raced upstairs laughing.

"Sorry, it was important." Ben got up.

Kitty's smile disappeared as she reverted back to reality.

"It's always important. When did we stop being important to you?"

"Never. I mean, you've always been. I'm just trying to straighten some things out. We've been through stuff before. You gotta trust me."

"*We've* been through it. Now, *you're* through it and I'm, I'm, I don't even know what I am . . ." Kitty tried to recover, "Ben, what do you want?"

"What?"

"What do you want? I still can't believe this—it's not going away. You risk the house, where we live, where your kids live, for what?"

What do I want? It's not about what I want; it's about what I have to do.

Telling her about Willie would just make things worse. She would think he was an idiot for bailing him out; he probably was. He probably should have let him take his medicine, lose the gas station and straighten himself out. He should have; but he didn't. And Kitty knowing about it wouldn't change anything. They would be right where they are—up Shit's Creek. He just had to fix it.

"I can't explain it all now. This isn't the time."

"This is the time. This is the only time."

A car horn temporarily broke the somber mood and gave Ben the out he needed. He didn't want to leave Kitty like this but this conversation needed hours and days to resolve itself—if it could be resolved. He knew that he had to fix what he had to fix and life would be restored. She was a great partner, but it was hate me now or hate me later. Better she loved him later, now is shitty anyway.

"Look, we're in a bind and I'll get us out, promise. And when I do, we'll be ok."

The horn blared again: two toots.

"Ben, I don't care if we live in a shoebox—"

Three toots.

"Look, gotta go." Ben kissed her forehead. "Trust me. Can you do that?"

He didn't wait for her answer; there was no choice; that hole wasn't going to fill itself.

The light from a distant street lamp filtered through the blinds as Kitty shivered off the chill that came from somewhere deep inside. She had been standing in her front room since Ben drove off, some time ago. Everything had just changed and she didn't know why. She hadn't envisioned a perfect life but, so far, it was not far off—until now.

She was elated when she found out that she was pregnant again. Contrary to the other two, which almost didn't happen, this one was not planned. They thought they were done: at least she did. She had some plans as the kids got older; maybe take a job, maybe college—something. Yet, she was so excited when she found out and planned to surprise Ben—she imagined his look on his face, the smile that would erupt and the passion that would follow. He loved the kids; she could have had kept popping them out as far as he was concerned.

That moment didn't happen; the next kid went from being a blessing to being a problem. Her anticipation of the pregnancy and everything that accompanied it evaporated—along with some stability and trust. The future had just become uncertain; her anticipation had become apprehension. For the first time, she felt alone.

She heard herself whisper: "I can't do this."

- 29 -

"What are we doing?" Willie's question startled Ben.

"What?"

"What are we doing? The second half of the Twin is starting. What are we doing?"

"I bought some tickets from a guy who had the first half." Ben looked around the grandstand trying to reorient himself. "Paid a little too much but there weren't any sellers around."

"And . . ."

Ben smiled at Willie's eagerness.

"And—we took Sandy's super sure thing in the next race," Ben said sarcastically to get a rise out of Sandy, "and wheeled him into six horses in the last race. If . . ." Ben hesitated, "if . . . his horse wins the next race, we've got six horses in the eighth race . . . a nice position."

"Six out of eight? Nice? It's a lock."

"They're off!"

Willie and Sandy ran ahead for an outside view. Ben slowly trailed.

"C'mon. Who'my I rootin' for?" Willie yelled back to Ben.

"Four."

"And what else?" Willie asked Sandy who paced alongside.

"Just four."

"Got it."

Ben never made it to the grandstand. Trots were boring—the sulkies were unnecessary and the race was too long. Two long slow laps around a half-mile track and everything occurs in the last sixty feet.

Whatever happens happens.

The crowd noise picked up, indicating that that the horses were in the stretch run—where the real race happens. He kept his expectations low—disappointment is the one thing he didn't need now. This wasn't his pick; it wasn't his choice; he relied on information from someone else. He had no idea if it was good; had no feeling for it. He would only know when . . .

"Four!" Willie's head popped over the crowd; his program waving back and forth to ensure that Ben saw him.

Ben slapped his program and clenched his jaw.

One down.

"Four, four!" Willie yelled as he jumped through the crowd back to Ben, Sandy trailing. "Didja see it? Four. Took it by a mile. Knew it. It was a lock."

Ben smiled his first smile in forever and hugged both guys. "Way to go. Half way there."

"More than half way: one race to go and we've got six horses in it."

"Good old Pacey Diamond," Sandy added.

"What do we need?" asked Willie.

Ben held up a stack of tickets and said confidently: "Either the one, two, four, five, six or seven. Take your pick."

"Holy shit." Willie took out a pen and wrote the numbers on his palm. "I'll go back the truck up to the Cashier's window."

"Don't count it yet," Ben cautioned. "We still have to win it."

"Benny, we got six horses. Six horses out of eight and the other two will be on a merry-go-round after this race! I like our chances."

"Me too. Be right back." Ben left.

Sandy smiled victoriously as he tried to figure the appropriate cut for Pacey Diamond. He calculated the possible payoffs for each of the six horses.

"Mr. Kane," a voice preceded a gentle tap on Sandy's shoulder. Sandy turned and saw an elderly man dressed in a black suit and tie.

"Rabbi Weinstein," Sandy hid his embarrassment but not his surprise. *What is he doing here?* "Hello."

"Mr. Kane, are you behaving? Better yet, are you winning?"

"So far so good, say hello to my friend Willie."

Willie was a little tongue-tied and shook politely.

"What brings you this far north?" The Rabbi asked.

"Well, right now, it's any one of six horses in the next race."

"Six horses? You have been behaving. I'll pray for you, as I am tapped out. I guess I'll have to hit the collection box again."

Willie was shocked.

The rabbi put his hand on Willie's shoulder. "A little temple humor; we don't have collection boxes."

"I knew that."

"I'll just cash the congregations' checks." The Rabbi looked to Willie to see if he got the joke. He did.

"The horses are on the track!"

Ben returned and Sandy introduced the Rabbi and Ben.

"Did you see the payoff?" Willie had to know.

"The *seven* pays fourteen thousand five and the *one* pays forty eight hundred. The rest are up and down the middle."

"C'mon seven."

The guys all waited silently, inhibited by the tension of the next race and his holiness standing three feet from them. An unwarranted wave of guilt penetrated the air. Ben watched the sulkies line up behind the start car.

C'mon, start the race.

"They're off!"

Everyone just stood silently through the first lap. Midway through the second, the horses started to spread along the rail at the back end of the track. A pack of horses separated from the rest. It was difficult to see who was up. The pack stretched out further. The *two* was ahead with the *five, six, seven* and *one* close behind. The first six horses were their six horses.

The noise from the very small crowd intensified; this was the last race and the tail end of the Twin Double.

"C'mon *two*, c'mon *three*, c'mon *seven*."

"Willie, we don't have the *three*." Sandy reminded.

Willie checked his palm. "C'mon *four*, c'mon *six*, c'mon. Did I say *seven*? C'mon seven."

Ben and Sandy silently watch. Rabbi Weinstein davoned; he raised and lowered his head in prayer—each time peeking out to watch the race.

"Rabbi," Sandy caught the Rabbi on the upbeat, "you're a partner when we win this."

"I shall pray extra hard then," the Rabbi davoned faster, "c'mon *seven!*" up, down, "c'mon *four*," up, down, "c'mon *six*."

The horses and sulkies bunched up as they turned the head of the stretch—the final sprint for the wire. The *seven horse* rounded wide and caught a wheel with the *four* who stumbled and broke stride. A synchronized moan filled the air. The horse righted himself and veered towards the inside and collided with the *five* and sent the driver over the rail. The *seven* kept going.

The *five horse* recoiled and sought a path from harm's way—into the oncoming horses. The drivers from behind tried to avoid the collision and created a second pileup, which sent their horses tumbling. A sulky turned upside down and two others veered right to avoid the pileup. The other drivers and sulkies collided in the dust into an indescribable muddle of carnage and metal.

There was chaos at the head of the stretch. The collision hid the identity of the horses—it was one twisted pile of horses, drivers and carriages. Nothing was identifiable.

Suddenly, three horses somehow emerged; instinctively their legs charged forward as they continued their rush towards the finish line.

"What's going on?" Willie frantically shouted, "Can you see? Are we alive?"

Ben looked but could not make it out. "Sandy?"

"It looks like the *three, four* and . . ." Sandy's voice pitched up, " . . . and *seven!* The seven!"

The *seven* lead the remaining horses down the stretch.

"We got two out of three! Two out of three!" Willie shouted.

The crowd's moan melded with their cheers as their collective attention was torn between the wreckage and the survivors who stormed down the last few feet of track.

"C'mon *seven*." Ben shouted, almost inaudibly.

C'mon seven.

Forty yards to go and everyone was standing on their seats as the *four* began to test the *seven*. The *three* was on the rail, one and a half lengths back.

It was *seven, four, three*. The seven held the lead.

It tightened: *sevenfourthree*. The *four* put on a final burst on the outside and the *seven* sensed it gaining. The whip cracked above its head and the horse thrust itself forward, fending off the *four's* challenge. The seven held.

The guys watched the two horse battle.

"*Seven four. Seven four*," Willie reported, "We got both! We got both! "*Seven four. Seven four*. We got both. C'mon seven. Screw the *four,* unless it wins, c'mon *seven*."

Hidden from view on the rail, the *three* closed fast: suddenly, it was tight three-horse race again. Ten yards to go. The *seven* held, the *four* in tight and the *three* closing ground. Half a stride separated the three horses. The noses bobbed.

Seven held a small lead.

"Seven, seven . . ."

"Seven four three. Seven four . . ."

"Three."

They all saw it at the same time and looked at each other for some disagreement. Something to say that they got it wrong, that they still had a shot, that they were still alive. But it happened; the inside nose peaked through, beating the others to the finish line, the nose belonging to the three. *Three!*

Fuck.

Sandy and Willie stood on their seats and stared at the track as the *three* took a victory lap. Willie's mouth and eyes were locked wide open. Ben sat stunned. There was an irreconcilable finality; there was no second chance; it was over.

"Sorry boys, I tried," the Rabbi consoled, "but apparently God liked the *three*."

The track had emptied. Everyone had headed back to his bungalow or hotel; or made the long drive back to the city. Tonight was just another night out on vacation, nothing serious—a little excitement, a little fun and a great story to tell at breakfast. It was a night where you made a few bucks or lost a few bucks but you took a chance and had hope on ten different occasions. Just guess right and get lucky. It was a night where you had a shot at the big one. A small shot, but a shot nevertheless.

Three men sat quietly in the empty stands and stared straight ahead at the barren track.

- 30 -

The white light that exploded in Ben's eyes couldn't be morning; he must have dozed. He had just looked at the clock and it was 5:15; he had guessed 4:37. It was a long night and the last few weeks continuously cycled through his mind—Kitty, Willie, Monticello, Yonkers, Sandy, Al, Charlie, Kitty. He did everything wrong and things that could've gone either way, went the wrong way. *A lot of mistakes, too many.*

This was more than a bad patch, a pothole in the road—this *was* the road and if he didn't get off of it now, he would be done.

He thought about Kitty and one of their talks in the last few days—one where he really wasn't listening. He was explaining and trying to make her understand and accept the situation and trust him to fix it. He really didn't expect her to understand—he's not sure if he understood. He wanted to be truthful, but gentle. She needed to know what she needed to know, but not more. He felt a responsibility to insulate her from the real bad stuff, more so with her being pregnant, which at another time would have been a joyous asset—now it loomed as another liability and complexity. For the moment, that had to take a back seat to higher priorities.

So he explained what he could, defended what he had to, and omitted everything else. He did everything but listen. Her words resonated days later.

"Whatever happened to 'get up in the morning looking forward to the day, go to sleep at night feeling like you've pushed the peanut a little further'?"

She knew how to drive her points—he didn't hear them then but somehow they lay in his head until they would be heard. *"Do you look forward to the day? Do you feel like you've pushed that peanut? Do you even remember peanuts?"* She added to drive it home. It was an unnecessary postscript, but she was frustrated and he deserved it.

He turned to hold her hand as she lay next to him. He loved her body, their sex, but strangely, he loved holding her hand most of all. He reached out to emptiness. He opened his eyes to an empty pillow.

He looked at the clock: *ten after eight*.

Shit.

He clocked in, made roster and hit the road for his ticket detail. Fridays were the best; for some reason, people are less concerned with breaking the law on Fridays. He could hit quota early. He patrolled mindlessly. This was better than fighting fires; he didn't mind the hard work, just didn't want to fight for his life every day. Soon the job would be gone along with his paycheck and car subsidy. Reality was getting closer.

Kitty was right: he wasn't pushing the peanuts, he wasn't building anything. He had just been maintaining for all these years. And now all of a sudden he fell into a hole abruptly and tried to get out just as quick. Shooting at shortcuts, that's not his style.

He drove down Ocean Avenue and pulled up to a Chevy convertible parked squarely in front of a fire hydrant. A block later, it was a brand new Desoto, the sharpest tail fins in Detroit, which was parked too close to a hydrant covered by an inverted garbage can: two tickets. Three tickets in twenty minutes; this was progress that he couldn't be proud of on any level.

Peanuts.

He'd been taking shortcuts. This wasn't him—this was not the way he operated. He had his toe in the water with the trots but Kitty was right; he should be building. She certainly didn't mean the horses, but that's what he can do best. The horses, real horses, not the trots. He did it once and he did it well. He looked forward to each of those days. They were provoking, stimulating. They challenged him and put him against the horses, everyone in the stands and himself.

Be a horseplayer, but do it differently. This time he wouldn't be a kid playing the horses, trying to beat the system, this time it would be work; this time it would be business. Hopefully, it would be a living. Kitty would throw a shitfit, but he would deal with that later. The list is long anyway.

He wrote eighteen tickets by eleven, three over his quota. He headed back to the firehouse but continued passed it and got on the Belt Parkway east—east, towards Aqueduct Racetrack. He was caught in some native current that swept him into its flow. It was automatic and natural—the most natural act he had done in a long while.

The size of the track awed him. This was not Empire or Jamaica; this was Aqueduct, a new game and a new place. This was a real track, thoroughbreds, the best of the best. This was a modern facility, automated tote boards where everyone could see the current odds. No books to dutch here. This was a well-designed system, foolproof and far beyond the schemes of a high school kid. He continued his reconnaissance; he studied everything—the horses, the jockeys, the trainers, the odds and the track. He absorbed, he refamiliarized, he learned through osmosis. But he didn't bet; he just soaked it in.

Everything was different, but a horse is still a horse and seven furlongs is still seven furlongs.

Every fifteen minutes or so, a race would go off and, for two plus minutes, thousands of eyes would be focused in one place with singular energy. The thousands of individuals became one contiguous amorphous rooting ball. Unconsciously, the bettors' hands would tighten around their programs, some rhythmically slapping it against their thigh or whatever else was handy. They began to mutter a small chant that collectively filled the space and gave it a strange spiritual feel, as close as they'd come to actual prayer.

They continually repeated the mantra of the horse's number or the jockey's name: *C'mon two, c'mon two. Diego, Diego Diego.* Occasionally, they would repeat the horse's name: but only occasionally because they'd have to remember it and those attachments only lasted for the length of the race. *Coldstream, Coldstream . . .c'mon two.* The tension built as the race progressed, becoming tighter and tighter as the horses entered the stretch run, the final sprint to the finish line. The track announcer picked up the pace as his voice rose to a vibrato adding to the intensity of the final thrust:

only to be drowned out by the thousands of worshipers praying to a four-legged god with his two-legged rider to beat the other sonofabitches to the finish line.

C'mon, I'm due. C'mon three! Three! A crescendo built as two or three horses battled out the final few yards and the volume increased to a point where no one could hear himself scream. And the ritual climaxed in a burst of energy and a vital but short-lived moan.

Then silence; and then the players performed the post mortem. The loser tore up his tickets, licked his wounds and quickly migrated to handicap the next race—that race was over, ancient history; don't even remember the horse's name.

The winner engaged in a small singular celebration, silently complimenting himself for being so fucking smart to pick that horse. And, just to make sure he wasn't celebrating alone, he would turn to the guy next to him. "Did you have that one?" he would ask, waiting for the return question to which he would answer matter of factly, "Yeah, I caught it", while biting the inside of his cheek to keep the nonchalant veneer intact while the celebration continued inside.

Then, the next race and the cycle repeated every fifteen minutes or so. It was exhilarating.

The next week, Ben did the same: exceeded his ticket quota, left early and went to Aqueduct. Each night he would go out for coffee with the guys; except the *guys* were the *Morning Telegraph* or the *Racing Form*. He'd wait for the papers to come in, around ten o'clock or so, get a cup of coffee and check the charts, the morning line, the odds and history of every horse on the next day's card. At first, he was overwhelmed at what was sure to be a long and impossible journey. But the challenge evolved into something stimulating and invigorating.

Those few days were like an amnesty on everything that had happened—Kitty was civil, Charlie didn't hassle him, he didn't see the guys, and the sun was shining.

It had been a few days of being somewhere else and someone else—a much-needed timeout from his life.

- 31 -

Ben cruised Kings Highway, picked off some early scofflaws and made it to Aqueduct for the noon post time of the Daily Double, a parlay of the first and second races. Over the past few days, Ben began to make small, disciplined bets, mostly two dollars, to get into the flow. It's one thing to pick horses, quite another to bet right: it was all about betting right. He was about even—actually down a few but one bet away from being up a few.

He should have done this sooner, work in the morning, track in the afternoon. But he couldn't and he didn't. No second-guessing; he had no control over yesterday.

He began to develop an approach to analyze the horses' chances of winning. It wasn't so much of a system, more of a way of evaluating a horse's performance in his class: against similar competitors. And, most important, he focused on the odds and the value of any bet. The pieces were falling into place. This was natural—it was coming back.

He was on his own private mission as he sat anonymously in the grandstand. He hadn't told anyone, even the guys, about this. He wasn't sure, when, or if, he would. So far he had taken some small steps towards a future. At some point, he would have to tell Kitty, then the shit would really hit the fan.

He walked to the Seller's window to make a very small bet; he alternated between checking his program and the current odds on the tote board. In the periphery of his vision, in his subliminal eye, he caught a glimpse of someone familiar. It was an image that sparked an emotion, a memory, a familiarity—but he couldn't identify him because when he looked up he was gone.

"Hey Benny." Ben was snapped out of his nostalgia by a more familiar voice. "Hey Benny, What're you doing out here?"

Ben turned. He knew that running into Willie was inevitable.

"Hi guy." *Shit.* He wanted his secret for a little longer.

"Shoulda told me you were coming, we could've come together. What're you doing here?"

Ben wanted to ask him the same question, but didn't. Initially, Willie was a welcomed sight, good company in this large cold place, but that wore off quickly. He's in this jam because he bailed Willie and now Willie is still pissing it away. Ben didn't know if he was more annoyed at Willie for being here or being caught here himself. It was no use to telling Willie to keep this to himself, so he didn't.

Willie noticed Ben's program and his scribbling.

"You're back?"

"Just taking a day off and getting some air."

"You're back."

"No."

"When you're back, let me know."

"Yeah. Who's watching the station?"

"Slow day and the books wouldn't . . ." Willie reconsidered his answer. "Just getting some air."

Ben hated to hear his own answers.

"How you doing?"

"Almost up."

"How much are you down?"

"A little, but I got something real good."

Willie discreetly glanced around him and moved closer to Ben for some privacy. He whispered unnecessarily. "You picked the right day to get some air. I got something goin'."

They looked at each other knowingly: Willie knowing that he had some real good, top-notch info and a can't-miss scheme, and Ben knowing that whatever Willie had was worthless.

"Got a minute?"

Ben nodded reluctantly.

"C'mon."

Willie led Ben away from the windows towards the upper grandstand. They walked up, and up.

"Where are we going?"

"Almost there. It's worth it."

Ben looked back at the shrinking track. *What am I doing here?*

"Better be."

"The horses are in the gate," the PA declared.

Willie, breathing heavy, became more excited as they reached the top of the grandstand. Ben continued to look back at the track knowing it was pointless because he couldn't see what he needed to anyway.

"Ok," Willie gasped as he reached the top with Ben right behind, "see that guy over there?"

Willie subtly indicated to his left with his nose.

"Where?"

"There," he nodded his head to the left, "Section C. That guy all alone up there at the opening."

Ben looked and saw a short, gaunt, badly dressed man standing alone at the top of the bleachers.

"Yeah," Ben's patience had evaporated.

"That's Ziggy."

"Ok. Who's Ziggy?"

"It is now post time," echoed through the grandstand.

"Don't look." Willie checked to see if anyone was eavesdropping as they stood alone yards from the nearest person. "Ziggy's a guy. When the horses come out of the gate, Ziggy goes to work. Watch."

Ben just stared at Willie in wonder.

"And, they're off!"

Willie turned away from the track and watched Ziggy. Ben watched Willie.

Ziggy went into action. He watched the beginning of the race through binoculars, put them down after the horses were several seconds out of the gate and turned towards the parking lot away from the track. He raised both hands and clasped them over his head.

Ben tried to see how the race was going and Willie nudged Ben with an elbow and a big smart victorious smile. Willie nodded outside towards the parking lot.

"See that guy in front of the candy store?"

"Where?"

"Across the street. The candy store."

In front of the candy store stood a tall man in a suit with too-short pants, a toothpick in his mouth and binoculars on his eyes aimed at Ziggy. Suddenly, he dropped the binocs to his side and ran inside the candy store.

"Yeah."

"That's my friend Ed," Willie declared proudly as the caper was unfolding.

"Not Ed the Brain? Drives a Chevy with rope on the doors?"

"Yeah."

"You hanging with Ed the Brain now?"

"He's got ideas. Now, when the horses leave the gate, Ziggy sees who's in front and signals Ed by the candy store.

Ben was dumbstruck and stared at Willie for what seemed like twenty minutes more than forever but was probably more like ten seconds. Willie proudly looked up at Ben and dissected the anatomy of the plan.

"Now the books don't close their action precisely at post time. Ed calls the book and bets on the lead horse. He puts the bet in after the race started." He waited to see if Ben got it and then spread his hands victoriously. "Ta-da!"

"And how do you know the lead horse is the winner . . . with a six furlongs to go?"

"Don't, but he's closer than the other nags," Willie offered with impeccable logic.

"Did you come up with this brainstorm?"

"Well, I did, actually, Ed did most of it. You want in?"

"Pass."

"Really, no prob. Say the word and you're in. After all, how many times did you—?"

"I said, pass. You're fooling with this shit." Ben grabbed Willie's arm firmly. "What's the matter with you? I put up my—"

"What's a matter Benny? Let go."

Ben slowly released Willie and pat him on the shoulder like a dog he had just scolded.

"Sorry."

"Why you do that?" a totally confused Willie asked, "Why're you so mad? You don't have to be in if you don't want. Just thought I would do you a solid."

"Sorry. Maybe you should be at the station. I mean, you said business was slow and you had that spill a few weeks ago. I just thought that maybe you should lighten up a bit, nothing more. Just lighten up."

"Just taking a break. You know, get away from the stink for a few hours."

"Forget it. Good luck with this. Let me know how you do."

Willie watched Ben walked down the long stairs towards the track. "I meant it," he shouted. "You can still get in."

Ben didn't answer.

- 32 -

Sheepshead Bay was the home of Brooklyn's fishing fleet, Manhattan Beach, Lundy's Restaurant and the Golden Gate Motel. Sandy tapped lightly on the door of room 219. He didn't like standing in the hallway exposed to whoever may chance by. Of course, anyone who would be in the same hallway would be equally as averse to seeing him. Nevertheless, he felt vulnerable. He waited for the door to open.

It did. A woman stood in the crack of the doorway offering just an eye.

"Yes?"

"M'am, I am Sandy Kane, legal counsel to the biggest and best. I have some briefs for you."

The door opened slowly.

"Well, I hope you do and I hope there's something in them." Eileen stood there wearing just a blouse. Her long legs ended in just the right place. "You're six minutes late."

"Seven." Sandy took off his suit jacket, grabbed her and kicked the door closed in one well-coordinated fluid move.

He had been anticipating this for hours. He prolonged the anticipation as he stared at her and rolled his hands up her sides and felt the outside of her breasts, just touching lightly, incidentally, teasing both of them. He still pictured her as the untouchable young secretary sitting outside of his office: much too young, much too close and much too desirable.

She put her arms around his neck and they drew into a kiss—a soft, gentle kiss. He stopped and looked at her again, checking to make sure that it was really her he was kissing.

They kissed again—slowly, a little deeper, more passionately. This was what it was all about: the challenge, the conquest, the seduction, and the fear that it would happen, or worse, it would not.

He had felt secure that she had paid no attention to him; she remained alluring, yet professional. She had kept her distance and that made his conflict diminish. She was unattainable, so he would not try to attain her; safely relegating her to some private moments of fantasy. He knew that the consequences far outweighed the benefits—but consequences are later, benefits are now. And now always wins over later.

It was about tonight, this hour, this moment, this kiss. They stretched it out, knowing it was not about where they were going but where they were. It was about savoring each moment and anticipating the next.

"Let me catch up to you," Sandy said, his lips a breath away from hers. "What are you drinking?"

"Chivas."

"Sounds good."

He undressed as she took an airline bottle of Chivas Regal out of her purse and fixed his drink. He watched the sex ooze from her blouse. He could see all he needed to and imagine the rest—as he had many times before.

"One Chivas, coming up."

She handed him his drink as he lay there and, in the same move, slowly slid on top of him. He balanced his drink on the unoccupied pillow next to him and unbuttoned her blouse. He savored the adventure of each button. He wasn't disappointed. She was everything he had hoped plus some; her breasts were bigger, rounder, and firmer than he thought—he caressed them. Reality exceeded fantasy.

She was *an old twenty-two, a very old twenty-two.*

He slowly traced the contours of her stomach down to her crotch as she sat on him. Her skin felt like beautifully soft twenty-two year old skin, softer. He reached the silk of her panties and slid his fingers underneath into the warm and moist homeland as they fixed on each other's eyes.

He was pretty lucky that Wasserman hired her—the niece of a friend or something. He hoped that Wasserman wasn't screwing her also. The old fart probably hadn't gotten it up in years. He wanted to think that she was a very experienced virgin that was exploding with him on her mind.

The warmth spread through her body as his hands explored inside her. She moaned and melted softly on him and locked into a long kiss that was the ultimate communication that two people could have. She had never been that wet before and it was far from over. She undulated rhythmically as if to keep pace with a hastening drumbeat. Her body surged with delight as her pace increased and her breathing became very heavy until she gasped, out of pleasure, and out of air. This was a new high for her, a new extreme, and a new definition of pleasure.

At that moment, they were as perfectly physically paired as any two people have been. Their bodies were amoebas that choreographically floated and joined together in all the right places. They were in uncharted territory.

They made love for over an hour. They couldn't get enough of each other yet they prolonged the inevitable until they exploded simultaneously into each other, leaving no sensation undiscovered or unexplored.

When they were through, Sandy reached back and grabbed his Chivas, still delicately nestled on the pillow, and downed it. He stayed longer than he thought he would. He lit two smokes and placed one in her lips. He realized that he had never seen her smoke, didn't know if she did. She exhaled smoothly, her smoke gently merging with his.

"Gotta go," he said softly.

She was glad he stayed longer than she thought he would. She watched him leave and thought about how wonderfully strange this was. He had surprised her. They were the only two in the office, not a rare occasion, and he came out to her desk and stood over her. He didn't say anything, he didn't have to; he just smiled and nodded. He walked behind her and leaned over to her typewriter. He typed:

Golden Gate 6pm.

He had had a bad day and was in a rare bad mood and she felt sorry for him. Bullshit. She had been baiting this for a long time but she had expected him to ask her for a drink and gradually work up to something more romantic. She looked up at him. They both knew where this would wind up, so why bother with the long route. Strange, but efficient, and very effective.

She would have to put an end this thing with Wasserman.

Damn!

Ben's head slammed into the visor as the car plummeted into a pothole and out again. His head connected on the same spot that he bruised in the fire. He checked the mirror to see if he opened the wound. It was a last reminder of another life, a life that he had led for the last twenty years and almost forgotten about, almost.

He had avoided the Belt and took the short way home through the Linden Boulevard minefield, choosing instead to navigate through this obstacle course than sit still in hot rush hour traffic. He rode the edges of the cracks narrowly avoiding a pothole, only to be positioned to face two more directly in front. Like a deft jockey, he swerved left and right and guided the car through the field and wound up straddling both potholes, missing by inches with both wheels. He didn't like driving, but if he had to, this would do fine.

Today's connection with Willie brought him back to reality. *How could he bet on that stupid shit?* He checked on the bruise again in the mirror and caught himself smiling. He hadn't had anything to smile about in a while. Maybe it was for Willie; he couldn't stay pissed at him. He loved the guy but he was such a fuck up; maybe that's why he loved him. No matter how many times he lost on his lousy horse picking or dim-witted schemes, he always came back for more. He was a resilient, dumb, lovable fuck up. His horse finished way out of the money, but not far enough out to keep him from trying the dumb shit thing again.

Maybe the smile was for his day; he came out ahead, cashed on two races, with long enough prices to cover his investment plus some. It was still lunch money but the feel was coming back; it felt natural. Maybe this was the answer, maybe it would work out.

But not in time to solve the Charlie dilemma. No use pressing and trying to rush it; that would only lead to bad decisions and, ultimately, worse than where he started.

Don't press.

No, be smart, make good bets, play the edges and maybe this would be an out. That's the long-term plan but Charlie was still out there and wasn't going away.

He had to give him five hundred tonight, which he took out of their savings; there wasn't another five hundred to take. He had won a little on the horses but it was test money, not real money, not enough anyway. Besides, he had an idea about tonight.

Ben pulled over in front of a florist on Flatlands Avenue.

- 33 -

Goodies was a little more crowded and noisier than usual. The leftovers from the after work crowd hung a little longer and crossed into the early arrivals of the late night contingent. Ben had stopped home to an empty house and left the flowers in a vase on the kitchen table. He was momentarily relieved that Kitty wasn't there; he didn't want to face her and lie to her about where he spent his day—much less where he would be tonight.

He walked into Goodies and stood behind Willie and Ed the Brain who sat at the bar. They were deep in conversation and didn't notice him.

"Maybe we should bet the *last* horse outa the gate," Willie lamented.

"Huh? Why?" Ed the Brain was focused on the Racing Form.

"Well, this isn't working."

"What do you mean?"

"We lost every race."

"So?" Ed didn't look up from the paper.

"So? What do you mean 'so'? So, we lost every race. So, my dog could've done better if I had a dog."

"You don't have a dog and even if you did, it couldn't read."

"Well if I got a dog and it could read, it would come up with better schemes than you."

"Maybe it could, maybe it couldn't."

"It could."

"Could've been worse."

"You can't do too much worse than oh-for-nine."

"Sure you can."

"How?"

"You can go oh-for-ten."

"You know," Willie looked at Ed as if he was looking at the dumbest sonofabitch on the planet. "You're a fuckin' idiot. No wonder they call you Ed the Shit for Brains."

Ed looked up. "Fuck you, nine fingered asshole."

"Fuck you, shit for brains."

This was heading south. Ben put his hand on Willie's shoulder. "Hi guy."

"Benny, how long you been standin' there?"

"Just got here," he held back a grin.

"Oh Benny, say hi to Ed Zally."

"Ed Zally? Ed the Brain, right? We've met," Ben said as they shook hands.

"Sure," Ed said, unsure.

"How did you guys do today?" In spite of how he felt about Willie's gambling, he couldn't resist prodding.

"Not bad." Willie jumped in. "Ed's got some pretty good ideas. Still working some things out. Beer?" He turned to the bartender, pointed to his beer, put up two fingers and turned back to Ben. "This is some day, saw everybody today—you at the track and you again now."

"That's everybody? Me twice?"

"Oh, Al and Sandy this morning. Didn't I say that?"

"I must have missed that. Where were they?"

"At the station, before I took a break and saw you out at the track. Al was filling up and I was shooting the breeze with him. You know, just this and that, nothing with nothing. What do you know; Sandy pulls up right behind him. He gets out and comes over, didn't say much of a hello, figure he's got something on his mind, and says to Al that he's trying to reach him, where was he and gets into Al's car."

"Both of them filling up?"

"Al filling up, Sandy parked behind him. Then another customer pulls in, wants his oil checked. This guy wants his oil checked all the time. So I check it, tell him he's a quart low and show him the stick like I do every week. I turn back and see Al and Sandy going at it in the car."

"Going at it?"

"Well they were arguing about something. I figure there's a few fuckin'-Paula-this and fuckin'-Paula-thats bouncing around the car so I'm better off pouring oil, which I don't do, but I charge the guy anyway cause he's a real schmuck."

"What happened?"

"Oh, he paid and left."

"No, with Al and Sandy."

"Oh, dunno. Things got real quiet and they talked. I stayed away, none of my bees. I got my own probs. Then Sandy gets out and Al pulled out like he's going to a fire, which he isn't because he just got off duty. Didn't even pay, but I put it on the tab."

"Sandy say anything?"

"Nah. Just left, didn't even fill up. Wasn't in a talking mood, I guess."

"Divorces are tough."

"Yeah, but Al's had plenty of practice. Beer?"

"No thanks, just passing through. Speaking of Sandy, seen him?"

"Right behind."

Ben turned and saw Sandy approaching.

"Night guys," Ben said as he intercepted Sandy, grabbed him by the arm, spun him around and exited.

"Nice guy," Ed said as he turned back to the *Racing Form*.

"Benny, the best. Known him all my life."

"Maybe you're right; maybe we should bet the last horse outa the gate."

Willie lifted Ben's beer and downed it.

Ben and Sandy crossed the street and both spied an old Chevy with ropes tied around the door.

"Ed the Brain?" Sandy asked.

"Yeah," The grin Ben had been sequestering exploded on his face as they got into Sandy's Olds and pulled out. "Willie's new girlfriend."

"What?"

"Forget it. Won't last."

"If you say so. Where am I going?

"Ocean Parkway. Charlie's apartment. Gotta make a down payment, less than what he wants but he'll have to live with it."

"Ok."

"And, it's Wednesday."

"So?"

"So Wednesday is payday at Charlie's."

"And?"

"And we need to get into the crap game and book the six and eight."

"Book them?"

"Book them. His game pays even money on sixes and eights. We'll be the house on this one and let the odds work in our favor for a change. Maybe put a little dent into Charlie."

"Sounds good. Ocean Parkway."

They digested the day and drove in silence for a while, the kind of silence that friends could be alone with and not be uncomfortable.

"Good day?" Ben asked. He decided not to ask about what Willie told him about him and Al. Willie was probably right; it's none of his bees. He also decided not to mention the track just yet. They'll be plenty of time to go through that.

"Not bad. You?" Sandy held back the grin as he thought about Eileen.

"Same."

- 34 -

Beefy Leonard's sweaty hand brought the dice up to his mouth, kissed them like they were his dying kittens and blew on them for luck. Spit sprayed across the makeshift crap table. Sandy and Ben watched as Beefy's nostrils flared. He was far uglier up close; his skin was small patches of alligator hide separated by islands of curly stubble. The furrow over his eyes undulated as it connected ear to ear and duplicated itself all the way to his hairline. He had enough skin for three ugly people.

Balls of sweat appeared on his chest as Beefy rolled. "Seven, fucker!" He drooled and unconsciously wiped his sleeveless arm across his mouth.

Seven.

He quickly picked up the bills on the table as if anyone else were about to lay claim to them. By the way the three other men at the table looked; he had been on a roll for some time. He noticed Ben.

"Want in?"

"Not right now." Ben turned to see if Charlie was available; paying him had to be the first priority. He was nowhere in sight. Charlie's apartment was an ordinary Ocean Parkway apartment: all the requisite furniture, a couple of stock oil paintings, a well stocked fridge and rolling bar cart. An aging brunette sat on the sofa looking bored. His house in Bensonhurst was much higher class, his wife saw to that. But this was his apartment—for business and pleasure, not for living. There was a lot of crapola, but no Charlie.

"How about you?" Beefy asked Sandy.

"Shoot."

Beefy Leonard scooped the dice into his clammy hand and looked at Ben once more, curious as if he should know him from somewhere. He didn't come up with the answer and turned back to the dice and began his foreplay again.

"Seven, you little fuckers." He snorted and rolled.

Eight.

"Twenty on the eight," Beefy Leonard threw the money down. "Who's going book my eight?"

"I'll take it." Sandy floated a twenty onto Beefy's twenty.

"Fresh money. Hope there's more of those Benjamins in your pocket."

"Jacksons." Sandy offered.

"What?"

"Twenties have Jackson, not . . . never mind, shoot."

The dice bounced off the wall.

Eight.

"Eight!" Beefy scooped up the money and picked up the dice once more.

He left a twenty on the table and Sandy dropped another to match it. Beefy rolled.

"Seven!"

Eight.

Beefy took Sandy's twenty and left his on the table.

"Feel lucky?" Beefy asked. "Wanna press? You got the odds."

"Covered." Sandy floated another twenty down.

"Eighter from da freighter." Beefy kissed the dice.

197

"Decatur." Sandy muttered a little louder than he intended.

"What?"

"Nothing. Shoot."

"No. What'd you say?"

"That's Decatur. Eighter from Decatur," Sandy corrected him wishing he hadn't.

"What?"

"It's eighter from Decatur, not the eighter from the freighter."

"What the fuck. Who the fuck cares?"

"Never mind, shoot."

Beefy set the dice on the table, side by side and positioned them so the four showed on top of each one. He moved them along the table as if he was playing with a model car. He slowly looked up at Sandy.

"See that? Hard way. Hard eight. From a fuckin' freighter. And that's where the eight is coming from. Forty four, mother fucker." His smile revealed a gold incisor. He picked up his kittens once more, slobbered on them and threw.

Ben turned as Charlie emerged from the bathroom. The brunette perked up and patted the sofa, inviting Charlie to sit. He ignored her and looked at Ben and nodded.

"Be right back," Ben said to Sandy.

Ben fixed on Charlie as he walked the few steps, leaving the dice game in the background. Charlie probably expected a lot more than Ben had in his pocket, but it would have to do. It didn't look like the dice were going to help.

Eight!

"Eighter from da fuckin' freighter!" Beefy echoed through the apartment. "Ain't your lucky night Jackson."

They silently drove down Ocean Parkway in the right lane where each corner offered a special dip to provide for water flow. The speed bump hit at exactly the wrong time and jostled Ben into the present.

"Should I ask?"

"Down three twenty."

"Figures. Ok if I give to you tomorrow? Charlie wiped me."

"No prob. Take your time. He press you?"

It took a long time for Ben to respond. He looked up at the huge maple trees that lined Ocean Parkway; their dwindling leaves leaving gaps for the night sky to pass through. It was a clear night for Brooklyn as a few stars dotted the sky. He suddenly felt small and irrelevant.

"I've got two weeks."

"How much?"

"A lot more than I have."

"Or what?"

"Or," Ben hesitated, "or, I could do him a favor and we're square." He kept looking at the night sky passing through the window of the Olds.

"What kind of favor?"

"The kind he's not gonna get." Ben opened the window and the side vent and let the cool fall air press against his face.

Sandy knew that if Ben wanted him to know he would've answered directly, so he didn't push it. The car rolled up and down, up and down in a predictable cadence—like his life until a few weeks ago. Now there's nothing routine about it.

They hit another bump. Ben wondered if Sandy knew what this would do to his shocks.

"Next time," Sandy said, "I'll bring my own dice."

"Wouldn't've helped."

- 35 -

The smoke meandered from Irene's mouth, up and around the contour of her nose, through her eyelashes, her hair and into the air, as she sat in her kitchen and downed her third cup of coffee.

"New?" Kitty broke the silence.

"What?"

"This," she ran her hand across the table.

"Yep. New dinette set. I treated myself, got it on sale, thought I'd pretty up the place. Sandy hasn't even noticed it."

"He will."

"Don't think so, hon. He's had coffee and dinner on it for five months now."

"It's pretty." Kitty absently scanned the kitchen which housed reminders of several attempts to pretty up the place: empty cartons, including the one from the dinette set, a tiffany chandelier, which had been lying on the floor forever and an unused bicycle, which she bought to trim down a few years back. A wooden box with silverware from last Thanksgiving dinner stood open on the counter.

"New chairs too?"

"That's why they call it a set, dear."

"Yes." Kitty looked at Irene's cigarette. "Give me one of those."

"You don't smoke."

"I do. Sometimes."

Irene slid the pack of Kent across the table.

Kitty very carefully chose one.

"They're all the same."

Kitty plucked one from the pack and awkwardly lit it—feigning smoker's aptitude, which made her appear even more awkward.

Irene watched. The problem with amateur smokers was they try too hard; the rest of us just smoke without knowing we're smoking. She wasn't being judgmental, she told herself, just observant. If she were a self-conscious smoker she would have flicked her ash long ago. Irene was a professional, a ranked smoker, a two-pack-a-day hard smoking queen. Poor Kitty—an amateur smoker, but a sweetheart.

Irene had a couple of years and a couple of pounds on Kitty. She was pretty, her face well sculpted, but her looks were evaporating at an accelerated rate. She was frenetic but without a mission in life.

"You're sure he doesn't have a honey?"

"No!" Kitty was emphatic. "I mean, I'm sure."

She knew Ben; he doesn't screw around. She wondered why she was so adamant, so sure. The smoke stung her eyes and she welled up and snorted in the unhappiness mounting in her nose. *Shit.*

"People change, you know."

"Huh?"

"People change. Maybe he's the greatest guy in the world for the first hundred years you're married and something happens or he just gets bored or he meets someone in a fire and suddenly Ben's not Ben. He's the new Ben; a nice guy, but a cheating asshole like all the rest of them. After all these years, you find out that, deep down under all that nice guy stuff, he is an asshole after all."

Kitty took a puff on the cigarette and held it between her two fingers defiantly as she stared at Irene trying to figure out if she was serious or just being Irene.

"You just think all men are pigs."

"Oink. Because they are."

"Not Ben."

"You're sure?"

"Pretty sure."

"Not a hundred percent?"

"Pretty sure."

"Ok. Just asking. Well this job thing's gotta be tough on him and maybe this is the real him. Oink. Or maybe he's not a pig right now but he will be tomorrow morning. They can't help it you know. God gave us eggs and them bacon."

Kitty laughed. It felt good. She knew that Irene didn't mean it. This was Ben we were talking about, not Sandy.

Irene wasn't always this tough; she was a pretty young thing when she met Sandy in the Philippines during the war. She had the distinction of being one of two nurses that Sandy did not sleep with in the Philippines; the other had braided armpits. She was interested but smart enough to hold out. There was no shortage of guys and if she were to get involved, it would be on her terms. Sandy pursued her when they arrived stateside and they got married three months later. She bounced from nursing to Phys Ed teacher, to school administrator, to receptionist; even sold Fuller Brushes door to door for a while. Turns out, her being outgoing and always on the move, the brush job suited her best. She convinced Sandy that with their two jobs they could buy a house. So they did, and hired a live-in maid and Irene quit work. She had energy to burn and nothing to burn it on so she has been moving in and redecorating ever since—packed boxes populated every room and the house was in a constant state of change.

As different as they were, Kitty and Irene became friends and stayed that way over the years. They didn't hang out together much, but they counted on each other at those crucial times when only a real friend would do.

Kitty appreciated Irene's raw candor and her ability to convince herself that life was tolerable when it wasn't. Irene deluded herself into believing she had control when she knew she didn't. Her life was always in turmoil and crisis.

Kitty, on the other hand, relinquished control to Ben long ago, and she was happy she did. She lived the Ozzie and Harriet lifestyle for so long—at least that's how it seemed to everyone, including her. *Was she fooling herself?* She didn't know if she was more afraid of losing the house or Ben or their lifestyle or just being humiliated.

What if Irene's right?

Kitty crushed the cigarette out so that there was no chance of it ever being resurrected, or even recognized as once being a cigarette. It was out, very out.

"I should go."

"You sure? The kids are sleeping out and the guys are out anyway. Stay a little . ."

They're out? He didn't . . .

Maybe she would stay a while. Not because she wanted to talk about anything with Irene. No, she was tired of talking.

She just wanted to get home after Ben. She wanted to be the one that was *out*.

"Ok," she picked up Irene's Kent that was burning in the ashtray, inhaled and held back a cough.

They talked about everything except what mattered and, a little before two, Kitty left.

Kitty didn't cry that night—she was proud of that—she was stronger than she looked. She pulled into the narrow baseball field that also served as a driveway and quietly entered the dark house. A smile erupted when she saw the flowers sitting on the kitchen table and somehow the troubles of the night seemed to evaporate. Maybe things would be ok.

She ascended the stairs quietly and gently opened the bedroom door. This must be the way Ben felt when he would come home late. She pictured him lying in bed and wondered if he was faking it the way she always had. She was strangely excited, almost guilty, as she felt her way to the bed in the dark room. Maybe she was too hard on him. Her clothes dropped to the floor and she crawled into bed.

It was empty.

The tears that she held back for forever erupted and she cried herself to sleep.

Al was shitfaced when Ben and Sandy got back to Goodies. They hadn't planned coming back, but a nightcap seemed in order after the fiasco at Charlie's.

"How long has he been drinking?" Sandy asked Willie.

"Dunno. He walked in with some broad over an hour ago. Beer?"

"Chivas rocks," Sandy said.

"Two," Ben added.

"What broad?"

"In the corner," Willie nodded towards a booth where a woman rested comfortably asleep, head on table.

"Miss happy face."

It wasn't long before the three of them approached Al's status in shitfaceville. It was unusual for the four of them to be drinking hard—the last time they did Sandy was headed to war. Now they celebrated that they were all going through tough times, didn't want to talk about it, and that they were still good friends. That's what they celebrated; they didn't say any of it, they just celebrated it and drank.

Willie turned to Sandy. It took several moments before the words formed.

"A question. What if you could bet on the lead horse in a race after the race started?"

Ben delicately edged his stool down the bar, just out of earshot and drew next to Al who, at that moment, was staring at himself in the bar mirror. It was a tense moment until they caught each other's eye in the mirror and, in a look, realized that they were on each other's back for no reason and they should patch it up. It was a particularly sensitive moment for Al who slurred his way through the conversation as he drew closer and closer to Ben. The more Al drank, the closer he would get. Pretty soon, he had his arm around Ben's neck and was speaking directly into his ear, imprisoning Ben in this slurring headlock. Ben immediately knew he wasn't going to like this conversation.

"Let me make it up to you. I know you're tight right now." Al slurred. "I've got some cash, a loan. Pay me whenever, doesn't matter."

"Thanks. I'm ok."

"Ok." He took a few moments to formulate his next offer: "I've got a truckload of smokes that lost their way. I need someone I can trust to move them with me. It's a fast thousand."

"Not interested," Ben said as he tried to pull away. "And you shouldn't be either."

"Well, I know you're—"

"Not interested. Don't ask me again."

"I'm a schmuck."

"Forget it."

"No. I'm a schmuck. I fucked up. Sorry."

"Yeah. Forget it."

"Benny, I'm sorry. Everything's been so fucked up. I'll make it up to you. I'll make everything up to you."

Ben figured they had patched enough for tonight and tried to break the headlock and the special relationship Al had with his ear, but he couldn't.

"Al, you've been through rough spots before. You'll come out of it, you always have. Right?"

"Ben. I'm sorry," Al said and his words broke up and became soggy as he started to shake and cry in Ben's ear. He just kept saying *I'm sorry* over and over. Somehow, Willie and Sandy missed this as Willie had Sandy captivated by his past-post scheme. Al sobbed like an out of control child and Ben just held and comforted him, not knowing what else to do. He felt for the guy, a three-time loser.

"Al, let me ask you a question."

Al dried his eyes on his sleeve and snorted up, ready to receive.

"Did you come here with anyone?"

Al didn't quite understand, suddenly did and looked to the corner.

"Angie. Nice lady, come and meet her."

"It's been a long day. I think I'm going to see my own nice lady."

"Benny, thanks."

"You ok?"

"Ok."

Al departed for Miss happy face and Ben called it a night. Willie ordered one more round and had Sandy convinced that Willie was totally out of his mind.

Ben pulled into the driveway.

Long day, good to get home to a little warmth.

- 36 -

Ben had less than two weeks left in the department but that was becoming less of an issue; that was the past. The challenge was to get good enough at the track to earn a living and find some way out of the box with Charlie.

He and Al were best of friends again, Sandy and Eileen were becoming better friends, Irene was up to two and a half packs, Willie continued to scheme his way to becoming the first gas pumping millionaire and Kitty and Ben hardly spoke. The kids went off to camp for a few weeks and Kitty was abruptly left without day-to-day chores.

He was at the track every day, including Saturday, an hour before the Double and sat at the same table. It didn't take long before he promoted himself to the Clubhouse, where the successful players play. It cost a few bucks more to get in but it was worth it. His system was working—he made careful, educated, bets. He watched the odds until a few minutes before post time and made his bet. The odds were the key; any good handicapper could pick the winning horse a reasonable percentage of the time. After all, Joe Schmoe could bet the favorite and probably win one out of three or four times. Of course, he would go home with less money than he came with.

Yeah, figure the horse's chances based on past performance, particularly how he did against other horses in the race. Check his class—was he racing against better or worse horses? Check the odds—was there something in this horse's charts that was clue to today's race? Check the odds again—eliminate the horses that don't have a shot. Throw out the favorite, the price is too short, no percentage in betting the favorite—ask Joe Schmoe. And, if you think the favorite's a lock, then sit out the race, have a beer, take a crap, figure the next race, whatever.

Put it together—make the selections based upon the horses' chances and the potential payoff. Narrow it down to one, two, maybe three horses that fit. If you're lucky, one will stand out and speak to you, only you. Is there a horse that has a shot whose odds are out of line? Check the odds again—are they better than what you figure the horse's chances are? Are they dropping too fast near post because late money is coming in? Is it smart money? Does somebody know something? Does somebody think they know something?

Check the odds once more. Remember the odds are figured based on other people's opinions—not on reality, chance, statistics, or quantitative physics. This is not Vegas, where the house bets against you—where they smile, get you laid and keep you around long enough to lose. This is parimutuel wagering. The house doesn't give a shit whether you win or lose—it gets a piece no matter what or who wins. The bets are all put into a pool, the house and the state get fifteen percent and the odds are figured based what's left and on how much is bet on which horse. It's you against every Joe Schmoe and his mother-in-law out there—the horses are almost incidental. If everyone liked the two horse because he won his last sixty three races or his purple polka dots or his Tuiti Fruity name, then the odds will go way down on the two horse. On the other hand, if everyone missed the seven because they can't see his potential or his name is Irwin, then the odds would be high. *You cannot be smarter than horses; you cannot know who will win. You can just figure the chances and see if it's worth the bet. If you can figure the horses better than the rest of the money out there, you are going to do very well. Then you bet. Maybe bet one horse, maybe two. You never know. If it's the Double, maybe bet two horses in the first tied into one in the second, or the other way around. Bet win, not place or show—no percentage there. Put your money where your mouth is. Do it well and you are a good horseplayer—you are a good handicapper.*

Ben was becoming a good handicapper—he wanted to become a great handicapper. He began to develop a sense of finding the *value* horse—the horse with a reasonable chance of winning with a big potential payoff.

Ben looked for *Irwin*.

He began to build the information resource by tracking the horses and recording his impression of their performance. He improvised ratings, which became his shorthand guide. Each night he would update the previous days ratings for each horse into a book, which he kept with him at all times. This was his bible—he would look up his ratings for the all the horses on tomorrow's card. He didn't win every day, but he won enough to give him encouragement to refine his skills further and to get him noticed.

The track was a clubby place for the regulars and it quickly became incestuous after the same guys see the same guys at the windows, at the table, on the floor and in the men's room. *Who do you like?* Everyone wanted another opinion, to corroborate his own or to get that special piece of info that would help them make those important decisions nine times a day. It didn't take long for the word to spread about Ben—*new guy, seems friendly, not a talker, knows his stuff.*

Translation: picks winners. The word spread. Willie helped.

Willie, a regular at Ben's table, subtly and discreetly told anyone who'd listen:

"Yeah, he's a good friend of mine, rode in together. Can really pick 'em."

"Who does he like here?" Big Jack stood over Willie with Little Jack at his side.

Ben never advertised his opinion, but when asked, he would normally take a conservative approach and hedge it a little.

"The three has a shot."

It didn't really benefit him to make his opinion known. After all, the more money bet on a horse, the lower the odds. But he figured, *you never know*. It's better to have allies than not. Besides, it felt good, real good.

"Benny, who do we like here?" Willie asked but Ben was lost in thought. He studied the program, the odds and the performances up the kazoo, but all he could think about was last night's conversation with Kitty.

"What are you doing to us?"

Her question cut right through Ben. It was a question, a statement and a declaration of mistrust. It cut right to the core of their relationship. They've had issues before, differences of opinion, but never about trust: trust they had, until now. He knew that he wasn't himself lately and it was probably difficult for her—not probably, definitely. But, she should have believed that he, they, would get through it—they always had. But, this time was different. This time, she didn't believe in it or in him.

"I'm not doing anything to us. I, we, have a situation that I'm trying to fix."

"With the horses?"

Now we're at the nerve, the real issue.

"Maybe, yeah, maybe. Got a better solution?"

"Solution? What do you mean solution? I don't even know what the problem is?"

"It's that we owe a lot more money than we have, it's that I'm trying to fix it, it's that . . . look, I know you don't want me to play the horses, never did, and I promised I wouldn't."

"So you lied."

"No. I meant it. But it was a long time ago and I had my whole life to do it. I figured I could always do it later, so I gave it up for you, and that was ok."

"And now?"

"Now, it's later."

"And we're not important now?"

"Look, I don't have other chances down the road. I didn't plan on losing my job, it just happened—maybe it's a good thing. If I don't do it now, I'll always wish that I had. It's my only chance of fixing this . . . and being something, standing out, of being special."

"Special?"

"Kitty, I'm good at it, maybe very good, I don't know. I just wish you'd trust me."

It was a long moment before she replied.

"So do I."

"Benny, who do we like here?" Willie asked again and interrupted Ben's distress.

"The *three* has a shot," Ben recovered.

The *three* lost—so did all of his other picks that day. Is it possible that the horses got wind of their conversation and just weren't up for running that day? Even winners have bad days.

- 37 -

The note kept slipping out of Ben's hand. This was another *I'm at Irene's*, except there was no *see you later*. Instead there was:

> *I don't know when I'm coming back.*

It said *when* but Ben read *if*. It went on about her needing time, space, universal good, and so forth. At the end, instead of *love K*, it said *sorry, K*.

If there was a time that Ben would cry, this was it. He trembled inside, felt weak and nauseated, welled up, but didn't cry. He couldn't seem to break his own strong façade. He didn't think she knew how much he counted on her; she was his inner strength, his resolve and determination. She protected his downside, no matter what happened he'd have her: until now.

For the next hour, Ben wandered aimlessly through the empty house. He picked up the phone several times but never dialed; if she needed time, she'd get time. Maybe this was good; maybe he could focus more on the track and fixing the situation with Charlie. Maybe this was the break he needed and there would be more time to concentrate; but he knew that she would be behind every thought.

The phone rang and resonated through every corner of the barren house. He grabbed it midway through the second ring.

"Hi . . . hey Al."

It was clear to Kitty that she had lost whatever control and faith she had in the marriage and Ben. Everything had eroded to a new low and she had to do something, something. She walked through the kitchen and made her decision. As she packed, she thought, if she left she'd have no control so she'd stay, but this wasn't working, so she'd leave. She made a lot of decisions that day—each reversed the prior. Until she realized that she needed to do something and this was the only something, she got angry with herself: *when did I lose my spine?*

She wrote a note, ripped it up and wrote another—hard, but not final; jeopardizing, but not threatening. It was a declaration—a note of assertiveness, meant to hurt but not harm—the gauntlet had been thrown.

Irene was no help.

"Hi," Irene greeted her, "now go home."

If Kitty expected warmth, solace and empathy, she came to the wrong place. Irene would give her shelter and food and honesty far beyond what she wanted. They talked all night, Kitty complained about insensitivity, selfishness, broken promises and loneliness, which seemed to be the real issue. Kitty was left out of the problem and lost any shred of control.

"Once you get used to the fact that men are pigs," Irene sniffed the cigar smoke emanating from the basement and went on in support of men, "they are easier to take. Roll with it honey. Say, men are pigs. Go on."

"Men are pigs."

"Good. Feel better?"

"Yes. No."

"Look," Irene decided to play her trump card. "You may not know this but Sandy flirts with everything in a skirt."

"Not with me."

"Well, you're family. But outside these walls maybe he's crossed the line once or twice in sixteen years. I mean if old Wasserman wasn't banging his secretary, then I'd be worried that . . . that's not my point."

"There's a point?"

"The point is I deal with it. I shouldn't tell you this but the boy who delivers my cleaning, well, I let him . . ."

"You didn't."

"Didn't what?"

"You know."

"Well I did. I fucked his sixteen year old brains out."

"No."

"That's how I deal with it. Men are pigs. Women are piglets. Try it. It balances things. I bet you never thought of cheating on Ben."

Kitty did not respond.

"Kit?"

"Once, in Stockholm; on a trip with my boss. He was so nice and authoritative . . . power is an aphrodisiac you know. I've never been with anyone else. I mean ever, even before Ben. Anyway, I felt so guilty after that I quit work."

"You didn't?"

Kitty nodded.

"Between us, please. Please. Now we know each other's secret."

"Not really."

"Huh?"

"Delivery boy, bad acne, wouldn't even let him through the front door. Wouldn't fuck him with your twat."

Ben hit his horn once and Al came out immediately and jumped in.

"What happened? Wreck your heap?" Ben feigned.

"Worse," Al replied in an unusually good mood, "Paula borrowed it and when she borrows things, I never see them again. Fuck it, the transmission's ready to drop. With my luck it'll fall out in a car wash and I know she'll just leave it there. Was thinking about a new one anyway."

Al went on about Paula in a tender way; he didn't call her a cunt once the entire ride. This wasn't the Al he knew but it was a pleasant change, although strange. It was good to hear him upbeat; it helped Ben forget about his own mess. Then Al abruptly stopped and stared out the window.

A morose silence replaced Al's non-stop chitchat and Ben once again bounced between the track, Charlie and Kitty. Then he sensed Al looking directly at him as he drove. It was a long uncomfortable stare.

"Benny, don't worry, I'll fix everything." His tone was serious.

"I know."

If he wanted to play God, it was Ok with Ben.

The card game was underway when they arrived—Sandy, Willie, Pacey Diamond, Doc and Phil, a new guy. It must have been cigar night: Doc always smoked them, Willie smoked one and Phil had one permanently implanted in the right corner of his mouth. Ben noticed later that when he was bluffing the cigar migrated to the left corner—it didn't help.

After the intros, Phil offered Ben and Al a:

"Cigar?"

Ben passed, Al didn't. It occurred to Ben that Kitty was probably upstairs with Irene, crying and slamming him from wall to wall with Irene cheering her on. One thing about woman, they always stick together. They are empathetic and team up quickly. Men, however infrequently the need arises, listen and then go on to talk about their own problems, then something safe, like sports.

The thought never occurred to Ben to go upstairs. After all, this was the card game, every week in Sandy's basement, just like always. If she wanted to see him, she knew where he was. *Deal.*

It was an uneventful game. Ben and Willie lost and Al was the big winner. Good for him, Ben thought, he needed it and I've been oh-for-everything today anyhow. It was uneventful except that Ben didn't know that he would soon find a clue his future.

The chips piled high in front of Al and he began to stack them in neat little piles, which Willie would regularly tip over. It didn't matter—it was Al's night.

"Three ladies, ladies," Al declared as he raked in another pot.

"Somebody's stepping in it," Willie said.

"Law of averages: long overdue my friend. An off night Ben?"

"Law of averages. I'm down."

"Me too," Willie echoed as he stacked his three chips.

"Hey, it's early. I finally get a run and everybody's a short hitter," Al moaned cheerfully.

"What's your line, Phil?" Ben asked as they settled up.

"Garment center—the elastic in bras? I make 'em. You?"

Now that was a simple question: *"you?"* Yet Ben had trouble answering. Good thing he didn't have to.

"Benny's the best fuckin' horse player in the state, maybe two states." Willie bragged, "Except today, but tomorrow'll be better, right Ben?"

Enough, Willie.

"Heard you been hitting pretty good," Doc added.

"Yeah, doing ok." He obviously didn't hear about today.

"You going out tomorrow?" Doc asked.

"Probably," Ben said, meaning definitely.

"I got a tip, do me a favor, make a bet for me."

"Sure."

Doc handed Ben a slip of paper and a twenty-dollar bill, which Ben glanced at and stuffed into his pocket. He looked at the door leading upstairs and thought: it's been a long day; it'll be a longer night.

- 38 -

Sleep wasn't happening. As tired as he was, sleep was on the distant horizon and every thought was an obstacle on the way. His mind raced and his body felt like each cell had an anchor dragging it down. He avoided the clock, which could only bring him bad news and closed his eyes for the nth time.

There was no escape from light of a full moon, which played across his eyes, and the street sounds which were too clear, too defined, too sleep depriving. This day needed to end.

When he heard the second loud knock at the door, he remembered that there was a first knock somewhere deep in his dream. It took a moment before he fully bridged into consciousness. *Kitty!* Ben threw the sheets off, jumped out of bed and raced down the stairs wearing just his briefs. He took the stairs two at a time trying to end this chapter and restart his life. He envisioned spending the rest of the night cuddled close to her in bed.

He unlocked the door and hastily threw it open expecting to see Kitty stand there sheepishly and, without unnecessary words, fall into his arms. When they fought which was very rarely, they both would realize that they were in it for the long game. The door swung wide and the cool night air blew in.

"What the hell are you doing here?"

"That's not the welcome I expected," Charlie stood there nonchalant as if he was a regular visitor.

"You're not who I expected. What do you want?"

"I was in the neighborhood. May I . . ."

"No. What do you want?"

"I don't usually visit clients," Charlie said casually as he peered over Ben's shoulder, "I just wanted to check on my investment."

"It's not yours yet and never will be. You want to check it, check it from across the street. You're not coming in."

"He's already in," bellowed a strong voice from behind Ben.

Startled, Ben swung around and saw the voice belonged to Beefy Leonard who stood in the hallway looking down on him. He stepped closer and made his threatening hulk seem even larger.

Ben went into defensive mode as he tightened up and stood ready to keep swinging until he couldn't. He only wished he had his pants on; he felt a little disarmed being in his shorts.

"Don't get nervous Ben," Charlie advised. "This is just a friendly house call and a reminder. You've got ten days and a big account to settle. The vig is mounting. Or . . ."

Ben didn't appreciate this way of doing business; a debt is a debt and he was committed to pay but *fuck you, Charlie*.

"Or?"

"Or . . . you can make this go away with the right phone call."

"Forget it."

"Or . . . you lose this beautiful house."

"Don't pack yet, you'll get it. Get out."

"Oh I'm not packing at all. I told you this house is too small for me. Too difficult, banks, mortgages, paperwork, a hassle." Charlie said as he slowly retreated, "I said you'd lose it, not that I'd necessarily get it."

"What does that mean?"

Charlie looked back at Beefy who took out a matchbook. With one hand he split a match, bent it and, while it was still attached to the book, struck it against the flint and lit it. He put the match back into the book, closed it and watched as the rest of the matches ignited sending a flare of fire out of each end. He lit the cigarette with the flaming matchbook and dropped it on the carpet. Beefy smiled, a big shit eating, gap-toothed, Neanderthal smile, and left, making sure to brush Ben as he went by.

"Ten days Ben," Charlie called out.

Ben picked up the matchbook and watched them leave as it burned out.

- 39 -

Morning broke to the sound of crackling timber and smoke filled hallways. An axe crashed through the front window signaling the first firemen to arrive. This was big. The neighborhood was asleep; it was called in too late to save the building but there must be someone inside. Hoses hit the second floor shattering the glass and sending steaming flames and smoke into the atmosphere. Sirens and chaos filled the air.

Ben was about two blocks away from the firehouse when he heard the sirens. He had stopped to pick up the morning paper and a quick cup of coffee; he felt uncomfortable having coffee alone in his house. From the sirens, he knew it was big; he could hear the shrill sounds from two different companies. Then he remembered Charlie and Beefy. He ran a stop sign and pulled up in front of the firehouse. The trucks had already left.

"What's up?" Ben yelled out his window to the dispatcher.

"Big one. Four-alarmer. Brighton First. Just follow the smoke."

A wave of relief shook through Ben. Pretty stupid, he thought, Charlie wouldn't do anything yet. Then, he didn't understand quite why, but he pulled out quickly in pursuit of the fire.

"Hey, where're you going? You're a short timer," the dispatcher yelled.

When Ben pulled up, the fire was out of control. The immensity of it awed him; he hadn't seen anything like this since Luna Park. A grocery store stood at the base of the building. There were eleven floors of apartments above it. The building was next to the El, the above ground subway, which complicated attacking the monster. Two hose trucks and a Hook & Ladder were already in position. They would not be near enough. Firemen had broken entry and had brought out at least a dozen people; no one knew how many more were in there.

Rampant destruction followed the fire as it crept up the sides of the building. Every window spewed smoke and small fireballs were catapulted onto the El creating additional blazes. At the same moment, morning rush hour, a train passed overhead and showered everyone under the El with fiery cinders and debris. The street ignited as a car exploded and shattered store windows on both sides on the street. Several storefronts were burning and several dozen fires lit the street and sidewalks. A second car exploded trapping onlookers in a circle of death.

Ben found himself looking for gear, which he found in the cab of the hose truck. He didn't know why but in a few moments he was fully dressed and ready to attack the monster—the same monster that almost killed him more than once. He shouldn't do this, he told himself—he shouldn't even be here. He was a short timer—days away from never wearing the uniform again, from never putting himself at risk. But he was here and he was doing it. Maybe he was trying to punish himself for the last few weeks—perhaps redeem himself. Or, he was trying to make up for all the fires he never fought, or retaliate for the ones that almost killed him. He didn't know why, he just suited up. The heat from the burning building singed his face and he was poised to attack.

Ben stood next to the captain who looked twice at Ben and knew all the reasons Ben should be somewhere else.

"You want in?" He never asked; he asked this time.

Ben nodded.

"Take the first floor relay. And stay there. I don't know how long we have."

Ben went in with two other firemen, relieving three firemen that were stationed on the ground to guide, retrieve and otherwise assist their brothers on the front line. They entered through the demolished grocery store and broke through a burning wall that led to the lobby of the apartments. Ben looked up and saw a fireman, Louis Realmuto, gasping for breath at the bottom of the stairs. Ben draped Louis' arm over his neck and began to walk him out. He reached the smoke filled lobby and looked up. Another fireman moved deliberately down the smoke-filled stairwell, a brother draped across his shoulders. Ben recognized that shape.

The flames became more intense as the fireman proceeded downward. Suddenly, there was a huge tearing sound from below him—the roar of the monster as it ripped the heart out of its enemy. The firemen looked at each other, fear in their eyes—the staircase ripped away from the wall.

There was a split second of amnesty from the fire, from the world, as everything moved in slow motion and the fireman knew there was no going forward and no retreat. The stairs gave way and the fireman looked down into an endless black abyss. The stairs beneath him were no longer there as he was suspended in midair for the rest of his life.

Another loud crack broke the silence and the men fell into forever. The men, a stairwell, a conflagration, a victorious roar from the monster and then silence. Nothing existed.

Nothing.

Momentarily paralyzed, Ben turned and made it out through the broken wall, Louis in tow. They kept running as they hit the street and the building imploded. The walls collapsed inward sending tons of century-old brick and mortar onto a pile of dust and bones.

Everyone outside retreated to safer ground; there was no safe ground inside.

- 40 -

It was a beautiful, sunny, cool and breezy day. For some reason, Ben felt he had to clean out his locker today. Maybe it was to officially close this chapter and move on or maybe he hated loose ends. The captain released him from all duties, so today was it. He sat by his locker in his dress blues and slowly packed memories into a duffel bag. He had said his goodbyes to the guys who were in the back catching some downtime after yesterday's battle. The firehouse was too quiet and the only thing left for him to do was to leave.

He walked to his car carrying a duffel bag over each shoulder and decided not to look back. He would remember what he remembered, not the final moment, just all the ones that preceded it. The good ones, he hoped. He would miss the camaraderie but not the fires. He reached down and lifted one of the duffels and pushed it to the back of his trunk ensuring that he would have enough room for the second. He turned and stared at the second duffel lying on the ground waiting for someone to claim it and take care of it. He looked at the name stenciled onto the duffel as if it was the first time he saw it:

Al "Bull" Goldman

It was a beautiful, sunny, cool and breezy day, and Al was dead.

Temple Avarath Shalom stood in the middle of Bensonhurst, a largely Italian Catholic neighborhood. It was unusually busy today as almost a hundred well-wishers gathered outside waiting for Al's final ride to the cemetery. Blue on blue uniforms dressed most of the men, black the rest. Everyone was there: Paula, Willie and Rowan, Sandy and Irene, Ben, in his dress blues, and Kitty.

Fragments of his eulogy echoed in Ben's head as he exited the Temple and rejoined his friends: *Spoke his heart, good or bad, right or wrong, whether he should or he shouldn't. He had no rules; he just did what he felt. Yesterday, he felt like rescuing a brother. It wasn't the first time.* Ben stopped to regain his composure . . . . *but it was the last. Many of us are alive because of Al, a brother, a colleague, a friend. Thank you, Bull.* Ben gave him a thumbs-up as he had a thousand times before: his last thumbs-up. *I'll miss you.* Then he saluted and a force of firemen, in their dress blues, stood and saluted with him.

Paula sat with the group during the service, crying throughout, and reliving many moments with Al. Some undoubtedly, she wished she could relive and change the outcome. She had been hard on him, probably much too hard and far more than he deserved. Truth is, he was a kind man, yet far from her image of her soul mate. He was there when she needed someone to be there and she could not offer the same to him. She never felt accepted by the group but did not let it show during the last few moments. She said her goodbyes, knowing that they would have nothing more than incidental contact in the future.

Ben hugged Paula and watched her leave. He faced away from the group as his eyes welled up again. Willie, his head buried on Rowan's shoulder, could not stop crying. Kitty touched his arm to comfort him and he squeezed her hand. She then walked over to Ben and placed her head on his shoulder. They looked at each other and said *I'm sorry* without saying it. This was one of those rare moments with perfect and precise communication. Words would just cloud the air. No one had anything to say. No one had to.

Sandy nudged Ben and motioned him to join him.

"Be right back."

Ben and Sandy walked along a cast iron gated fence that surrounded the Temple. They stopped. Sandy lit a Lucky and offered one to Ben. As Ben lit up, Sandy said, "Willie's taking it hard."

"He lost a sparring partner, those guys fought like they were married."

"You Ok?"

"Good as you. I'll miss that prick."

"Listen," Sandy searched for the right words, "this might be the wrongest time, but I have to let it go."

The tone of Sandy's voice told Ben to pay attention.

"Al . . ." Sandy stalled as he took a long drag and let it out slowly. He leaned against the fence and talked to Ben without looking directly at him, the way they would talk if they were at the rail at the track and the horses were parading by. Only, there were no horses, just a stone building and a shaded lawn. "Remember getting bounced for our Twin Double by the Pinkies?"

"Like I remember breakfast." Ben's anticipation grew. Sandy had never been at a loss for words before. The silence heightened the impact of whatever was to follow.

"Al," Sandy took another drag and another as he stalled for time.

Ben sensed that this was not just an idle conversation. He had seen this before, Sandy had something to say; when he's ready, he'll say it.

One more drag and Sandy flipped the cigarette onto the small pristine lawn surrounding the Temple. He looked directly at Ben, "Al was behind it."

What?

"What?"

"Al was behind us getting ripped off that night."

"Bullshit."

Sandy's look told Ben that it was anything but.

"How do you know?" Ben asked.

"I know. Some people repaid a favor."

Al's betrayal felt worse than his death. Ben's knees weakened and nausea rose from within. He looked at Sandy for confirmation.

"That night," Sandy explained, "he was the only one that could have done it. The Pinkies didn't have the balls. He was the only one alone with them. He set it up in their car. It was the stupidest thing that stupid bastard ever did."

"I don't believe it."

"When I found out, I tried to get to him but he was nowhere. I caught up with him filling up at Willie's and called him on it. He didn't deny it. It was spur of the moment, he didn't plan it. He was desperate and angry."

"At us?"

"At the world." As he explained what had happened, Sandy found himself in the awkward position of defending Al. But Sandy had had the time to hate him already and now the guy was dead—so he continued.

"Look, he was fucked up. He didn't even know why he did it; just happened. He was sorry . . ." Sandy hesitated, " . . . bawled his eyes out—right there in his car. He tried to get the money back but turns out they screwed him also."

"Why didn't . . ."

"I love the prick, just like you. He asked for some room to set it right. He would've . . . he wanted to tell you but only after he could repay some part but he just ran out of time."

"Ran out of time? He ripped us off. Goddamn you, Bull. Goddamn you."

Sandy let Ben digest the news—the same news that he had to digest on his own. It felt no better to have company. They both stood there for a long moment.

"How come I didn't see it?"

"Nobody saw it. He was screwed up. His head wasn't on straight."

"Ran out of time," Ben said, and in one sentence concluded that all he believed in had vaporized. He weakened as the impact of the last two days finally hit. At that moment, he wished that Al were alive so he could hug him and hit him and hug him again. But he couldn't.

- 41 -

Ben got right back into action after Al's death; he had the rest of his life to mourn and digest Al's deed. It had been a bad few days and he knew that if he didn't move forward, he'd move backwards. First he had to clean up some old business.

He walked past Eileen, who sat in front of Sandy's office both as an assistant, a protector and an adornment. She watched him pass and smiled a small smile. On another day, he would have small-talked and taken her in a bit—but it wasn't another day. He stepped into Sandy's office.

"They didn't have too many of those at the Fire Department."

Sandy jumped, startled by Ben's unannounced entry.

"Yeah, she's supposed to protect me from the riff raff, like you."

"Fire her. I know a nice old lady that needs a job, can type too."

"I'll think about it. What's up?"

"You have some union contracts coming up?"

"Yeah, most of the time."

"I mean something substantial."

"Yep, the biggest in . . . why?"

"Charlie . . . he wants your access to the union." The words just flowed out. Ben was not going to tell Sandy, hoping that it would go away. After all, he was in deep enough, why drag a friend in with him. But Al's death changed everything. Everything out, nothing left on the table. There was nothing to protect. If he was going down, it would be swinging.

"What?"

"Yeah. He wanted me to get to you and get you to intervene for them in the contract negotiations. He didn't give me any details but I figure he wants the contract, say, shaped a little. Nothing that'll hurt, just edge things towards some of his friends' projects. He wants me to get to you, you play ball and he lets me off the hook."

"Charlie?"

"Yeah and whoever his friends are. I guess he's just trading up. Doesn't matter, he's not going to get it."

"Why didn't you tell me before?"

"Because I didn't want you to do anything about it. It's not your problem. Fuck him."

"Ben, I can't—"

"I know. I don't want you to; I wouldn't let you." Ben leaned across the desk for clarity and emphasis. "Listen to me. I'm telling you because I think you should know. That's it. Nothing more. I don't want to fuck this up any more than it is."

"What do you want me to do?"

"Not a thing. You're out of it. Fuck him. I've got to stop the bleeding; it's gone far enough. I just owe him money, not my life, certainly not yours. He's going have to hang in there and they will get the whole nut, plus the vig . . . and a turkey for Thanksgiving."

"You're bluffing, right?"

"How's Kitty?" Ben sat.

"I guess she's doing ok. She's a sweetheart and I love her company but I want to be able to wear my skivvies around the house When are you guys going to end this? Kiss and make up and take her home."

"Not yet. She's still mad at me, let it cool down a while, start fresh. Boys'll be back from camp soon and you'll have even more company." Ben made sure that Sandy understood, "I don't want her in the house until this thing is settled. We've been having roach problems."

"Charlie?"

"And a big slab of Beef."

Ben headed out to the track early today: no tickets to write, no scofflaws to harass, no bad guys to nail, no fires to fight. He sat at what had become his usual table in the Clubhouse and checked through the program for late scratches when Willie put his hand lightly on his shoulder.

"Who do we like today?" Willie said; his gentle tone reminded Ben of yesterday.

Ben just looked at him with a mutual understanding of the pain they were both going through and how they were not going to talk about it.

"The *two* and *six* in the first with the *seven* in the second," Ben said, "want to make some of Double bets?"

"Sure."

Ben pulled some cash out of his pocket and noticed a small note wrapped around a twenty-dollar bill on his money clip.

"Shit, Doc's bet."

In the confusion of the last few days, he had completely forgotten about the bet Doc asked him to make. *I'll book it myself; he probably lost anyway.* He grabbed an old *Racing Form* and checked the results.

"You believe this? The horse wins . . . paid $10.40." He said incredulously. "I owe Doc a hundred four bucks."

"Why? You didn't bet it, you were . . ." Willie didn't want to finish—he didn't have to.

"I took the bet, win or lose; it's on me to make good. Shit."

"Just give him his twenty back."

"And if he lost, do I keep it?"

"Yeah, he lost."

"And if was your twenty, what do I do?"

"That's different."

"No, not really."

If Doc had lost, Ben would've kept the twenty. He won so Ben had to pay him off at track odds. Twenty bucks invested into a horse paying $10.40 equals $104. No shades of gray—there was no question in his mind that was the right and only thing to do. *Shit.* But it got him thinking.

Willie went to make the bets and Ben took a stroll to the men's room; his selections for the first two races were in and he could relax a little now. He thought about booking Doc's bet—bookies are like the house, except that the house, the track, gets its take off the top, the handle. The house doesn't care who wins.

Bookies on the other hand, take a position on a bet—they don't care who wins as long as you lose. They assume that if you bet on horses, you are a long-term loser. If the bet is too big or the risk is too high, they will try to lay off part of the bet on other bookies just to keep the risk in check. Generally, though, they will take a bet on a horse and pay off at track odds.

In other sports, such as football, except for pushes, there are only two possible outcomes: win or lose. They charge a *vigorish*, a premium, of ten percent if you lose—so, bet a hundred, lose a hundred ten. As long as the bets are balanced and there is roughly equal action on both sides, the bookies win because they collect the *vig* from the losers. They are like big banks except that they don't give away toasters.

Ben thought about it as he stood over the sink. He just booked Doc's bet. Unintentionally, but he did. Interesting business, but the problem with bookies was that they could not control the bets. They had no influence over the outcome; they weren't doing the picking, their clients were. They just had to wait for them to fail in order to win—and they will fail. There's got to be a way to do this differently. Besides, he wasn't a bookie, he was a handicapper. It sounded good, *a handicapper*.

Ben left the men's room and stopped when he saw that familiar figure again, only this time, he knew him: Caz Frankel. Ben froze as a thousand memories flashed in a second. Caz Frankel, much older, about sixty Ben figured, but everything else looked the same: the entourage, snappy clothes and, of course, the handkerchief. Caz Frankel. The last time he saw him was the day Willie's finger was turned into soup. Ben just stood and stared as the memory just walked by.

He got off his schneid like a rocket—he won the first, and then the second and the Double paid fifty-six dollars. The memory of his oh-for-everything disaster a few days ago was totally obliterated.

The fourth race had passed and Willie walked away from the Cashier's window and counted up. He walked straight into Big Jack.

"Hey where you been?" Jack needled.

"Around." Willie just didn't want to deal with him.

"What happened to wonder boy? That three horse the other day cost me."

"Hey, no guarantees."

"How's he doin' today?"

"So so, he caught the Double and the fourth." Willie added just a delicate touch of sarcasm. "Missed the third though."

The Jacks looked at each other and Willie in disbelief.

"He caught three out of four?"

"Yeah, he's slippin'." Willie bit the inside of his cheek. He wasn't used to playing dumb—it felt good. The Jacks couldn't figure if Willie was serious or playing them or what. Willie started to walk away wanting to end this non-conversation ASAP.

"Who does he like here?"

Too late.

"Dunno. Why don't you ask him?"

Big Jack's look told Willie that doing a good deed was probably the best course at the moment.

"Or I could find out for you." Willie brandished as insincere a smile as he could and walked towards the table. They watched.

"Hey Benny," Willie approached Ben who was deep into the program at the table, "who do we like here?"

"The *two* has a shot," Ben answered without looking up.

Willie turned to Jack and raised his right hand with his middle finger and index finger stub raised.

"I'm not sure . . ." Jack said to Jack. "I think he likes the one and a half horse."

Willie was having a good day. So was Ben. He caught the ninth race that day, a good way to close a good day with four wins including the Daily Double—a real good day. Ben felt like celebrating.

"Got plans for dinner?"

"Well, I'm sure Ro is about to burn something real special to a crisp and serve it with a boiled potato or spaghetti and ketchup unless you got something better."

- 42 -

Rowan was preparing a salad when Willie walked in.

"Hey chicken."

He kissed the back of her neck. This was their daily greeting since they got married. They were a uniquely balanced and totally mismatched couple, but they gave each other what they needed. He gave her stability and love and she gave it back. She was religious and went to Church several times a week; he went to that big church near the Belt Parkway, where thousands prayed nine times a day.

"Hi handsome. Hope you're hungry. Cooking pork chops the way you like and pasta marinara. Ok?"

"Great. I'm starved. Gonna go out after with Ben and Sandy. Had a good day. Our system is working. Think we're onto something. I told ya', I told ya' my plans would work."

"Yes, you did. Now wash up."

Garguilio's Ristorante, a beautiful, romantic, old country Italian restaurant with slate floors and stucco walls, stood just off of Surf Avenue in Coney Island. Ben sat there alone and recapped the plays of the days for the hundredth time and figured how he almost had the sixth and if he did what a day it would have been, when Willie walked in.

"What happened to Sandy?"

"Had a prior," Ben offered without the details because none were necessary. "He'll catch us later."

They had a nice dinner, Willie's second. Willie repeated his encounter with the Jacks three times. Ben laughed the first time. It was an extra hard laugh because today was an extra hard laugh day.

"To a good day," Willie toasted.

Ben raised his glass and looked around: Garguilio's, Ben and Kitty's favorite place. Tonight he wanted to celebrate a good day—a rare good day these days. He wanted to share the moment, toast, laugh and feel good. This is what winning was about.

He wanted to do all that with Kitty, not Willie. Kitty's the one that should be here.

"To you," Ben toasted.

"To us," Kitty clinked glasses.

"Did you ever think we'd be here, I mean together?"

"After you didn't speak to me and turned me down three times because of some phony goldfish . . ."

"I resent that."

"What?"

"I turned you down twice. I just avoided you after that."

"OK. Twice. After all that, yeah, I knew you were playing hard to get."

"I wasn't playing. I am hard to get." She raised her glass to toast again.

Sandy walked back from the men's room and Eileen gave him the high sign. He saw Wasserman's office door was open and looked in.

"What are you doing here so late in the day?" Sandy stood in Wasserman's doorway. "In fact, what are you doing here at all? It isn't Wednesday."

"Hello. I had to come in." Wasserman welcomed him. "Sit."

Sidney Wasserman, other than his plaid sport coat and open shirt, fit a lawyer's image precisely: receding gray hair, distinguished, careful and deliberate mannerisms and long and slow speech. He went on about a case that needed his attention and he felt that certain people should have been contacted and that the office was looking a little shoddy and that Sandy should have updated him on the union contract and several other items of no importance.

Sandy was used to this. He felt that Wasserman used his long talks as ways to pump up his billable hours. He used to call him Phil, for Philabuster Wasserman, until he found out. Sandy used charisma and guile as his tactics and Wasserman used long talks and endurance.

Sandy glanced out the door and saw Eileen slowly and dramatically put on her jacket and get ready to leave. Her look said: *what's the story?* His return look said: *I don't know, be out of here as soon as I can.*

Wasserman was still the senior partner and they were in his office and he was sitting behind his desk, so Wasserman had control. He went on about another client, reaching no conclusion and having no point. Sandy compared him to Al. When Al had a thought it immediately dropped to his mouth and out. Wasserman's thoughts were more like pinballs in a pinball machine. The thought would emanate in his brain and get bounced from bumper to bumper taking the most circuitous route possible until it eventually, perhaps forty-five minutes later, was spoken. Sandy rarely knew the subject of any conversation until they were far into it. He wondered when he'd get to his point.

Wasserman meandered on about his eventual retirement and how they should plan to discuss financial arrangements—a plan to plan the discussion. Sandy thought this was it; this is why he's here. It wasn't.

"Irene called me."

At last.

"Irene? My Irene?"

"Yes. She sounded very distressed. Wanted some legal counsel on divorce."

"Shit. Kitty's staying with us; she must be—"

"No. Not for Kitty, for her."

"What?"

"I couldn't really help. A conflict of both interest and friendship. I probably should not be telling you but I referred her to Jack Kaplan."

"Jack the Ripper?"

"Yes. He's very good. Don't you agree?"

Sandy sat there mortified. He thought things were ok. *I mean, we get along. Shit.*

"Are you Ok?"

Sandy nodded absently.

"Come to think of it," Wasserman got up to leave. "I may be mixing up Irene with another client. My mind is just not what it was. Forget I said anything. There was one other thing." He put on his hat and walked to the door. "Oh yes . . ."

Sandy looked up.

"I would appreciate it if you would stop fucking Eileen."

Sandy didn't remember the drive to the Golden Gate motel as he replayed his conversation with Wasserman. He opened the motel room door totally confused and off balance. He felt as if he was about to be stabbed in the back from the front.

Wasserman, that old prick.

Eileen must have had some sense of it. She sat fully clothed in a chair in the corner reading a TV Guide. There were three airline Chivas neatly lined up like little soldiers with their caps directly in front of each one. They were empty. She didn't look up when he entered or as he stood over her.

This was it. They both knew it. It was over.

They talked for a while saying nothing and feeling detached. Then they shook hands and hugged and kissed for the last time. It was a requisite cordial and unemotional goodbye. After all, it was what it was, nothing more. Their entire relationship was clearly defined by the four walls of the motel room—a defined space with clean boundaries and no entanglements. Simple and uncomplicated. There was no history to lament, no future to hope for and nothing to regret. There was only now—the last now. They were filling a void and the void had been filled. They had reached the point they knew they would reach—that unplanned, predictable and inevitable last time.

They hugged once more for old time's sake and kissed again: a tender and gentle kiss. This time there was some universal silent decision to make this the very last kiss—the kiss that conveyed every word that they never spoke to, and about, each other. All the shielded feelings and unsaids floated to the surface. The walls were down and the passion flowed through their mouths and into their bodies and suddenly they were one again.

Somehow they had ascended to another level, as if they had collectively survived some crisis and bonded closer in the process. They were not using each other now, they were each other and their familiarity lived at another depth that far exceeded sex. His hands traversed her body as they dove into a passion that neither had felt with each other or anyone else. They made love like never before.

They agreed not to see each other again, until next week, maybe sooner.

- 43 -

Ben and Willie nursed beers at a table in Goodies as Sandy stood at the pay phone. They were caught between the mood swings and wondered whether this one good day was a signal that would eradicate recent events. They knew better but they needed something to carry them forward.

"Betcha he's on with a honey," Willie said as he threw a buck on the table.

"You're on," Ben added his buck.

Willie saw Angie, Al's last date, sitting at the bar. She wiped out the good day. He drifted back.

"Not bad, your next ex?" Willie goaded.

"You can't get to me tonight," Al smiled back; "I'm in too good a mood. First of all, my company's a lot softer than yours and she doesn't have hair on her chest."

"You sure?"

Sandy sat down and Willie snapped back.

"What's the Yankee line tomorrow?" Ben asked.

"Six and a half, five and a half," Sandy answered as Ben looked at Willie and whisked the two dollars off the table.

"Ben was a king today."

"Good day?"

"Yeah." Ben changed up. He was thinking about tomorrow.

"Ok. If you were a bookie, what's your biggest problem?"

"Credit," Sandy snapped back. "Getting guys to pay up."

"You just break their legs or fuck up their lives," Willie added.

"But, you break too many legs you run out of customers. It's a fine line."

"Ok, second biggest problem?"

"Not being able to lay off enough, getting hit too often in a short time, not having enough action across the board to let the losers lose." Sandy rattled off.

"Stop there," Ben had heard what he needed to. "What if you could cut your exposure, from eight or nine horses in a race to two or three? And, the best bet in the race isn't one of them?"

"Good position to be in. What're you thinking?"

"Just thinking."

Sandy knew different.

"You gonna take book?" Willie asked. "Be one of Charlie's guys? Good, cause he won't take my action."

"Because Ben stepped up for you." Sandy said and tried to pull the words back in.

"What do you mean?"

Ben knew it had to come out—he would rather it just go away because no matter how much good he was doing, it would not come out that way.

"What do you mean?" Willie alternated looking at Sandy and Ben.

"I took on your line to Charlie. Stepped up to what you owed."

"Why?" Willie didn't know if he was hurt, embarrassed or happy.

"Because you were . . . I just felt I had to. You were in deep and weren't stopping. You couldn't see it. You were about to get real hurt."

That was it; he was embarrassed.

"It was none of your business. My problem, not yours." Willie slammed his beer down splattering beer on his pants and the table. "Did Kitty put you up to it?"

"No."

"She doesn't know," Sandy was pissed at himself for leaking it.

"It was none of your business, Goddamn it," Willie said as he stomped out of the bar.

"Sorry," Sandy said. "Never seen him so angry."

"It had to come out sooner or later. He'll get over it."

"He should. You saved his ass."

"I should go after him."

As Ben started to rise, Willie came back in through the front door.

"That didn't take long," Sandy said under his breath.

Willie appeared indecisive as he entered the bar. He hesitated, and then approached the table, still fuming. He stood and looked down at Ben.

"How'd you pay him?"

"Didn't."

"Good. How're you gonna pay him?"

"Don't know."

"Good." He looked at Ben and Sandy for a long moment. "Want another beer?"

Willie bent down and hugged Ben. "You shouldn't have done it. I mean, it's my problem."

"Now it's our problem".

"Thanks. I'll make it up. I promise. I'll sell the station."

"What do you live on? Besides it probably won't cover it."

"I know."

"Benny, I'll make it up to you."

"I know." Maybe he has a place for me to sleep at the gas station, Ben thought.

Willie sat down and stared at his friends. He took stock of the moment.

"To Bull," Willie toasted.

"To Bull."

- 44 -

The next few days Ben continued his run at the track. He picked winners, more importantly, winners with prices, and even more importantly, ended each day with a profit. There was not enough to pay Charlie by a long shot, but it was growing. The buzz on him grew as well. Aqueduct closed for the season and the action moved to Belmont. The tracks alternated sessions instead of competing head on and diluting the handle.

The same crowd, players and horses moved to Belmont as well. The tables at Belmont were bigger and couple of new guys joined Ben's. They didn't say so, but they had heard about Ben and his prowess and they wanted in. Lou "Chalk" Weinstein, semi-retired with beer distributorships in Brooklyn and the Bronx was a pretty good horseplayer—self-proclaimed. Georgie Toro, a quiet cigar-smoking guy, didn't say much but he would always offer to run Ben's errands. Willie, of course, was a fixture and every once in a while a new face would plant himself at the table. On Saturdays, Doc Brodsky, and, occasionally, Sandy would show.

The sixth race had just ended; nobody had it, a twenty-six dollar horse that just didn't figure. Ben checked his notes to see what he missed in the calculations. There must have been something he showed before that was a clue to his win today.

"Hey Caz," Lou said as he waved to someone walking by.

Ben looked up. *There could only be one Caz.*

"Lou, you know him?"

"Chalk. Everybody calls me Chalk."

"Chalk, you know him?"

"Yeah, Caz Frankel. Has one of the best stables in the east. Just moved them up from Hialeah. Nice guy."

Ben checked the program. Sure enough, one of his horses is running later today. *Missed that.*

Lou earned the nickname Chalk because he loved to play the favorites. Money was not really an issue for him; he just liked to win and favorites win. They're not profitable, but they win. So Chalk picked winners, which would have made him a winner except he lost. He also followed the tout sheets like a lot of other players. For five bucks anyone could buy any of a half dozen brightly colored tout sheets and get expert handicappers' picks for the day.

Ben checked the lineup for the seventh and feature race. The way he and everyone else figured it, the one horse, the favorite, was a lock. Sit this one out, he thought.

Or maybe not.

He had been waiting for the right moment, the right situation. Chalk studied his tout sheets and came up with the obvious. Ben waited for the question.

"Who do you like here Ben?" Chalk asked right on cue.

"The *six* looks good. You?" Ben answered without looking up from his program. The *six* did have a shot, Ben figured, but not a good one and, ordinarily, he would sit this one out.

"The *one*. He's a lock."

"How much you betting?"

"Twenty."

"Tell you what," Ben feigned figuring out something he had already figured out. "I'll book your *one* horse and you book my *six* for the twenty. Save us a trip to the window."

Chalk thought for a moment.

"You're on. You probably didn't think of it but this is pretty good for both of us because if another horse wins, we are both off the hook."

Didn't think of it, my ass.

"Yeah. Didn't look at it that way."

They shook.

The *one* horse won as Chalk, Ben and everyone else on the planet figured it would. Ben paid Chalk track odds, which came out to a sixteen dollars profit for Chalk on the twenty-dollar bet. Chalk was happy. Ben was happier because his little test worked. He knew he would lose that bet. It wasn't a bet to him—it was an investment for the future. It was a new way of betting which he filed away. *Cultivate it.*

Ben broke even that day. Not bad. Breaking even is not losing; not losing is good because it preserves capital. *Live to bet another day.*

Willie drove today as he had for the past few days. The car stopped and started in the Belt Parkway traffic.

"Not for nothin', but thanks again for the Charlie thing."

"No sweat. Thanks for your finger." Ben wanted to forget this already.

"This little ol' thing?" Willie held up his right hand. "If I had it I probably would've gone into the Army and lost the whole hand right up to my shoulder; wouldn't've had it anyway. Besides, I save on gloves."

Ben was thinking; Willie was talking.

"We're doin' pretty good." Willie broke the silence.

"So far." Ben didn't want to get into the impending big black hole with Charlie.

"Just heard of something."

"Not with Ed the Brain?"

Willie looked hurt and Ben picked it up.

"I'm listening."

"You know Johnny Bates?"

"*Bet for Show* Johnny? Lives with his mother?"

"Yeah."

"That guy couldn't smell shit if it floated in his soup."

"Maybe. But he's got ideas."

There was no way out of this conversation now: "Go on."

"He's come up with a wind machine. At least that's what he calls it."

Ben was deep in thought about the bet with Chalk Weinstein and was only half listening to Willie. Willie went on.

"It calculates a horse's chances based on the wind that day."

That got his attention. He looked at Willie and waited for the next incredible proposition.

"It's only supposed to work at Pimlico where the stretch is longer."

"Pass."

"I know it sounds crazy but—"

"You never learn. I'll spec on something crazy but right now we need to lock something up. I'm passing and you are too."

Ben closed his eyes. This was the kind of driving he liked—somebody else's. The car was quiet.

"Do you know anyone at *Lawton's?*" Ben asked without opening his eyes.

"*Lawton's?*" Willie was glad Ben broke the silence, "You mean the tout sheet?"

"Yeah."

"Not at *Lawton's*, but I know a guy who works at their printer. Why?"

"Even better."

When Ben got home there were two messages waiting for him. The message outside was wedged into the front door: a burnt-out matchbook from *The Gravesend Bar, a family place.*

Ben wanted to throw the matchbook on the floor and stomp it along with the guy who put it there. But he realized that he would only have to clean it up so he stuffed it into his pocket.

The message inside was from Kitty—saying that she stopped by to pick up some things and the boys were coming home from camp tomorrow. They will stay with her at Irene's, she hoped he would be there to greet them, had been trying to reach him, but it seems he's never home and hoped he was happy, which Ben read with a strong dose of sarcasm and bitterness. *Hey, you were the one who left.* It was signed with a definite non-committal, plain vanilla:

Take care, Kitty.

Ben decided that he had to make two visits, but tomorrow was Saturday and he needed to be out at the farm—he wanted to try something and Saturday drew the right crowds and races. The visits would both have to wait until Sunday. He'd call the boys tomorrow anyway.

Tonight he had plans: a short nap, a quick dinner, and homework—then run out at ten for the *Racing Form* to see tomorrow's entries, more homework, maybe turn on Jack Parr and turn in.

- 45 -

Ben and Willie got an early start to beat the late summer beach traffic and give them a little jump on the day. The Saturday crowd filled the place with people criss crossing, checking the tote board, making and cashing bets and just gabbing. Saturday was as much for socializing as it was for serious bettors. The handle was bigger which filled the track's coffers. It didn't do anything for the payoffs except attract a better class of horses which made handicapping a bit more predictable.

Ben's table was full up as well: Chalk, Georgie, Willie, Sandy and Doc. After the normal morning chitchat, which Ben participated in only to the smallest degree, and intros and cross table handshakes, everyone got down to business.

The Double had just completed and Ben had the first half, missed the second by a mile—an eighth of a mile actually. It didn't take long before Chalk hit the bid again.

"Ben, who do you like?"

"The *five*. You?"

"The *two*. Twenty five?"

"You're on. Twenty five, my *five*, your *two*."

Ben made sure everyone at the table caught the action.

The race went off, and the five won, paying eight dollars even. Chalk caught Ben as he was coming back from the outside track and handed him seventy-five dollars.

"Better you than the track."

"I feel the same way. Hang onto it. Let's settle at the end of the day. Who do you like here?"

Ben knew that settling at the end of the day implied trust and it would assume more action between them throughout the day. And, the fewer the exchanges, the less chance that someone would pick up on it. Just then, Caz Frankel walked to his box with a small entourage in tow.

"Caz."

"Chalkie."

"Hey Caz, meet Ben Collesano, good guy, real good horse player."

"Nice to meet you." Ben extended his hand.

"Heard a lot about you."

"You can't believe Lou, er, Chalk."

"Chalkie? He didn't say anything. People talk. Who do you like here?"

This was the question Ben was asked a dozen times a day, but from Caz Frankel, it became more than a question—it was a test. Ben had been hoping and preparing for this test but he didn't expect it so soon. When he heard that Caz had his stable here, he studied every horse, their records, their performances, their ratings, their tendencies, their breeding, everything. He knew what conditions they liked, what jockeys performed best and what class they ran in. He knew who was moving up in class, who should move up in class and which horses are over their head.

He vigorously focused on any entries on today's card. Ben figured that Caz is a player and he must know the players and the plays—and they've got to know him. So when Caz asked the question *"who do you like here?"* Ben knew that he had a horse in this race.

"The *two* has a real good shot."

Chalk jumped in, "Caz owns *Cupid*, the *seven* horse."

"I know, good luck."

"You don't like him?" Caz asked.

"He's a good horse, good line, but this isn't his race. When he runs a mile and a eighth, he should really show himself. Even in better company." Ben spoke with confidence and authority. "This race is a tune up. I'd even move him up in class after he has a good showing at a distance."

"Two minutes to post time," blared over the loud speaker.

Buddy Catalano, a forty-year-old man with slicked-back hair that smelled of an overdose of Brylcreem and a loud plaid sports jacket, stepped up right behind Caz and nudged him.

"Post time."

Caz was still fixated on Ben's answer. Right or not, he did his homework.

"Interesting advice," Caz said and turned to Buddy. "Buddy's my trainer; he'd be interested in your opinion. Buddy, say hello to Ben Collesano."

"Hiya doin?" Buddy offered a quick hand and turned to Caz, "post time, let's go."

"Gentlemen." Caz said as they left.

"Who's that?" Buddy asked when they were almost out of earshot.

"Someone who thinks he knows more than he does."

Ben and Chalk just watched them disappear into the crowd as Sandy, who had been watching this from a short distance away, joined them.

"Is that . . . ?"

"A guy who thinks he's better than us. Caz Frankel. Remember him?"

"Holy shit. Couldn't forget."

Then Doc Brodsky joined the group.

"Ben, who do you like?"

"The *two* has a shot."

"Do you want to, uh, exchange . . ." Doc Brodsky had caught wind of the action and wanted in.

"Swap bets? Sure."

"Twenty on my number *one* and I'll take twenty on your two horse."

Chalk and Ben swapped bets almost every race except when they liked the same horse. Ben had won two bets and Chalk had won one. Neither of them won three other bets; but neither of them lost those three either. Both men were happy they made the arrangement.

Ben waited for Willie to ask. They had been sitting in traffic for a half hour since they left the track. Ben was getting some shuteye and breathing in the success of the day. *It was working*—not only that, he met Caz Frankel and showed his stuff. What the hell, he wouldn't wait for Willie to ask.

"It's a horse swap."

"What?"

"A horse swap. Chalk and me, we swap horses. I book his pick and he books mine. He wins, I pay him. I win, he pays me. Simple . . . I'm the track."

"What if another horse wins?"

"That's the best part . . . nobody pays anybody. It becomes a two horse race . . ." Ben turned to Willie for emphasis, ". . . with the payoff of the full field."

Ben figured he'd close his eyes a bit to give Willie time to digest it. It didn't take long.

"Benny, you're a fuckin' genius! It's beautiful. You eliminate all the other horses. You eliminate all the other horses."

"The only way to lose is if his horse wins . . . it's man to man."

"My money's on you." Willie's mind raced. "What if you both want the same horse?"

"No bet. We pick other horses or wait for the next race. That's where your friend at the printer can help out."

Willie's appetite for details jumped dramatically as Ben went on.

"If I know what Chalk's picks are, I'll just say I want that same horse before he does and cancel his out. Then, if he wants to swap with me, he'll go to his second choice. If I can do that before he makes his selection, he won't pick up on it."

"I don't follow," Willie's heart was pounding.

"It gives me the edge to eliminate his top horse, Ok? This guy follows *Lawton's* tout sheet, so do most of his buddies. If I know *Lawton's* picks before he does, then tell him they're my picks. They will be his picks too and we'll cancel out that horse. I'm eliminating his number one choice."

"So you're putting your best pick against his number two."

"Bingo."

"So you need to know what *Lawton's* picks are before it hits the stands?"

"By eleven if possible."

"Should not be a problem."

Willie drove, his mind tied in happy knots—the possibilities were endless. Ben was making book, using his own picks and eliminating most of the other horses in the race. He ran through it a dozen times, looking for holes or something to add. Why couldn't he have thought of that? He would've . . . maybe. What he didn't know, what Ben omitted, was the best part was yet to come. But Willie knew one thing for sure.

"Benny, you're a fuckin' genius."

- 46 -

Ben called the kids last night; it was too difficult to explain on the phone so he didn't say anything. He just reinforced what Kitty had told them earlier—that they were going to stay at Uncle Sandy's and Aunt Irene's for a while. He'd explain later. Later was coming up fast and he tried to think of something rational; the truth was not in play. Ben pulled into Sandy's driveway and saw the boys outside playing with a new hula-hoop.

The hugs and kisses felt better than Ben had imagined. They grounded him—the only bit of sanity in the last few weeks. He told the boys to get ready to take a ride and he went inside and found Kitty and Irene in the kitchen.

"Am I interrupting?"

The reaction was something that skirted between surprise, awkwardness, and elation.

"No," Irene, who had plenty to say, didn't. "Gotta go and iron my entire wardrobe," she left.

"Let's go outside." Kitty led him onto an open porch that was cluttered with boxes.

"How are you?" Ben wanted to know.

"Fine. Doing Ok. Ok. You?"

"About the same. Look. I miss you and the boys."

"Me too."

"I left the department."

"I know. And you're still . . ."

"Kitty, you should see me out there. I'm really good at it. I have a feel for it. I know you don't want me to go to the track."

"I don't care if you go to the track, just not every day. Not as a way of life."

"I'm a horseplayer. That's what I am. It's something I'm really good at, something people look up to me for. You should see how they treat me. They want to know what I think, who I like. Not just the guys, strangers. Out there, I make an impact. I feel important." He didn't know if she got it. He didn't know if she would ever get it. "I want you to come home."

"I don't—"

"But not now."

"Huh?"

"There's something else . . . I took on Willie's debt to some guys."

"Bookies?"

"Yeah. And until I fix it, you can't come home."

"Is that why you've been so . . . Why'd you do that? I mean, he's my brother and I love him and . . . Why'd you do that?"

Ben didn't have an answer, at least not one that made sense.

The firehouse was half empty when they arrived. Two men washed the Hook and Ladder truck as it stood half out of the building and into the driveway. The dispatcher sat in a small office at the entrance, reading the paper.

"Cap around?" Ben startled him.

"Benny, thought you'd be off fishing somewhere."

"Never liked fishing. Just taking it slow right now. Cap around?"

"On a call. Some schmuck left a pile of leaves to burn out by itself; caught a tree, demolished a tree house and a car. He should be back any minute. Who're these guys?"

"Rick, Scooter, say hi to Doug, he runs the place." The huge truck mesmerized the boys.

"Hi Doug." They said politely.

"You guys want to take a tour?" Ben asked.

Ben had brought them to the firehouse a couple of times; mostly on quick visits on their way somewhere else. This was a part of his life that he never felt comfortable sharing with them; perhaps, he never felt comfortable doing it himself. They walked through the bunkroom, which was lined with twenty or so beds.

"This is where I slept when I worked nights. Unless there was a fire."

"Have you ever saved anyone?"

"I guess I helped a few people out when they were in trouble." He tensed as he remembered pulling out a fireman the day Al bought it. He closed the image down but the vision of Al lifting him out of a pile of burning debris immediately replaced it. His chest tightened as he took a breath and quickly returned to the present. "And some helped me. But I'm not a fireman anymore. I just retired."

"Mommy told us." Scooter said.

"Oh?" *Of course she did.* "Good."

"So you'll be home with us all the time." Scooter added.

"He's still going to have to work, dummy," Rick jumped in.

"But I will be home at night."

"Are you getting a divorce?" Rick looked him right in the eye and would accept nothing less than a direct answer.

He didn't know how he would explain this situation to them and didn't even know how to open the conversation, until Rick did it for him. Ben sat on the bunk with the boys.

"No, I love mommy and she loves me. I just have to work some things out around the house and I need to be alone in the house for a while to . . ."

"Promise."

"I promise." It was a promise he hoped to keep.

"Told you." Scooter said.

"I knew, just making sure."

"You guys ok?" Ben didn't want to leave any more open ends than he had to.

They nodded.

"You sure?" Their nods were more vigorous but no less sad. "Then who wants to slide down the pole?"

They spent over an hour playing in the firehouse. They slid down the bright brass pole several times until they got tired of walking the stairs. Scooter had a fascination with the Hook and Ladder, an elongated vehicle that carried telescopic ladders on a turret. Ben lifted him onto the tiller, the position for the second driver at the rear of the truck, and Scooter mocked driving to every fire in the city. Rick climbed up behind him to direct his driving and provide crash and tire-screeching sound effects as Scooter narrowly avoided major collisions at every turn.

This was the first time Ben laughed in days. He held the moment as long as he could, carefully embedding it into deep memory.

Ben hadn't been back to the building since Al's death. In a sense he missed it: the camaraderie, the security and sense of belonging to something larger than himself. But he also felt a strange sense of relief that it was behind him. The burden of his narrow path had a bigger impact than he had realized. Somehow, he felt more comfortable with a future that was yet undefined, a future that he could shape. Ben missed the firehouse, the men, but not the job. When he was one of the team, he gave everything that he had, but he hated the peaks and valleys: either waiting for disaster or in the middle of it. There were few rewards, other than knowing that you had helped someone, somewhere, and made it out alive. Ben loathed the events that ended that career, but he was somehow on his way towards a better place—if he could only get there.

In that moment, Ben remembered the somber truth of the building; that they had just lost one of their own. The firehouse was hollow with the reality of the vulnerability of the job. There was no control; no matter how many precautions, no way of predicting who would turn up dead next. He was glad that was his past. His sense of belonging was becoming more remote: the last eighteen years here seemed like someone else's life. He took one last look at the building. He didn't plan to see it again.

Ben felt better about having told Kitty the truth. If they were eventually going to put it together, he didn't want any secrets or guilt gnawing at him. He felt that he only let her down if she felt let down. But if she could understand how Ben felt, then she would come around. Ben was convinced he had done the right thing; if only Kitty felt that way, he'd be more convinced. Kitty could handle it, he told himself, she just needed time.

Somehow the boys understood it better. They didn't get mired in all the ugly details, which Ben didn't share. They just took him at his word—Dad needed to work some things out, there was nothing wrong that wouldn't be fixed soon and most important, Mommy and he love each other. Kids are funny, Ben thought; if they know that there is a happy ending, they could put up with all the uncertainty in between. As long as they believed there was a happy ending.

It was a good day that Ben wanted to extend as long as possible, but he couldn't.

He took the short way to the Gravesend, punishing the shocks for something they could not have possibly deserved. He took every bump and pothole head on as if it would toughen the car to get it ready for the ride of its life. He planned to take it into Willie's tomorrow to get new ones anyway. He was beginning to feel optimistic—maybe there is an end in sight—hopefully, a happy one. He'd just pay Charlie down a bit and hold him off. After all, if Charlie burns the house down, he has no more leverage. As a precaution, he had Kitty take all of her valuables and the boys' winter clothes out of the house: no point in losing everything if Charlie suddenly got irrational or if Beefy got match-happy.

Yeah, Charlie's not doing anything as long as I keep showing him I'm working down the nut.

Beefy was in his regular slot at the bar practicing his one-handed match lighting. He greeted Ben with a broad, almost friendly, gap-toothed, idiot smile. Ben ignored him, for now. Charlie was also happy to see Ben.

"Sit, want a drink? An iced coffee?"

Three televisions were on at the next table. Their rabbit ear antennas giving them varying degrees of snow obscuring the two baseball games in progress.

"Both games in the ninth inning. What are the chances of that? You like baseball, Ben?" Charlie didn't wait for a reply. "Ninth inning, crunch time. Just when you think you've got it won, you lose it."

"Or vice-versa."

"Or vice-versa. It's the ninth inning Ben. You winning or losing?"

Ben took out several bills.

"I've got five hundred for you now, and I can give you five hundred a week."

Ben had more but he needed working capital.

"That's nice but that only covers the vig."

"What vig? We didn't talk about the vig."

"Ben, there's always a vig. Money is my business. There's a cost to doing business. The vig gets turned on when you don't pay. Even a bank charges a vig, mercenary bastards. Your payments are just meeting the vig; you're just treading water. You've gotta work the number down in big chunks—very big chunks."

Charlie looked over Ben's shoulder and Ben looked back to see Beefy continue his fascination with lighting matches, reminiscent of a Neanderthal discovering fire—only the Neanderthal was smarter, and better looking.

"I'm still interested in your house. You see, if it should suddenly disappear, you'd collect insurance and that should cover my end nicely. Of course, then you would have no place to live but I know you thought of that. You've got ten more days."

Ben got up quickly and began to storm out of the bar.

"Ben, you like football? The football season starts next week."

Ben stopped and looked back at Charlie. *Is this guy nuts? I'm into him for more than a year's pay . . .*

Ben didn't answer and turned toward the door, not noticing that Beefy, the load of Neanderthal shit, was no longer at the bar. Ben blew through the front door and to the car. He reached into his pocket for his keys and, suddenly, the car took off by itself.

Jesus!

It pulled out of the parking spot and screeched right into the street and kept going. Ben stood there a moment, surprised by the car's sudden exit. It took off all by itself—with Beefy behind the wheel. Ben felt the heat rise through his body and rushed back into the bar and stood over Charlie who anticipated Ben's return. Before he could speak, Charlie did.

"It's a down payment, a security deposit Ben. You know, collateral. That's how you got the extension. Bottom of the ninth, strange things happen."

Ben hung onto the strap as the subway threw him from side to side as it screeched around turns and abruptly lurched into and out of stations. Now he had another issue to deal with, a car, or lack of one. *If I was still in the department, Al could pick* . . .

The train screeched so loud that it obliterated his thoughts. It had totally controlled his body—and now it was working on his mind. Ben decided not to think of anything and go with the flow of the New York Transit Authority. He had to change twice to get home from the Gravesend. Since it was a Sunday schedule, he didn't make it in until after nine.

Ben wondered if Charlie knew about the bad shocks.

- 47 -

Willie drove for the next few days as he had in the past. Ben preferred to sit shotgun and concentrate on the day ahead anyway. He also had let Ben borrow a clunker that he had at the station, a 1953 dark blue Olds convertible with a mismatched white door that didn't quite fit and a top that wouldn't go down. It wasn't pretty, but it ran—just like Willie. This was the least of Ben's problems

The next few days were pretty much the same. Ben came out ahead on most days and he continued his horse swap with Chalk—and he found out that he didn't really need the tout sheets to give him that extra edge.

Ben stood at the urinal focused on something remote.

"Who do you like in this race?"

Georgie Toro stood two urinals down. This startled Ben who was using this time as a one-minute vacation from the cerebral work of handicapping.

"Oh, the *three*."

Georgie Toro became a swap partner; it turned out that Chalk convinced him that it was a really good deal. *"You cut out the middleman, the track."*

That's just what Ben was counting on. First, it *was* a real good deal because you narrow your chances of losing to only one horse—the one Ben had. Second, he wanted the *bet swap* to sell itself so that guys approached him—it put him in a stronger, more trustworthy, position.

Willie spread the word and helped, sometimes.

"It's simple," he said to the Jacks. "You pick whatever horse and he'll pick whatever horse and whoever wins, wins, unless nobody wins then you don't lose. Get it?"

"What's the catch?"

"He has a secret." The Jacks listened attentively as Willie looked around then whispered discreetly. "He's smarter than you."

Now Ben's plan was really kicking in—he had Chalk, Georgie and occasionally one or both of the Jacks swapping horses with him. It was a good deal for everyone, he reminded himself over and over. This was what he was shooting for: several regular customers or swap partners. He wanted the word to spread but discreetly. Too many players will screw up the game, the business. He just needed four or five regulars to make this really effective. Over time, he'd weed out the right ones and increase the stakes. He thought about Charlie's chunks.

Sandy, Willie and Ben sat in Goodies. The guys got together more often these days. Maybe it was because of the void Al left, maybe because Ben was flying solo and maybe because the action created another bond. It didn't take Sandy long to figure the swaps. He had seen it in action last Saturday and he pieced together the rest. Willie helped.

"You see, Benny picks his horse and the other guys pick their horses and whosever horse wins, wins."

"Got it."

"He doesn't have to beat the horses, just the other guys."

"Like the guys with the bear."

"Huh?"

Sandy had to grab control of this conversation. Willie was driving him nuts. He was beginning to see why Al and Willie fought all the time.

"Two guys are in the woods and one is wearing new sneakers, Keds, I think." Sandy went into character. "The other guy says 'how come you're wearing new Keds in the woods?' He says, 'in case of a bear.' The other guy says 'stupid, you can't outrun a bear no matter what you're wearing.' And the first guy says . . ." Sandy broke up at the impending punch line, " . . . the first guy says, 'I don't have to be faster than the bear, I just have to be faster than you."

They all grabbed onto the much-needed laugh.

"I'll lay three to one on the bear," Willie added.

"Ben is not only beating the horses, he's beating the other players."

"That's what I said."

"I know. But you missed the best part."

Sandy and Ben exchanged looks. Ben knew that Sandy would pick up on it right away.

"May I?"

"Be my guest," Ben offered.

"The best part is when Benny swaps with one guy . . . it's his knowledge against the guy. I'd go with Benny any day."

"I know that. That's what I said. Isn't that what I said Benny?"

Ben nodded.

"But," Sandy leaned forward and lowered his voice to a strong whisper, "When he swaps with two or three guys and Ben wins . . . he gets paid from each of them. And if he loses, he only pays one."

Willie thinks about this new angle.

"What if they had the same horse?"

"I don't let that happen," Ben interjected.

"So," Willie surmised, "When you win, you're getting paid off two or three times and if you lose, you pay once."

Ben and Sandy smiled.

"Put that together that you can handicap the shorts off these guys . . ." Willie accentuated a shiver running up his body. "I'm getting a chill. Benny, you're a fuckin' genius."

Willie turned to the almost empty bar.

"This guy's a genius."

Then there was an awkward moment—unusual for these three.

"You guys want in?"

"Sure," was the immediate response.

"Good. I want to raise the stakes. You're in for five hundred each. Ok?"

They both nodded.

"My take's going to pay down Charlie, that rat bastard," Willie said, remembering that he was the one who got them into this in the first place.

Ben had hoped Willie would step up.

"Same thing goes for me," Sandy said.

"You're sure?"

"Sure."

Ben felt a sudden surge of strength knowing he's not alone in this challenge—it's good to have partners.

"Ok. Everything goes to pay down Charlie. After that, we split."

They nodded

"You know that even if we win—"

"We'll win."

"Even if we win," he continued. "We don't have enough time. The vig will probably just suck up anything we make. He wants it in chunks."

"How many chunks?" Willie asked.

"One."

"Then we'll just find another way," Sandy said.

It's good to have partners, good partners.

"To the Syndicate," Ben said as he raised his glass.

"The Syndicate."

- 48 -

Ben saw Caz Frankel a couple of times that week and they just nodded. He also saw Buddy Catalano, who ignored Ben completely. Ben wondered if he made any impact at all with Caz after he told him his horse was in the wrong race. *Cupid*, Caz's horse, lost that day—rallied much too late. Ben's pick ran a photo for second. Ben also wondered if Caz had any memory of him at Jamaica. Probably not—he was just a kid and Caz was a player back then.

It was Friday when Ben ran into Caz, literally. He was coming out of the men's room deep in thought as Caz was entering.

"Excuse me. Oh hiya Caz."

"You should be a little more careful."

"Sorry, didn't see you."

"I was talking about your play."

"What?"

"Never mind."

"No. What?"

"Ok. You're a smart boy Ben; you're just not playing it smart. I know what you're doing and I don't like your action. You're looking for the angle and a shortcut when you should be playing for the long haul. You've been that way since Jamaica."

"You remember me from Jamaica?"

"That's what I mean; you underestimate people. You're a good judge of horses; you need to work on people a little. You learned some since Jamaica but not enough."

"I'm not following."

"Come talk to me when you want to get serious. Right now, I've got priority business."

Caz went into the men's room and left Ben speechless. *What was that about?*

The next day Ben saw that *Cupid* was running in a mile and an eighth race—longer and up in class just as he suggested. Either Caz was bullshitting him or it was just coincidental. Or maybe, he really was listening to him. Buddy Catalano wasn't.

"Hi Buddy," Ben said offering a hand.

Buddy knew he knew him but didn't want to give him the satisfaction.

"Ben, Ben Collesano, we met with Caz."

"Oh yeah."

"I see you've moved Cupid up, how does he look?"

"Been wanting to move him for a while. Looks good."

"Well, good luck."

Ben left accomplishing what he intended to; he wasn't going to let Buddy ignore him. He could deal with him as an asset or a liability but he'd have to deal with him.

"Who do you like here Ben?" Chalk asked.

"The *four*."

"The *four*, yeah me too. We'll sit this one out. That's Frankel's horse, *Cupid*, remember?"

"Yeah, I noticed." He said as he looked around for Willie to make the bet.

Willie paced through the Grandstand looking for Ed the Brain, partly to see how he was doing and mostly to gloat over Ben's success. Of course he couldn't tell Ed the details—the schmuck wouldn't get it anyway. He couldn't find him and stopped for an afternoon beer when he noticed that *Cupid*, Caz's horse was running in the next race. *I wonder if Benny caught that?* He looked at the tote board and saw it was ten minutes to post. *He probably did, doesn't miss much.* Willie checked the program to figure how he could pick a horse that would save the day, which wasn't lost. He figured, maybe I can pick a few that Ben can't, maybe. Then he remembered Charlie, the chunk, the Syndicate and all of that. *I'll stick with Benny . . . the best on the planet and the entire country.*

Willie rose from his bar stool and saw a face across the Grandstand that froze him—a face from another time, another hell. He fell back down on the stool as his hand clasped tightly on his bottle. He had only seen this face once but he remembered the helplessness he felt as his hand was pinned to the anvil. He remembered the long anticipation and fear he felt as the hammer was raised and stood there poised to strike for what seemed hours. He remembered not feeling anything until he looked down at his bloody mess and the pain kicked in and lasted for days. He remembered screaming awake with this vision night after night for years.

The man sitting there held that hammer; Zito. He couldn't see him clearly, but he was sure. The bottle somehow lifted off the bar with Willie as he walked toward the man, the guy who deformed him, made him a freak. He joked about his finger, but the guys never could understand how ugly it made him feel. This was the prick that did that.

He approached the man from the back, partially obscured by other players. He wanted to make sure of what he was already sure of—that this was the guy. Willie didn't know what he was about to do but he was about to do something. He'd find out when it happened. Hatred and vengeance rose through his body now. It didn't matter that this guy was twice his size and towered over him—there was nothing but vengeance fueled by anger burning inside of Willie. There were no consequences to his action, as he saw himself smash the bottle across the guy's face over and over to repay him for all those nights and all that fear. The bottle transformed into a weapon as Willie approached behind the unaware man sitting there.

As Willie approached, his body trembled and he grasped the bottle tightly in his hand and raised it to shoulder height. It cost him a finger, it would cost this guy his head: fair trade. In a moment, he would be vindicated; the score would be even, no matter the cost.

But, he stood there and looked down at him—he was not the beast who savored in the thought of maiming him years ago—instead, there sat a washed out shell of a man in a wheelchair. Willie stood there trembling. Someone, something had already taken his vengeance. Someone had robbed him of the satisfaction of paying off this ancient debt.

He just stared for a long moment and walked away.

Ben bet on *Cupid* the traditional way because everyone he knew had him. Cupid won, paid a very decent sixteen dollars, sixty cents. Ben looked over the railing onto the field and saw Cruz Santiago, the jockey, dismount and walk the horse to the Winner's Circle. Caz and Buddy joined them and put on their best smiles for the photo. Buddy couldn't do anything about his loud jacket—guess he didn't expect to win, then again, maybe he did. Ben watched the proceedings: the handshakes, the official whatevers, the pats on the backs and the respect that both Buddy and Caz received. They were kings of the moment.

There was something about that episode that sparked envy, a feeling that Ben rarely felt. And, for a moment within that moment, it was Ben who was getting his picture taken with the winner.

The Winner's Circle photo was special; it outlived the race and even the horse. They all look the same but different. The top half of the photo had the finish of the race and the glorious moment of victory. The bottom half showed the horse, the jockey, the trainer and, of course, the owner standing proudly in the Winner's Circle. In between the two images, in bold letters, were the names of all the victorious parties.

The photo would be framed and placed on his wall alongside all the others until there was no more room. He would give copies to his friends, the barbershop, Goodies, Sandy's office and even down at the firehouse. His Winner's Circle photo would say:

Owner: Ben C. Collesano.

Caz and his entourage blew right passed Ben. He didn't think Caz heard him say,

"Good race, congratulations."

But he did and responded, "Thanks."

Ben may have read too much into the word but he was sure Caz acknowledged him. The *"thanks"* was more than thanks for the congratulations—it was thanks for the advice. Buddy nodded a polite nod that Ben interpreted as meaning nothing.

Ben just noticed Willie standing quietly by his side.

"Hey, where you been?"

"Took a walk."

- 49 -

Swaps became a small annuity and the Syndicate was netting several hundred dollars a day. It wasn't big money and it wasn't going to pay off Charlie but it was far better than losing. Some days more, some days Ben went oh-for-the-card. He was prepared for those days—days when the horses wouldn't cooperate or only the chalk horses finished in front or days when his picks just got nosed out. The swaps helped minimize his losses on those days and maximize them when he had the winners and two or three partners were not as lucky.

The formula was: *Win big; lose little.* The betting scheme focused on preserving capital, managing the money and the downside. *Live to bet another day.* Still, a couple of hundred a day was good but it wouldn't add up to a chunk.

Sandy's words echoed, "Then we'll just find another way."

That's what he liked about Sandy, always upbeat, always looking for solutions—the path of least resistance to the goal line. Don't beat your head against the wall; if going left isn't working, go right. The clock was still ticking and going left wasn't working—he had better look for another path or his house would become one big ashtray.

Sandy's motel routine had become old. This was supposed to be a one-nighter; he had far too much at stake to let this screw it up. He broke it off with Eileen several times and each time they screwed like it was the last. The office became more complicated as well, as Wasserman's weekly visits became daily pop-ins. The old man continued his filibusters and delicately probed into areas that were none of his business. Of course, he didn't see it that way, but fuck him; he's on the way out anyway.

Sandy knew that he would have to do something because Irene seemed to have smelled something and was acting strange. And Ben's kids, he loved them just like they were his own, but they weren't. At least Irene had some company when he wasn't there which was more often than not these days. It was time to get some order back into his life. *Enough's enough.*

Willie had found new strength and resolve. Perhaps it was Ben and his success and the Syndicate being back in operation or maybe it was a lifelong debt that was marked *paid in full*. Maybe he grew into the void left by Al. On Thursday, he brought flowers home to Ro.

"*Not for nothin', just felt like it.*"

She gave him that special back rub that she used to give him as a customer—the one that kept him coming back week after week. They made love that night for the first time in six months. The next morning Willie slept in.

"You getting up?" Ro gently nudged him.

"Nah," he slurred. "Day off. It's national gas station day," as he pulled her into bed with him for another round.

Ro made him a big breakfast and he just spent the rest of the day in front of the TV watching soaps and doing Jumbles. He wondered how he had gotten himself into this mess—it was only small time betting and he swore it was the only way out of pumping gas for the rest of his life. He knew he'd hit the big one. Maybe when this is over and he parlays his piece of the Syndicate into the scheme that he'd been working on but hadn't quite figured out yet, he'd find a way out and sell the station or maybe just give it to his daughters and move to Connecticut with Ro or just stay here and play the ponies with his extra cash. Of course, he'd let Ben and Sandy in on it.

Friday had started out good. Willie was home sick today, so Ben drove the clunker in and made the bets himself, regular way. The fourth race had just finished and Ben had two winners already—both long shots. He was feeling very comfortable at the track, as if it were home—much like the firehouse had felt some weeks earlier. There was twenty-five minutes until the next race and Ben took a short walk towards the field; maybe he could catch a few rays between races. Caz and Buddy were involved in an animated discussion near the entrance; Ben veered away, politely nodding as he passed.

"Hey, Ben." Caz summoned. "A question for you."

Ben walked over.

"Why're you . . .?" Buddy was somewhat put out.

"Ben, you looked at the card for the next race," Caz accurately surmised. "Which horse would you claim?"

"Well, I haven't really looked at them from that angle." *Why is he asking me that?*

"I know, an unfair question. But if you could claim one now which would it be?"

"Ok. Give me a moment."

Ben reviewed the entries quickly. He had done this several times before but not with a long-term head on. He was always looking for who would win this race, not next year's races. In claiming races, a price is put on each horse's head—presumably a fair price—and any qualified owner could claim, or buy, the horse for that price. Now the question was much different: *"which horse would you like to own?" Another test.*

"I would have to go with *TJ Parker*, the *four* horse." Ben looked at Buddy, then Caz and continued, "Good lines and workouts are decent and improving, blinders may make a difference. Of course, if I had time to really study it and knew what kind of stable I wanted to build I may see it differently."

"Thanks, that was one of our top three also."

"No problem." Ben said as he started to walk away. *What was that about?*

"Ben," Caz called and walked up to him out of Buddy's earshot. "Take some advice. Be careful."

"With what?"

"Just be careful." Caz made eye contact to punctuate his warning and walked back to Buddy.

"Why did you tell him that was one of our three horses?" Buddy was frustrated. "That's the horse I been telling you about."

"I know."

Ben was still replaying the conversation with Caz as he entered the men's room. There were no swap partners in this race and he was debating his next selection. *Six horse—seems like the price horses are up today, not that one race has anything to do with another, but you never know.*

He stepped up to the urinal lost in his figuring. A small man in a suit grabbed the urinal on his right. *Plenty of pissholes, why pick this one?*

"You like pissing here?" The man said as he looked straight ahead. Ben thought he was talking to himself when a voice came from the other side.

"He asked you a question."

Ben turned and there was another man in a suit and skinny tie taking a leak on his left; he was also looking straight ahead. It was not the appropriate moment for Ben to leave so he continued his business while looking left and right at the flanking and peeing suits. Ben didn't answer; he didn't know what the real question was.

"Well how about if we pissed all over where you live," the right suit said. "Just came over and pissed. I mean, on the furniture and the house that you probably built and your car and everything that took you years to get."

"I wouldn't like it," he figured they needed some response and they had a point to make somewhere before they all zipped up.

Just then, the left suit swung over to Ben's urinal and started pissing in it alongside Ben. Ben stepped back—he had had three cups of coffee this morning and figured that he could make the distance. The right suit joined in and now three men pissed in the same urinal.

"Didn't think so. It gets pretty uncomfortable when you use something in a way that it was not intended to be used."

"Yep." It was either piss on these guys' pants, which would probably go downhill from there, or keep pissing until the last drop of java left, no matter how much company he had.

"Then we agree. Then stop pissing in this pot."

"What do you mean?" Ben asked, knowing exactly what they meant. He wondered how much piss they had left; this buddy system did not do it for him.

"You know what we mean. You stop now or you will never be allowed to piss in a track Men's Room again."

"In all Men's Rooms," the left suit added.

There was no point in debating the issue or denying accusation; he was nailed. Apparently, the track figured that his swapping bets were encroaching on their turf; of course, it was. Whatever meager bets Ben was swapping reduced the track's handle. His bets really didn't make a difference, but if it caught on, everyone would do it, reduce the handle to squat and there would be no more track. He knew it had to end sooner or later; just like at Jamaica, it was a matter of time. He had hoped that this would have a more businesslike ending.

"I'm done." Ben decided against a last shake and zipped up.

His buddies followed suit.

He washed up and the two suits flanked him at the sinks. They talked through the mirror but never looked directly at Ben—never made direct eye contact.

"It's over," the left suit said as he combed his hair.

"You've pissed for the last time," the right suit added.

He was getting a little tired of the analogy but sensing that they would not leave without some affirmation, Ben nodded. "I said: I'm done. I'm finished."

They seemed satisfied and left.

Ben stood staring at himself in the mirror. *"Be careful,"* Caz's words had a little more meaning now.

- 50 -

Ben drove Willie's clunker down Flatlands Avenue looking for a smooth road without traffic; he found both. To keep from stalling out, he threw it into neutral at every light. *You'd think that Willie would adjust the carb or whatever he does; he owns a goddamn garage. What a day for him to get sick.*

He drove with mixed feelings—swaps were dead, kaput, over. The cash cow rolled over and died. His win-win scheme, his brainchild, was gone. He knew that it couldn't go on forever but he had expected, had hoped for, a longer run. Rest in peace, swaps. This would really affect his betting and his cash flow but not his horse picking—that had been pretty good lately. Today, he wound up with four winners, with mostly good prices. He felt good about that. But he lost the annuity.

He was still caught between being pissed about losing the swaps and being upbeat about his selections—even Caz Frankel had asked his opinion. He had mixed feelings, but that soon changed.

A hose truck had just finished packing up as Ben arrived. The sight of a fire truck in his own driveway startled him. He bounced the clunker over the curb and into his driveway—almost hitting the truck and sending a garbage can onto his lawn. The driver's door wouldn't open so he exited via the passenger's side.

Instinctively, he flashed his badge to the first fireman he saw. "What happened?"

"Not too much, somebody got real careless with some paint rags in the garage; could've taken the garage and the house if we got here any later. You live here?"

Ben nodded and looked over to the garage, a mess of water and wooden debris that used to be a garage door. "But you got it in time."

"Yep. Got it in time." Sorry about the door, didn't want to . . ."

"No problem. It's just a door. Origin?"

"Don't know, strange. As I said, paint rags in a bucket. Anyone painting here in the last few hours?"

"No." The pieces weren't hard to put together. But he wasn't going to escalate this and bring in the department and maybe the police; life was complicated enough. "I'm the only one here and I wasn't."

"What about the kid?"

"The kid?"

The fireman looked towards the house. Rick stood on the front porch just behind the screen door. Ben wasted no time in getting to him. He was shaking. Ben held him tight.

"It's ok, I'm here now. Are you ok?"

"Yes." Clearly he wasn't but he stayed strong.

Ben held him to comfort him and to apologize for putting him in this mess and screwing up his life.

"You ok?" Ben asked again.

Rick parted from him. "I'm fine," he said with a little more credibility.

They looked at the garage and surveyed the damage. The cinder block walls of the garage had been seared; they probably inhibited the fire's ascent. Clearly the fire was climbing: a little more time and it would have hit the rafters and the roof, then the house. Was that what they wanted? Pretty stupid, the fire takes the house then I have nothing but the insurance. But they'd never see it. Never. I lose, they lose. Maybe it's a warning that could have gone bad.

"Good thing you were here. You called it in?"

"What?"

"The fire. Did you call the fire department?"

"No. I heard the sirens and came outside. Then the fire truck came into the driveway and I saw the smoke from the garage."

Then it was clear; it had been a warning. They started it and called it in, knowing that it wouldn't do too much real damage. But it could've.

"Hey, champ. What were you doing here anyway? You should be at Aunt Irene's"

"I was down the street and saw your car in the driveway . . ."

"My car?"

"The Buick."

Beefy.

"I thought you were home. And I went inside. When I came out the car was gone. Were you . . .?"

"No. The car was," Ben reconsidered complicating the situation with a lie on top of everything else. "Somebody has my car, a guy I know. He must have seen the smoke and called it in. Lucky he was around." But sometimes the truth is a lie. "Rick, I want you to promise me that you won't come home until I say it's ok."

"Ok."

"And everything will be ok. I promise you." He pulled Rick to him held him close to him to protect him from a danger that had already passed. He looked him in the eye. "Promise me you won't come home."

"I promise. Promise me that everything will be ok."

"Promise a thousand times over." Ben hoped he could keep it.

They looked at each other and fear slowly turned to smiles.

"Hey, how about the park tomorrow? Throw the ball around."

Ben hugged him again—not only to comfort him for today's experience but for not being around, for the situation they were in, and for everything else that had happened in the last few weeks. As he held Rick, he felt the heat rise inside and consume him. That Beefy prick crossed the line—by a fuckin' mile. Ben wished that he was here right now and, as big as he was, face to big ugly Neanderthal face. Anger was something Ben rarely experienced—this was one of those rare occasions. His chest began to rise and contract as his breathing became more labored.

"Dad, you ok?"

Ben looked at his son once more and remembered that *this* was what it was all about, not Charlie or that piece of shit Beefy, not the horses. It was about his kids and Kitty and as long as he had them, everything would work itself out. Everything.

"Fine." He kissed Rick on the forehead. "C'mon, I'll take you to Aunt Irene's. You want to ride in the coolest car ever?"

The tire grazed the curb and the clunker stalled to sleep as Ben pulled up to Goodies. Still fuming about Rick and the house, Ben kicked open the passenger's door, got out and slowly walked to the bar. They were way over the line. This has just escalated into something else; his debt to Charlie and the big piece of shit just grew. Ben walked into Goodies and directly over to Sandy sitting at the table. He didn't sit.

"Is Pacey Diamond in town?"

"I think so, why?"

"It's payback time."

Willie walked in behind Ben.

Ben sat and tried to calm down. He decided not to tell them about the garage fire; it was time to focus on business.

"The swaps are dead."

Sandy and Willie just looked and listened.

"They closed us down."

"Who?"

"I'm not sure. The track, maybe some others. Don't know. But we're down. If you guys want out of the Syndicate, just say so."

"We're in," they both echoed without hesitation.

"Good." Ben knew that, but he had to ask.

"The Syndicate has fifty two hundred."

"Wow."

"I want to roll that into Charlie."

"What do you mean? Pay him off? That's not even a quarter of what I . . ." Willie said. "We owe over nineteen grand. You more than tripled the Syndicate so far, just do the same thing."

"Can't. Not by Monday."

"Why not?"

"Because there are no more swaps to protect us or maybe the horses aren't there to bet on or maybe I have a bad day or maybe . . . I could lose it just as easy as winning. It's just not smart to press—that's how you wind up getting into situations like this in the first place. That's how you got here and that's why we're all here now. You can't play for all the marbles all the time."

"Sorry."

"Don't be sorry. It's time to be smart." Ben cooled down "I want to use the entire fifty two hundred to stake a different kind of bet to pay down Charlie. I think that we can do it."

"I don't get why we can't just . . ."

"Because it's a stupid idea. I have something else. It's risky; it may not work and we will be back where we started."

"Minus a house," Sandy added.

Ben just looked; it didn't need a reply. He looked at Willie and pat the back of his head. "Sorry."

"No prob. I earned it," Willie said.

"I thought you weren't feeling well."

"A twenty-four hour thing. Better now."

"Good. Sandy, see if Pacey Diamond can meet us."

"Will do," Sandy said as he got up and walked to the phone.

"Ben, sorry about this whole—"

"Willie, shut up. We're in this together. It is where it is."

Willie nodded; he didn't have to say more. "First round's on me." Willie got up and went to the bar.

Ben sat alone trying not to regret everything he had done in the last few weeks. It made sense, he backed a friend; any of them would have done the same. It didn't matter how he got here; the only thing that mattered was how to get from here to somewhere else.

Willie dropped three beers on the table. "There's some giant by the door he must be six foot a hundred."

Ben turned. A familiar big ugly figure hovered in the doorway. Beefy stood there lighting matches, flicking them into the street. The heat began to rise again—Ben pictured the fear in Rick's eyes. He had always been able to take the emotion out of gambling and business; that was one of his unique strengths, an advantage over the other players. He did that now; talked business and put aside the fire that was building inside of him.

But this time, the fire had its own momentum; it had fuel and if he gave it air, there would be no controlling it. His instincts, his experience, has taught him that sometimes you do not have the control that you thought you did; sometimes you have to step aside and let the fire have its way. The more he visualized Rick earlier, the angrier he got. He pictured him sitting in the house as it went up in flames. His fire had air—all the air that it needed to burst into an inferno. Suddenly, he was seeing white as the blaze inside consumed every rational thought that surrounded it.

Ben abruptly stood up and walked towards the front door.

"Where're you going?" Ben didn't hear Willie's question.

From across the room, Sandy stood at the phone and saw Ben make for the door. Something about his stride, his pace, his demeanor, something was different; and it wasn't good. "Shit." Sandy hung up.

Beefy slowly moved his large frame out of the doorway before Ben converged. Ben walked outside and saw him leaning against a car, lighting a smoke. Ben didn't break stride as he approached. There was no sign of Charlie; maybe he was waiting in the car with another wake up call.

He approached and they stood face to face; Ben wasn't a small man but he had to look up to meet Beefy's eyes. He looked right through him. If Charlie was nearby, Beefy was here to protect him, if he wasn't, he was here to intimidate, not do serious damage. *Pound the shit out of me now and you'll never see a nickel. You know that, I know that.* He hoped he was right.

"Charlie says to remind you that Monday is moving day. Three days. Monday." Beefy straightened up and blew smoke out of his nose the way fire-breathing dragons and assholes do. Beefy enjoyed his power—Ben amused him. "And I'm the mover," Beefy said as he took another deep drag and brought the smoke down into his belly—challenging Ben with a display of arrogance and invulnerability. He flicked his cigarette and it exploded on Ben's chest sending sparks flaring in every direction.

Ben reached somewhere deep inside and swung. There was no thought behind it, no plan: just raw emotion. One solid fluid movement that started low and arched upwards as every cell of every muscle in his body powered his fist as it plowed into Beefy's crotch. Beefy never saw the crushing blow as it rose into his groin; he had no time to defend or retaliate.

He never knew he was hit; only that his body was immersed in a searing flash of pain that crushed his balls and radiated throughout his entire mass like ten thousand volts. He knew that it would only get worse, a lot worse, before it got better. He also knew that there was nothing he could do about it as his legs left him as if they had been detached. The immense hulk doubled up, crumbled to his knees and hit sidewalk like ten tons of shit in a sack. He quivered as he lay there whimpering like a little girl.

Ben, consumed in a white heat, towered over the trembling mass. He stood ready to continue inflicting pain but he had won already. Beefy was crippled. Ben bent down and looked him in the eye, real close, and whispered.

"Stay the fuck away from my family."

He got the message, no point in prolonging it. Ben started to stand up then remembered Rick's face earlier. It was as if his body was being controlled by someone else; as if the fire had not been satisfied and had more destruction to deliver before it died. He raised his fist and crashed it square into Beefy's nose and felt cartilage shatter under his hand as Beefy's head slammed onto the concrete.

"And my house."

He pulled back and brought his fist into Beefy's face again.

"You like playing with matches?" He pried open Beefy's jaw, picked the still burning butt off of the ground, shoved it in and slammed the jaw shut. "Here's fire."

Beefy's eyes glazed as smoke lazily floated out of his bloodied mouth and nose. Inside his tongue and gums seared. He would remember that.

Ben stood and walked past Sandy and Willie who remained gawking at the motionless hulk, oozing smoke and blood. They followed Ben inside and joined him at the table.

Ben let out a sigh as if he had just rid himself of some serious weight. They sat there for a long moment. Willie and Sandy waited; this was a guy they knew their entire lives and they never saw anything like this; but they also knew that never to underestimate Ben. They gave him his space and waited for him to speak.

"Where were we?" The fire was out; back to business.

- 51 -

Ben explained in as few words as possible that he wasn't swapping bets any longer. The guys at the track didn't ask too many questions and seemed to understand. Chalk thought about swapping among themselves and perhaps bringing in a couple of new guys. After all, it's a good deal for everyone. He couldn't pull it off—he wasn't organized and didn't have the credibility that Ben seemed to acquire in a very short time. So, bet swapping died in New York, except for the occasional friendly wager.

Saturday blew by quickly. Ben wasn't as focused as usual considering all that was going on around him; he had just a couple of days to fix the Charlie situation. After Beefy's beating, Ben was sure that if he were a minute late, his house would be a cinder. He also knew that Charlie would not bother him again before Monday. This was more than just money; the line was crossed and Ben wanted to cross back. It wouldn't be enough to just get out of the predicament and pay off Charlie, which was a stretch no matter how you figured it; no, he would have to clear the financial debt and nail Charlie's ass to the wall—and do it in the next couple of days. He knew how to do it—he needed the right information, the right situation and a lot of luck—and Pacey Diamond was key.

Ben had plans and he left after the seventh race, finishing the day with two winners. The Syndicate had a few more dollars for ante. He took the clunker today so Willie wouldn't have to leave early with him.

Sandy was taking in the garbage cans when Ben pulled up in the clunker. He kicked the passenger door open and got out.

"Nice wheels. New?" Sandy ribbed.

"Speak to Pacey Diamond?"

"Everything's on. He'll know tomorrow morning if he has something . . . or not. What if he can't come up with anything?"

"Then we'll think of something else. Got another idea?"

"No. I'm with you; just thinking about a backup plan."

"Backup plan is we move in with you permanently."

"Speaking of that, when are you guys moving out?"

"Ask me tomorrow."

"Good 'cause I keep finding Cheerios in my shorts."

Small loud voices carried the sound of the boys as they ran out of the house and jumped him.

"Dad!"

"Hi guys."

"Hey," Ben said to Rick, "Listen, something important came up and we can't go to the park today but how about if we do something even better tomorrow?"

"Like what?" Rick was disappointed.

"I don't know, maybe . . ." Ben pulled three tickets out of his pocket. "We can go to the Yankee game."

The boys lit up and hugged him and knocked him to the ground.

Sandy watched. This is what he was missing.

"Kitty inside?"

As if on cue, Kitty came out.

"Ready?" Ben opened the passenger door as she approached the car.

"Well, things are looking up. New car?"

Ben grimaced. He got in before her and slid over. She stood outside the car perplexed.

"Coming?"

"Want to take my car?"

"Nah, I'm beginning to like it. Get in."

"Neat car," Rick said.

Ben wondered if nine year olds knew about sarcasm.

Some things hadn't changed in twenty years; the ocean was the same, the people were the same and the boardwalk was the same. Ben and Kitty were not the same—at least not right away. It took a little while before they could break through the awkwardness of the last few weeks. She hadn't crossed over to where she could fully and completely trust him yet. The boardwalk helped.

The summer crowd was long gone and just a few locals populated the boardwalk. The smell of the moist air coming across the sand revitalized old memories and connections to a purer, more innocent, state—a state where they were still learning about each other and themselves—a state where everything was in front of them and was exciting, adventurous and unknown.

Somehow, as they walked together on the boardwalk, the sound of the sea, the smell of the salt air brought much of that back and melted some of the new walls. They were beginning to know each other again the way they did in the purest of times. Trust would follow.

"Did you ever turn your head sideways while riding through a tunnel?" Ben didn't wait for the answer. "Well, it looks different, and a little scary."

"What are you trying to say?"

"I cooked. I mean, at home. I mean, without you."

"So?"

"You said that if you weren't home to cook, I would starve."

"Oh. I knew that you could get along without me if you had to. You just had to. What did you make?"

"Toast."

"I'm proud of you."

"Kitty, I miss you and I want you to come home. I miss you. I miss us."

"I thought . . ."

"That's just it. One way or another, this will be over soon. I'm not sure if we'll have a house, but—"

"I told you. I don't care if we live in a shoebox."

Ben hugged her and held her. He thought about her understanding and support. This is what he really appreciated. This is Kitty.

"I know that we have, well, we just existed for a while. Just accepted what we had as what we had."

"What was wrong with that?"

"Nothing, except I wanted something more. Not from you, from me." He might as well get it all out and away. This was the time. "And . . ."

"I know. You are going to play the horses."

"I . . ."

"Everyday."

"Yes." He waited for a reaction, which didn't come. "Kitty, I've always been missing something, some commitment, other than you and the kids. I need a goal, other than just survive. This is it. I'm good at it, real good."

"Ok."

"I've always been afraid that when I'm older I'll look back and regret not doing something, not taking the chance. Now, it's here. You and the kids have always come first; nothing will change that, horses or no horses."

Kitty got in front of him and walked backwards in step.

"You're just following the instructions on the box."

"Huh?"

"One, do you know where you want to go?"

"Yes."

"Well, where?" She prodded.

"I want to be the best horse player in the business and maybe have my own stable someday."

"Two," she poked her finger in his chest playfully, "and are you doing the things that will get you there?"

Ben smiled as he realized that Kitty was throwing his own words back at him.

"You're ok with it?"

She stopped walking and he walked into her. There was no space between them.

"I said ok. I'm ok. I believe in you." Her tone softened. "I have always believed in you."

Ben looked at her for a long moment.

"For a guy who doesn't believe in luck, I'm a lucky guy. I love you."

They kissed a long comfortable secure kiss; a kiss that held passion, respect, love and trust.

"Would you love me if I wasn't ok with it?"

"Of course." There could be no other answer.

"Tootsie Pop?" She held a cherry Tootsie Pop in front of him.

He took it.

They just walked arm in arm for the next hour absorbing this new place they were in. Not too far in the distance, the waves gently crashed onto the beach and carried in the cool sea mist. The smell of the salt brought back memories of childhood, of play, of peace and of starting fresh with their lives in front of them. Words were superfluous, time was not present.

He called Pacey Diamond as soon as he got home. It wasn't that he didn't trust Sandy to follow through—he trusted him with his life. He just needed to make sure that everything was covered, that Pacey knew what he needed and when. He did.

Ben slept that night; the horses had left the starting gate, the dice were in the air and he had no decisions to make.

- 52 -

It was a beautiful Sunday morning: one day to Charlie's moving company. It was perfect for a ride in the country, a Yankee game and taking care of old debts—if things go well—one day early. Ben met Willie and Sandy for breakfast at Cookies.

"We ok?" Ben said to Sandy as he returned from the phone booth.

"Golden. Big money is coming in on the Colts at about noon. They're six point favorites over the Giants."

Ben guessed nine forty-five and checked his watch.

"Quarter to ten."

Sandy waited as Ben thought for a moment and Willie chomped down his hash browns and eggs.

"Call Charlie and bet ten thousand on the Colts, minus the six."

Sandy nodded, took a sip of coffee and left the table. Ben started to eat as Willie polished his plate with a roll.

"Why'd ya do that? Does he know something?"

"Doesn't matter. Pacey Diamond is a commissioned merchant. You know what that is?"

"Sure . . . No."

"He runs big bets between the bookies to lay off their action. So he gets a lot of information." Ben looked behind him to see how Sandy was doing—still on the phone—Ben continued. "Our ten thousand will get their attention. Charlie may try to lay it off—he won't be able to."

"How do you know?"

"Trust me, I know. In any case, he will try to attract Giants money by pumping up the odds. Add that to the big Colt money coming in at noon, it'll move the line on the Giants-Colts. Then we'll bet ten thousand on the other side."

"Wait a sec. Where'd we get twenty grand?"

"Didn't," Ben said as he dug into his eggs.

"Don't get it."

"Sandy's betting ten grand on the Colts, on credit."

"On credit. What if he doesn't get the credit?"

"He took a short term loan from his business."

"What? What if we lose? Where's he gonna . . .?"

"Can't lose. We may not win, probably won't, but we cannot lose—we're betting on both teams." Willie looked as fried as Ben's eggs; Ben went on. "After the line moves, we're going to bet another ten on the Giants. Doc Brodsky will bet five . . ." Ben looked Willie right in the eyes. "And you will visit Charlie and bet another five grand on the Giants."

"Charlie won't take my bets."

"He will, if you put up cash up front."

"I don't have five grand. If I had five grand. . ." Willie decided not to finish.

"The Syndicate does." Ben said with a mouth full. He reached into his pocket and came up with a stack of bills, which he handed to Willie. "Fifty-five hundred, including the vigorish. Count it."

"I thought we only had fifty two."

"I added three. Doesn't matter. Listen." Ben held back the money to get Willie's full attention. "You don't bet until the line is over seven and Sandy gives you the go-ahead."

"Got it," Willie said, proud to be part of the caper but not exactly sure what the caper was.

"Sure?" Ben saw the familiar look on Willie's face.

"No."

"Remember Jamaica?" Ben started to explain and interrupted himself as Sandy returned to the table. "We ok?"

"Bet's in." Sandy sat. "We have the Colts minus six for ten thousand."

"Charlie give you any grief?"

"Nope. He seemed to know who I was. Said 'hello counselor.' I was a little surprised."

"Don't be. I was counting on that. What about Doc?"

"Spoke to him earlier; he's waiting for my call."

"Great. Thanks. You'll watch the line? I won't be near a phone."

"I'll watch it like it had tits. My coffee's cold." Sandy signaled the waitress.

"Jamaica. What about Jamaica?" Willie wanted to know.

"What?" Ben asked.

"You were saying. You said 'remember Jamaica.'"

"Oh. Ok, we've got ten thousand on the Colts minus the six points and later we'll have ten thousand on the Giants plus, hopefully seven and a half or eight. We'll have both sides of the bet, sound familiar?"

"Yeah," Willie said still uncertain.

"Jamaica? *Dutching the book?* We played the difference in the odds. This is the same thing."

"Yeah!" Willie got it.

"We've got a *middle*—the best bet never invented. We can win but not lose. We can win both ends if the Colts win by seven. Otherwise, we lose one side, win the other and we're out the vigorish."

"And a house." Sandy reminded.

"Benny . . ." Willie hesitated, "What if we don't win? I mean . . ."

"We have tomorrow to come up with something else. Anyway, we do nothing and the house is gone. This way, we have a chance to pay the Charlie off with his own money." Ben looked to Sandy. "What about the Union?"

"They are on board, mucho happy to help." Sandy said.

"With everything?"

"Everything; they have some skin in this also."

"Good." Ben stood. "Gotta go."

"Enjoy the game."

"Thanks," he left.

"What's with the union?" Willie said as he reached across for Ben's uneaten toast.

"Just cleaning up some old accounts."

"Huh?"

"They owe Ben a favor."

"He did them a favor?"

"Yep."

"What?"

"Nothing."

"Hey, you can tell me."

"I did. He didn't do a goddamn thing. And they're grateful." Sandy enjoyed building on Willie's confusion. "More coffee?"

- 53 -

The clunker rode down the Grand Central Parkway in the right lane. The boys really loved the car, bouncing on the huge back seat in some kind of Mighty Joe Young versus Godzilla wrestling match. Their sounds felt good. He missed them.

"How much longer?" Rick popped up with Scooter in a headlock.

"We'll be there in plenty of time for the game. We're going to make a short stop first."

"A Scooter?" Rick blurted out. "You're making a Rizzuto?"

"Huh?"

"A shortstop. You said you were making a shortstop, a Rizzuto." Rick said as he exploded in laughter, Ben and Scooter joined in.

"We'll do both. We'll make a short stop, then we'll go see Rizzuto," Ben enunciated his words, "play shortstop."

The laughter subsided as the anticipation of seeing the Mick drained from their faces.

"But first we are going to see some horses."

"All right!"

The clunker wheezed into a long private road flanked by tall white wooden fences and meticulously manicured pastures. It was clearly out of place among the straight clean lines edging the flowing green, as if disturbing a serenity of a time long gone. Horses that were quietly grazing in the pastures moments ago looked up to see the clunker disturb the tranquility and esthetics of their paradise. At the end of the road stood several white buildings, stalls, and turnouts. The sign at the entrance said:

Carillon Stables, Caz Frankel, Prop.

A day or two ago, Ben would have been too embarrassed to drive the clunker in front of Caz Frankel, but it wasn't two days ago. Caz stood there apparently directing a stable hand when he saw the car trudge down the drive. A lost soul, he thought, or a sightseer. He didn't get too many because he was so off road but when they showed up, they were usually very lost or very curious. He was about to tell his hand to deal with it when he saw Ben sliding out of the passenger's door.

"Stay in the car. I'll only be a minute," Ben said as he quickly surveyed the place and walked deliberately towards Caz. He looked different here without his entourage: more at home, more natural, more human. He never thought of Caz that way, human. He was always an iconic figure that stood way above him in the Clubhouse at a considerable distance.

Caz dismissed the hand and stood alone.

"New car?" Caz seemed to be in on the same joke as the rest of the world.

Ben smiled; he didn't think Caz knew how to joke.

"Yeah, like it? Gets no miles to the gallon but I like the look."

Caz looked behind Ben and saw the boys in the car.

"Yours?"

"Yeah. Rick and Scooter." Ben said proudly. "My guys and one on the way." Until Ben said that, he had almost forgotten that Kitty was pregnant. The words echoed inside of him: '*one on the way.*' It felt good for the first time.

"Why don't you let them out? How often do they get to see horses up close?"

"You sure?"

"Sure."

Ben walked back to the car and the boys flew out and huddled up to the fence to watch the horses. He stopped for a minute to take it in. He had never introduced his guys to what he was doing. Of course, it had only been a few weeks. It felt good to share it, be open about it.

He approached Caz again.

"I hope I'm not interrupting something."

"Just doing my day to day. Nothing that couldn't go on without me."

"I don't think I had it wrong but the other day were you giving me an invitation to talk?"

"You didn't have it wrong. I don't suspect that you're the kind of guy I have to mince words with."

"You either."

Caz nodded and smiled as he watched the boys beckon a horse to come closer. They walked towards the turnout pasture and leaned against the fence. Caz watched his horses.

"See them?" Caz nodded towards a group of horses. "They are compatible. You know why? It's the company they keep. Boys with boys, girls with girls. I don't turnout the stallions with the mares unless they bred together.

Otherwise, they can hurt each other. It's the way it is in nature, as if they were wild. I don't mess with that."

"Did you close me down?" Ben asked.

"Ben, you overestimate me. No. You closed yourself down. You were playing a crack in the system, and cracks usually close, particularly if they're costing someone money."

"You?"

"Me? No, not me. I could care less. The track. If you find a way to end run them they lose a lot of money and it doesn't look good. You do it, then someone else does it, pretty soon, it's serious dollars. You became their competition in their own house. You were the stallion in their pasture of mares. Besides, it was a loophole. Remember, the track's not your competition; you're your own competition. The track is just your arena."

Caz seemed to be more interested in the boys than in Ben.

"You have kids?" Ben asked.

"A son. Went to Korea . . . never came back."

This was an interesting side of Caz. Ben never thought of Caz with a family. He was always the upscale guy with the followers and the big stable. They both stared at the boys who ran up and down the fence line for a long minute.

"Look Ben. It's ok to beat the system. I've done it many times. Anyone who's successful finds some way through it. But if you want to beat the system, beat it. Don't look for little cracks in the wall and squiggle through. Beat it like a man. You don't have to bend the rules; you can do real well inside the rules. You've got the talent, go through the goddamn wall."

The boys suddenly remembered that they were going to see the Mick and they waved furiously at Ben.

"I'll be right there," Ben shouted, then turned to Caz. "Taking them to the Yankee game."

"Nice. Ben. Why are you here?"

"Not sure. Maybe to find out where I stand. And if you are in front of me or behind me."

"Now that's not mincing words. I'm not in your way, if that's what you mean. There's plenty out there for everybody—everybody who earns it, that is. What is it that you want?"

"The question of the week. I want to be a horseplayer, not just get by. I want to be really good. Maybe someday have a small stable. I want to be at the top of the game, like you."

The boys jumped up and down.

"So do it. Come to my box tomorrow, we'll talk. Now go. You have higher priorities at the moment."

Caz offered his hand and they shook. Ben turned to join the boys and stopped.

"One more thing."

"Yes?"

"Remember Jamaica?"

"Certainly."

"Did you close me down there?"

"Jamaica?" Caz smiled. "I was wondering about that. Actually, I admired your ingenuity, the way you had your friends race from book to book. Great little scheme. Wish I had thought of it. No, I had nothing to do with it. But it was inevitable; I wasn't the only one who knew what you were doing. The track—"

"I know. The cracks."

Noon took forever to arrive as Sandy waited by his phone; he'd give it a few more minutes then call in.

The house felt a little strange, almost too quiet, with Ben's kids not there. They'd only been gone a couple of hours and he missed them already. Maybe if he and Irene had gone that route, things would be different now; maybe this would feel more like a home. She wanted to at first, he didn't. Then they both reversed positions but it was too late—wasn't practical any more. He had made his choices long ago and he was on this road until the end.

He thought about Eileen. There was something about her that really intrigued him, more than the sex. But, like the kids, it's too late for that.

Might as well clean that up also. Enough daydreaming. Time to call.

"Line on the Colts-Giants?"

He wrote something on a phone pad—unnecessary, but he wrote anyway.

"Colts, seven and a half." *Whew.* "Thanks." Ben was hoping for more than seven. He hung up and redialed with one hand.

"Doc, Giants plus seven and a half. Put it in now and don't take less than seven and a half. Call me when it's in. Thanks."

One more call.

"Willie, you're on. Bet the Giants plus seven and a half. I know you know. Just go. Giants plus seven and a half, nothing less. Call me when it's in."

Willie stepped into the *Gravesend Bar* and slowly looked around. He had never been there before and never met Charlie; he had only dealt with Charlie's guys on the phone. Beefy, jaw wired, bandage on his nose, limped very slowly to the men's room. Willie turned away so Beefy wouldn't notice him; just in case he wanted to take out a little of Ben on him. Charlie was easy to spot with his gray hair shining in the single ray of sunlight that somehow broke into the otherwise dark bar. He was smaller than Willie imagined.

Charlie slowly looked up at Willie standing over him.

"Yes?"

"The line on the Giant game."

"Do I know you?"

"Willie Urbanski."

"I know the name. I don't think you have a credit line."

"Don't need it." Willie dropped a stack of bills on the table.

Charlie looked suspiciously. "Does your friend Ben know you're here?"

"Ben who?"

"Colts are seven and a half."

"Five thousand on the Giants plus seven and a half."

Charlie nodded and counted the money. "It's a bet."

Sandy picked the phone mid-ring.

"We in?"

"How'd you know it was me?" Willie asked.

"Are we in?"

"We have the New York Giants plus seven and one half points for five thousand. I left fifty five hundred with Charlie the putz. We're in."

"Good work. Go watch the game, root for . . ."

"Root for the Giants to lose by seven, not six not eight. Seven. Got it."

"Willie, good work."

"Yeah."

Doc had called a few minutes earlier with the same info. Only one thing left; wait for Ben's call to check up on the action. Then it's out of their control. That was one thing he could rely on—Ben's call would be right on time. And it was.

"We ok?"

"Willie's in, Doc's in. Giants plus seven and a half. Enjoy the game."

It was short and to the point business, the way business should be conducted. When it was chat time, they chatted. When it came time for business, they were efficient.

Sandy made one last phone call to his friends at the union, more business.

"Murph? Sandy Kane. That transaction we talked about. It's a go."

He hung up. Everything was in motion; the bets are in, might as well clean up some of his old business as well. He reluctantly picked up the phone one more time and dialed slowly.

- 54 -

Yankee Stadium was predictably crowded. The Yankees were in their annual pennant race versus the Orioles, Whitey Ford was pitching and it was a beautiful fall Bronx day. Ben had made his call and everything was in place. It was a rare moment within a tumultuous time. Everything was done and now it was Sunday—it was really a day off, a day to spend with the boys and relax. And wait.

A curious bit of scheduling, the Yankees playing at home against the Baltimore Orioles and the Giants playing football away against the Baltimore Colts. He wondered if they planned it that way. No. It couldn't be; they are just not that organized.

Charlie flipped on two TVs and waited for the games to start. It was strange that the phone hadn't rung in the Gravesend in quite a while; that he should have had another update by now. Maintaining a balanced book was critical to his business so that he did not get burnt. He didn't want to get caught being too heavy on one side or the other of a bet—after all, he was a businessman, not a gambler like his customers.

He picked up the phone to call his bookies—dead. He tried his other lines, dead also. A lot of action came in earlier and he needed to lay off some to keep his exposure low. Charlie was always concerned about his bets, about his customers, about his collections. But now, he was exposed, and even more concerned. He looked for Beefy to go out and make a call; the bar was empty. *How could that stupid piece of shit get the crap kicked out of him by some guys? He was supposed to be the crap-kicker. Where the hell is he?*

Beefy liked to keep his equipment clean and ready: a full tank of gas and now a wash. He even put in new shocks; he wondered if Collesano knew the car needed shocks. He had some time to kill because the afternoon bets were in and there would be no more action until the first football games were over. It didn't really matter because he had nothing to do with the betting or the money; that was Charlie's job. He was just insurance. Not much to protect today, a quiet day: the phone hadn't even rung. The bar was empty when he left and Charlie was busy doing whatever he does with the books. He wouldn't miss him for a little while.

He waited as Ben's old Buick Century exited the car wash, the sun gleaming off its squeaky clean exterior. One of these days he would trade this in for a new one; maybe a Caddy. He watched it being dried and carefully lit up and inhaled a small drag. He slowly exhaled through his left nostril because the other one had collapsed. He took another drag, carefully guiding the smoke around the hole in his tongue. It only hurt when he smoked or breathed; it would for a while.

Turning his attention from the pain he harbored in his mouth, he absently admired his shiny wheels. *Yes, someday, a Caddy.* He watched as a man tipped the car wash guy, thanked him and got in the car and closed the door. And he continued to watch as the car engaged into gear and took off.

"Hey, that's . . . Ouch," the pain seared through his mouth " . . . my car."

"Phones are dead." Kass, one of Charlie's guys, said as he rushed into the Gravesend.

"You too?"

"Not just me, I just saw Itz and his lines are out, all of them. Can't reach anybody."

"Call the fuckin' phone company."

"Did. Had a guy there in minutes."

"When will it be fixed? We're on the line here."

"Dunno. Told me that he doesn't know what's wrong. We're the only phones that are out; everybody else in the area is ok. He'd never seen this before and it might take days to track down, maybe weeks."

"Weeks?"

"Yeah, I greased him twenty bucks and he said no thanks, something or other with the Union."

"The Union?" Charlie's concern just jumped a notch.

Ben and the boys sat just behind third base, behind Clete Boyer; the boys recounted every diving stop and throw that he made. The game was a slugfest and a crowd pleaser. The kids loved it except when Casey Stengel pulled Whitey Ford in the sixth inning. *Whitey Ford, never on a Sunday.* Ben should have bet on this game also but how could he bet against the Yanks while he and the boys were sitting there rooting for them?

Roger Maris, Yogi Berra, who was playing left field this season instead of catcher, and Moose Skowron all hit one out. The Mick had a couple of long drives but they fell short; he made a spectacular diving catch to end the top of the eighth inning and shut down an Oriole rally. He came up limping from that catch but he stayed in the game.

Baltimore 5, Yankees 4.

The boys were having the time of their life.

Not too far away in the Bronx, a husky black man leaned proudly against his new Chevy Impala—a shiny red convertible. The sticker was still on the window to prove it was new to anyone who didn't know or didn't care. He circled the car; checking it for dings or spots and anything else that might mar its surface. He paraded, letting everyone know that he was the owner. It was time to cruise his neighborhood once more.

It was a sunny day; a good day for a ball game. He considered cruising by Yankee Stadium but didn't want to ride under the El with the top down. No. He'd just cruise slowly in the sunlight. He rode down East Tremont, his old neighborhood, and stopped at a traffic light behind a huge garbage truck. The late summer heat made the smell less tolerable than normal. Hopefully, it would not stink up his new upholstery.

He slammed the automatic into reverse, tires squealing, as he nudged back a couple of feet, maybe edge out and go around the truck. After all, it was Sunday and traffic was light; and what the hell was a garbage truck doing out on Sunday? He checked his rear view mirror as another garbage truck pulled up behind him and slowly inched forward, filling the mirror. He threw it into drive and squealed forward to avoid the second truck, but there was nowhere to go.

The rear truck kept coming as he waved his arms frantically to get the driver's attention. But he went unnoticed the truck nudged the brand new steel bumper of the shiny Impala and pushed it into the first truck. Then it mounted the convertible's trunk as the front truck backed up and caught the brand new Chevy Impala convertible in an unbreakable garbage truck vice. Both trucks accelerated as the vice slowly closed crushing the car.

The driver scrambled out, fell to the ground and crawled away; in his haste, he left his freshly laundered Pinkerton uniform lying in the rear seat.

Willie planted himself about three feet from the television and the Colt/Giant game. He didn't move except for two pee breaks and beer and popcorn refills—and only during time-outs. He had to get up to adjust the rabbit ears a couple of times but he didn't count that because he was still watching the game. He wanted to catch it with Sandy but he was busy with something or other.

So he watched, paced, looked for fingernails to bite and rooted for every inch, every first down. Trouble was, he didn't know whom to root for. He wanted the Colts to win by seven, the magic number—not eight, not six. Just like he told Sandy. So one minute he's rooting for the Colts, the next for the Giants. It was tough keeping it in check, continually adding and subtracting the score to figure out what the next best play would be: a touchdown, safety or field goal—any combination that would put the Colts up by seven.

He knew that the final outcome would be a direct result of his rooting and he took it very seriously.

Sandy told himself that this was the last time; he opened the motel room door. Today, he was here on business—close this thing down and move on. No sex, nothing.

Eileen looked particularly good today. She was dressed casually, a skirt and loose-fitting but revealing sweater, not in her business clothes that he was used to seeing her in or without. This would be a difficult, but obligatory, road to cross.

As he walked in, she knew this was it. Not like the other times when they seemed to work through it—when their passion exceeded their reason. Today would be the last day. No sex, just a short conversation and goodbye. Sandy told her it couldn't go on and she agreed. She was smarter than she looked but she couldn't help the way she looked. Sometimes pretty and sexy is a disadvantage, she thought. Sometimes they just see the packaging, not beyond.

"I'll resign tomorrow."

Resign?

Somehow the finality of the moment penetrated Sandy. This was it. This is what he wanted. It was over. Once she quit, there would be no more opportunities to rekindle it. It was really over. Not only wouldn't he see her behind closed doors, he wouldn't see her out in the open. No more quick glances, no more anticipation of being closer, no more smelling her as he walked passed. This was the end; there was no coming back.

The pressure was off and the walls came down. They were less guarded and shared some honesty and openness they hadn't before.

"I broke it off with Wasserman." She confessed.

Sandy was surprised she said that, as they had never spoken about her thing with him. He was never completely sure that she had had a thing with him, never struck out the possibility that Wasserman fantasized about her and wanted her, but never had her. He was wrong.

"And," she continued. "I broke up with my fiancé."

"Fiancé? What fiancé?"

"I told you about him."

"I'm pretty sure I would have remembered that."

"We were going to get married on Christmas day."

"What fiancé?"

"Doesn't matter. Anyway, let's go."

"Wait a minute. Why'd you break up with—?"

"It doesn't matter now."

"It matters."

"Because I'm completely in love with you."

Suddenly, he saw her differently—as someone with vulnerability, warmth, a past and a future, not just an incredibly compelling body. She had dropped everything for him, even dropped him. He looked in her eyes for the first time and every resolution he had recently made became undone. He brought her close to him and consumed her. He wanted every part of her, all the time. She had awoken feelings that he thought he had never had.

They made love. Only this time it was making love, not just screwing. He kissed her, caressed her, touched her gently and protectively and penetrated her eyes as if he could see inside of her. In that moment, he owned her: her skin, her body, her soul and her mind. It was beautiful, passionate and fulfilling.

When they consummated, she put her head on his shoulder and he held her tightly, safely. She closed her eyes, secure.

He lit a Lucky and turned on the Giant game.

"One minute, fifty seconds to go," the announcer said, "and the Giants look like they may win their first opening day game in two years."

Shit.

He turned the sound off and Eileen snuggled in closer. He lay there with her resting on his shoulder and took a drag. He didn't want to think about tomorrow or plans or issues or dealing with Eileen, Wasserman or Irene.

He thought about Ben.

- 55 -

Ben resisted thinking about the Giants until now. It must be late in the fourth quarter, he thought. He noticed a fan with a transistor radio to his ear. Ben tapped his shoulder.

"Giant game?"

"A minute to go. They're tied 17-17." The fan was jubilant. "Giants have the ball. Looks like they're gonna score. They're in better shape than the Yanks."

"Thanks."

In spite of all his preparation and planning, Ben knew that he would need a lot of luck to win this bet. This was an intelligent, no-lose bet but what he really needed was a sure thing. He needed a win. In any other circumstances, he would be ok—but this was a long shot. He needed to get lucky and luck is something he never counted on before. Still, it was exactly the right thing to do.

Normally optimistic and positive, he resigned himself to lose this bet. He knew of no better way to prepare himself for the large probability of a loss. If he had expected to win, a loss would be much too devastating. He would be mentally out of trouble and then thrown back into it. No, think loss; it's the likely outcome. Prepare for the worst. But he was ok with that; he was ready for the consequences because he had Kitty and the boys and *one on the way*. He also felt good about his handicapping and his short chat with Caz. There was hope; there was a future. He just didn't know when it would begin.

The bottom of the ninth and the Yanks were still down 5 - 4.

Rick saw Ben's concern.

"Don't worry dad, Mick will hit it out. I just know it."

Ben smiled, "You bet he will. C'mon Mick!" *This is what's important . . . nothing else, this.*

"Strike two!" The umpire's bellow echoed through the almost silent stadium. A soft moan fifty thousand strong immediately followed.

Ben turned to the boys: "Mick lives for this. Where are we?"

Rick looked at him incredulously. "In Yankee Stadium."

"Right. And what inning?"

"The bottom of the ninth."

"And who lives in Yankee Stadium in the bottom of the ninth?"

"The Mick." Rick shouted. "The Mick lives in the bottom of the ninth."

Rick smiled and they shared a look for a long moment. It started as a look of concern for the Mick and the Yanks but it soon became something else. Scooter must have sensed it because he turned around as well and joined in. The game was out there but they just held each other's eyes.

CRACK!

The sound could only be the Mick's bat smashing a ball. They all turned as the crowd rose to see Mickey Mantle finish off the final arc of his swing and stand there as the ball sailed straight up towards the top tier of the right field stands. This ball was not arcing; this ball was never coming down. Mick just stood there and watched. The crowd fell silent as they rose to their feet and watched the ball shrink into an invisible dot that sailed over the stadium roof and into the vastness of the Bronx.

Arms flew in the air in victory and the stadium erupted into a harmonic cheer as Mick began limping into his home run trot. Bobby Richardson stood on second base waiting for Mickey to join him on his journey to the plate. This was the *Yankees*—the bottom of the ninth Yankees.

"They did it!"

Rick hugged Ben as he hoisted Scooter on his shoulders. The crowd stood for a moment to savor it; after all, this is what they came for. The whole day led up to this moment of glory. The tension of being down only served to feed the exhilaration of winning. Mickey came out for his second standing ovation and graciously bowed to the crowd. The game was over. Good game, real good game. They began slowly filing out and Ben saw the fan with the radio planted next to his ear. He was about to ask when:

"Goddamn it!" The fan threw his radio to the ground and put his foot through it.

"What happened?"

"Colts intercepted."

"And?"

"And they ran it in. Giants lose. Had it on the six-yard line, six-yard line and muffed the goddamn thing. Jesus."

The words penetrated Ben's consciousness.

"Score?" He looked up at the fan and waited for the verdict. It seemed like an eternity had passed until:

"Twenty four, seventeen."

"By seven."

Ben took a deep breath. The Mick, the bottom of the ninth, Mick did it.

"Let's go home."

Sandy opened one eye and saw the television graphic:
Final Score Colts 24, Giants 17.
"Way to go Benny." He whispered.
"What?"
"Nothing," he said as he kissed her gently on the mouth.
They made love again.

Willie sat paralyzed in his chair in front of the television. His hair was standing straight up, his shirt was half buttoned and popcorn was strewn all over him. He breathed heavily and his eyes were frozen open as the announcer said: "Amazing. Guess the Giants won't get the opening day win this year."

The Gravesend Bar was dark, closed for the night. A wrecker pulled around the back, out of the light and out of street view. Willie stepped out of the driver's door, quickly surveyed the area and retrieved a tire iron from alongside the driver's seat. He nonchalantly walked to the building, raised the tire iron and punched a hole in the bar's rear window, not caring to muffle the sound of shattering glass. With his sleeve, he swept away any shards that remained ensuring that the opening was smooth. He looked inside and, once satisfied that there were no obstacles that would imperil his mission, he drew a long hose from the wrecker's rear and carefully fed it through the opening.

He checked the other end of the hose which was connected to a barrel of oil sitting in the rear of the wrecker. He turned on the pump and sat back. He felt like a cigarette but he promised Rowan he wouldn't smoke, so he bit his nails. He watched as the barrel emptied its contents onto the floor of the Gravesend Bar. He tapped the barrel to see if it had been completely emptied, no sense in wasting it. He then removed the hose and connected it to a second barrel and turned on the pump again. He calculated that it would take about an hour and a half to empty all four barrels into the Gravesend. Plenty of time, it wouldn't be daylight for hours and he had nowhere to go. He also calculated that there would be no square inch of the Gravesend that was not covered in thick oil.

Maybe when he got home, Rowan would whip up some eggs, sunnyside up, and bacon, his favorite.

- 56 -

Ben felt strange driving his old Buick again, particularly with new shocks; it was nice of them to take care of it, washed it also. *Damn nice guys, next time I want to fix my car or lose a house, I'll go through them.* He had developed a special affection for the clunker though and thought that he would miss it. Perhaps he'd take it out once in a while when he filled up at Willie's. Maybe he'd buy it from Willie and save it for Rick, and then Scooter, maybe. Right now, business.

Ben walked through the Clubhouse and returned to Caz's box. He was there with Buddy and Arthur Shulty, who Ben figured to be one of Caz's lackeys. Buddy was just sitting down as Ben arrived.

"How do we look?" Caz asked.

"So, so. I don't give us much of a chance," Buddy answered.

Caz reached into his pocket and came up with cash and handed it to Arthur.

"Put another five hundred on *Celestra*. Thank you." Arthur left and Caz continued to Buddy: "Every time you knock our horse, the price goes up. What do you think, Ben?"

"I think it has a real shot. He's in with the right company."

"I mean, what do you really think?"

Ben reached in his pocket and came up with two twenty-dollar win tickets on number *seven, Celestra.*

Caz nodded.

"Gotta go to the paddock," Buddy said as he stood.

"See you in the winner's circle," Caz said.

"Good luck," Ben added.

Caz watched Buddy leave.

"What do you think of him?" Caz asked.

"Well," Ben hesitated. "He knows horses and . . ."

"Hang on. Unfair question. You are going to be tactful. Let me answer my own question." Caz looked at Ben for a reaction, didn't get it. "He's a good trainer, maybe one of the best, time will tell. But I don't trust him. He doesn't have values, treats his family like shit, would sell them out in a minute."

"Why do you keep him?"

"I said . . . he's a good trainer. I'm not going to marry the guy. Besides, there are degrees of trust. Some people you trust with your money, some with your car, some with your life and some with your horses. You just have to know who's who and what's what."

"It is now post time," the PA broke the conversation, ". . . and they're off!"

Caz picked up two pair of binoculars and handed one to Ben. They watched the race through the binocs.

"I trust you, Ben."

"With what?"

Ben's response brought a smile to Caz.

"What are you doing Saturday night?"

"Got a date with my wife, why?"

"Good. Tell her to dress pretty. We'll have dinner."

Ben's week continued on an uptick. He rejoined his old table populated by the usual guys and it was business as usual. And even more frequently, guys stopped by Ben's table, unaware of his last few weeks in hell, and made the usual inquiry. "Who do you like?"

The only difference for some of them was there was no bet swapping, which the players soon forgot about anyway. It was back to old fashioned, pick your horse, make a bet and try to beat the track—actually, try to beat everyone else. Ben's reputation continued to spread and it was beginning to become a bit of a nuisance—a good nuisance, he thought. It wasn't that long ago that no one knew who he was.

Occasionally he'd stop in Caz's box and join him for a race or some friendly handicapping. Caz would increasingly ask his opinion on a horse, a race, or a nuance. Anticipating Caz's style, Ben had prepared for this, studying the charts in greater detail every night and asking himself questions that he had never asked before: questions that Caz may have asked, questions that a horse owner asks. When he would answer Caz, he would just take it in without reacting.

The Syndicate was still in full operation, relying now on Ben's prowess as a horse picker and skilled bettor—most days they did fine, some days not. They didn't have the swaps to protect the downside and pump up the upside—they just had basic skills and homework. That was enough.

Ben was in deep thought all the way home. Even the Saturday Belt Parkway traffic didn't bother him. He felt like he'd driven through a tunnel without end and somehow it ended. The action of the last few weeks had come to a screeching halt just as the next wave was kicking in. He wondered what lie in front of him now. The thought of the adventure excited him and created new energy and infinite possibilities; and there was dinner with Caz tonight.

As he pulled into the driveway he saw Kitty, the boys and Willie standing around a big blue car—it was the clunker, freshly painted with a big red bow on top.

"Doors all open, top goes down," Willie said as he stood proudly next to his creation. "Even tuned it."

"Didn't know you knew how."

"Don't, had my guy do it."

Kitty kissed Ben: "Gotta finish getting dressed."

The boys jumped in the back seat and started their King Kong wrestling match. Willie and Ben watched, relieved.

"It's yours. You earned it."

"Thanks," Ben did not disagree. "Hey, did you hear about Gravesend?"

"Gravesend?"

"The bar. Charlie's place."

"What about it?"

"Seems like they had an oil spill. The whole place was covered in motor oil. Had to close down."

"No kidding."

They avoided eye contact knowing that it would take this conversation deeper, a place neither wanted to go.

"Yeah, a shame," Ben mocked. "Willie, one thing I need you to promise me."

"You want me to stop betting."

"No. Wouldn't ask and you couldn't, if I did."

"Yeah. Then what?"

"You're a C.O.D. bettor from now on."

"Huh?"

"No more credit. You want to piss away what you earn, that's your biz. But don't piss away what you don't have. I don't have anymore houses."

"Deal. But I don't have to worry about that anyway."

"Why?"

"Because I got a sure thing." Before Ben could react, Willie said: "You. I'm in the Syndicate."

- 57 -

Garguilio's Restaurant felt a lot warmer with Kitty by his side; Willie was great company but a lousy date. She looked ravishing; she could not have been more beautiful, tiny baby bump and all. They had just sat down as Caz arrived with Vivian, his wife, about fifteen years his junior. The introductions were made all around and, after a wine toast, the four of them became fast friends, business friends. This was another Caz that Ben was seeing—a husband, with an adoring partner. Caz seemed enchanted by Kitty who radiated beauty as only a slightly pregnant woman could. Clearly, whatever Caz thought of Ben, he thought better of him with Kitty at his side.

Dinner was unexpectedly smooth and social—as if they had been old friends getting reacquainted. Ben wondered when Caz was going to reveal the reason that they were here—friends, dinner, and all that are fine, but there's more to it. The conversations finally segued towards the business.

"Now what can I say about Buddy? When he says it doesn't look good, send it in." Caz teased a little. "But you have to know when he means it and when he doesn't. We had a pretty good week, right Ben?" Without waiting for an answer, he asked Kitty, "Did you have a good week?"

A slow smile grew on Kitty's face: "Very."

With that one word, *'very,'* she lit up the room.

Caz could not take his eyes off of her. It was less of a flirtatious look, than a look of admiration. Ben couldn't take his eyes off of her as well, *"very."* A moment of beautiful silence captured the table, as everyone seemed to be captivated by the same sentiment.

"And," Kitty continued after what seemed like forever, "it was good to finally meet you. Ben's said so much. You even surprised him."

"Oh?"

"He found you to be a nice person."

"And that surprised him?"

"Very much. I think he's always been a little awestruck by you—or your image. Now, I think he's a lot awestruck. Actually, he's said some very nice things about you."

They all laughed as Ben wondered how she knew more about him than he admitted to himself.

Caz raised his glass: "To Ben and me . . . for being the luckiest sonofabitches in the world for having the best ladies in the world." They clinked. He turned to Kitty. "Is he a good man?"

She just smiled.

"I'll take that as a yes because I'm about to offer him a chance to build a new stable for me."

"What?" Ben was shocked.

Caz went right to business; the flow of wine did not impair his business.

"You pick the horses. I'll finance it. You get twenty percent of the purses. No winners, no purses." Caz looked at Kitty for approval of his offer and his style but mostly just to look at her again. "Think about it."

"Been thinking about this all my life. I'm in."

Caz didn't or chose not to hear Ben's reply as he continued to look at Kitty. He went on.

"We'll do it for a year then we'll re-evaluate." He turned to Kitty. "What would you say if we named the first horse after you? *Sweet Kitty*."

Ben just absorbed. A few weeks ago, he was fighting fires, fighting for his house and fighting for his future. Twenty years had transpired as if it was a day and the last few weeks covered a lifetime. The future had begun.

Epilogue

Las Vegas, 2000

Sandy Kane leaned into his desk in his small mundane office. Las Vegas was that way—keep the opulence upfront for the customers and keep the management digs barebones, not unlike any other retail establishment. An unlit cigarette hung from his mouth and several more crushed cigs, all unlit, filled the ashtray. Vegas was doctor's orders; well, not Vegas, just a drier climate. Vegas had been an opportunity Sandy couldn't pass up. *Manager of the Las Vegas Hilton Sportsbook* was the perfect job at the perfect time. Yes, at seventy-eight, it was a plum and fitting coup.

He stared at one of the many monitors on his desk that enabled him to keep tabs on the activity in the Sportsbook, a huge Vegas-style betting den where you can bet on anything. Hundreds of bettors, mostly men, sat, stood, leaned, paced and alternately focused between their programs and the tote boards displaying the odds for the current race at racetracks throughout the country. They drank beer, diet Coke and coffee. They rarely conversed; if they did it was in short, non-informational conversations, trying to get, but not give, information.

Today was special:

> *The $1,000,000 National Thoroughbred Horse Handicappers Tournament.*

Sandy watched the action through his monitors while on his break from the floor. This was it, the event he had focused on all year. *The event.* The best horseplayers from everywhere were here because of him—and the one million bucks.

His eyes landed on one studious old man in the crowd whose emotions did not swing as high or low with each race. *Still at it. Not too many like Ben.*

He couldn't help but smile as he checked the monitor with the standings to see where Ben stood in the competition. It was the last day of the tourney and only the top twenty-five or so had an outside shot of finishing in the top three. There was still time left but not much. Realistically, only the top half dozen had a reasonable shot of walking away with the million and the crown: *the best fucking horseplayer in the country.*

He hoped that Ben finished respectably so he could hold his head high. After all, at seventy-nine, he was lucky to make it through the grueling three-day tournament, much less finish in the top one hundred.

Ben's name popped off the list as if it were blinking:

BEN COLLESANO...4.

Jesus fucking Christ, fourth place, three hundred and twenty guys and you're in fourth place Ben! Jesus!

Sandy flicked a non-existent ash into the ashtray and took an unsatisfying drag on his unlit Merit. Old habits, yeah. He looked at the Merit and thought that maybe he should go back to Luckies. No, Merits seemed fitting. Lit or not, it was as unsatisfying as his life. He stuffed out the cigarette and glanced at the monitor, reminding himself that he should go back down to the floor of the Sportsbook and put in some face time with the players. Ben came into his field of vision and a smile grew out of an ancient love and renewed pride. *Fourth place.* He gave a thumbs-up to the monitor.

He absently took another Merit out of the pack, put it in his mouth and down on the ashtray next to the other unlit Merits. He looked down one more time at the monitors on his desk, his eyes wandering from screen to screen catching different views of the action, which was basically three hundred plus men in various stages of concentration.

The crowd had thinned a bit since some of the players who were out of the running had taken off; but it was still a good showing. A million bucks—somebody's going to win it and everybody wants to see whom. He looked at the standings once more not only to make sure he got it right but also to enjoy the sight of it.

Fourth place, Jesus Christ Benny, fourth place among the best of the best. No shot at the win here but fourth place out of three hundred plus of the best in the country is incredible.

It was time to put in some quality face time with the players. He got up and walked over to a single framed photograph that hung on his almost barren wall and looked at it closely: a solitary moment of captured time that exploded into so many memories.

It was a winner's circle photo:

Woodmere Stakes

Sweet Kitty

Owners: Caz Frankel and Ben C. Collesano

Trainer: Buddy Catalano.

Surrounding *Sweet Kitty*, the winning horse, stood Ben and Kitty, Sandy, Willie and Caz. That was the moment, the breakthrough. Ben had transcended lives—a fireman one moment, a horse owner the next. It was so many years ago but it seemed like the two events were just a moment apart. Back then there were so many moments in between when it didn't look like it would ever happen, like everything was eroding and heading straight downhill. Time has a way of eradicating all of those moments and selecting only the highlights to replay over and over. Funny how life tricks you into thinking you know where you're going and you wind up somewhere else. And just when you think you've lost, you find more than you hoped for.

Those were good years, a little adventurous, a little change: but again life takes strange twists. After Sandy and Irene split, he had lost touch with Ben. Wasserman finally kicked off and he had the practice to himself—but gave so much away that he never really got ahead of the game financially.

He moved to Jersey with Eileen for a fresh start. Kitty and Eileen didn't really hit it off that well. *They might've under different circumstances.* But it wasn't different circumstances, it was these circumstances and change drives change.

He looked again at the photo once more; Willie stood there smiling as if he had ridden, trained and even sired the winning horse. Ben's moments were his moments. He'd be proud to know that Ben was here today, still trying, still handicapping, and still looking for the recognition that he earned so many times over among a small elite group of nobodies. He was king of that world, king of the table, the Clubhouse, the track.

Sandy had seen Ro a few times after Willie's accident. It caught everyone off guard because things were going so well. It was strange that Willie just didn't see the hydraulic lift descending. It was tough on Ro because she relied on him so much for sanity and stability. He heard that she turned completely to the Church and withdrew from any normal functioning.

Sandy was sure that Willie ran into Al where he was and they're fighting as usual. Willie was around long enough to see Ben team up with Caz for a few good years. They turned out to be good partners and good friends; they didn't even have a formal contract, just a gentlemen's agreement, both being gentlemen.

After Caz died, Ben managed a stable for Red Carlson, a kingpin in the garment district, a player. Ben was off to a great start, selecting quality horses and built a stable of force. He even picked up an unknown two-year-old filly; Carlson named her Chris Evert, after the tennis player. She was later named Filly of the Year in 1974. His relationship with Red Carlson did not have the underpinnings of trust that he eventually earned with Caz. Ben thought he did have it and, as a gesture of professionalism and good will, he let Red keep all copies of their contract, which said Ben owned ten percent of the horses. It was an unfortunate mistake because, after a bad turn, Red Carlson suddenly didn't remember a contract. *What contract?*

Ben tried his hand at running his own stable for a few years but didn't have the capital to keep it going during the dry spells. He gave it up for the simpler life of handicapping.

That's life, Sandy figured, you just need some good shocks to get through. Ben had good shocks.

The photo showed the winning horse and the owners but it was Kitty who was the centerpiece. She stood under Ben's arm and, while everyone else looked pretty for the camera, she looked proudly up at Ben, glowing. She was the magic elixir that kept Ben whole and motivated and safe. Sandy put on his readers to see her radiant smile more closely.

Kitty, sweet Kitty. Everyone loved and was in love with Kitty, the peasant queen.

The kids had grown and moved out into their lives and Ben and Kitty stayed in Brooklyn, in a different house, and better neighborhood. They would winter in Miami Beach when the horses moved to Hialeah and Gulfstream and they lived off of Ben's Fire Department pension and his earnings from handicapping. They lived well, didn't save anything, but lived well.

And, Benny—he stood there so proud. The first milestone in his life's dream recorded in the single snap of the shutter. At that time, he knew clearly the road he took to get to this exact moment. Many of the routes were the result of decisions, many by circumstance. There was no straight line to where he wanted to be; he wondered if there was any line at all. He figured that life dealt him cards and he had to play them—just like any poker game. What makes one guy a consistent winner? It isn't the cards; you can't control the cards. He often thought about the years he wasted in the fire department. What if he had started with horses earlier? Would he be the king of a bigger horse world now? Would he be the best in the business? Would he have Kitty? There are no ifs; only what is and what you do with it.

Sandy looked at Ben once more on the monitor. They used to be so close before the years eroded their relationship. It didn't diminish the love they had for each other, it just diluted their proximity and reliance.

Face time.

The Sportsbook was down to the few potential finishers and a bunch of onlookers. This was the finish, the end. The competition was drawing to a close and it looked like any of the first three contenders could take it all. Others had a shot of improving their position and catching a bigger share of the consolation prize, but not the million bucks and the bragging rights that accompanied it.

Ben was in deep concentration as Sandy approached.

"You always were a strong closer."

Sandy startled Ben.

"Yeah, not enough time to make up the shortfall. I need a real tail wind and a big price."

"Sounds familiar. You've been there before."

"Yeah," Ben smiled. He, they, had been there many times before. But he was realistic, this time there wasn't enough time or races to close the gap on the leaders. If he lost before, he had his whole life to make up for it. This was not before, this was now his last chance. Now, everything was finite. He knew it. Sandy knew it.

"Hey, you're in fourth place. There's over three hundred guys behind you licking their wounds."

"And three in front. And there's only one race left on the card."

"Fourth place is twenty five grand, not too shabby."

"Not bad at all. It won't change my life, but what will?"

Sandy put his hand warmly on Ben's shoulder.

"Good luck pal. I'm rooting for you."

Ben placed his hand on Sandy's. "Thanks."

"Attention," the announcement blared over the loudspeaker. "There are two minutes to the last race in the

National Handicapper's Tournament. Get your pick in now."

Ben rose and walked to the window and left his selection card with the Seller. He took a slow walk, a little hunched these days, to the men's room.

He returned to his seat and thought about Sandy. The warmth of an old friend felt good and brought back a simpler yet more complicated time. No relationship he has had since had brought him the same level of trust or oneness that he had with Sandy. He had many friends, not so many these days—but over the years, many. They were good friends, sociable friends but not childhood friends that understood everything real friends understand about each other. There were none that he could have a conversation with without speaking—none that he could trust with everything. None that knew what he meant even before he did.

He had Kitty, his life. She stood by him and believed in him all those years; he would've been someone else, taken a different course without her. But he didn't have Sandy—seeing him again reminded him how much he missed him.

But right now, he needed a long shot. On his program, he circled the *four horse* over and over:

    4 Blue.

He put the program down gently. No stress now; all of the decisions have been made. There was nothing else he could do. The pick is in and now it was up to the horse. He closed his eyes for a brief moment before post time.

Sandy watched from his office. No matter what happened he couldn't be on the floor at the time Ben lost. It was his job to celebrate with the winner and he knew he'd look at Ben: proud that he made it so far; sorry that he didn't make it all the way. Maybe he could catch a winner and move up to third place and the fifty thousand dollar prize. Not likely, but possible, and he knew not to count Ben out of anything. He wondered if Kitty would make it down for the final race. Probably not, Ben liked to keep these worlds separate; it worked better that way; she would be bored by the activity or lack of it and he would be conscious of her feelings. He needed to concentrate and get the job done.

Through the glass of the monitor and the crowd looked quiet and tense—everything was at stake here. Ben rested; anytime he could catch a catnap or, preferably, close his eyes in the sun, Ben would.

"And they're off!" The announcer shouted with extra enthusiasm that further intensified the moment. "It's *TheSchneid* out in front with *Jicki-Jacki* on the rail and *Donnyboy* going wide in third position."

Ben looked again at the program and *4 Blue* circled in pen. He checked the tote board for the final odds—thirty-five to one. This outing was beginning to work on him—it's been a long three days and he felt the weight.

"At the far turn," the announcer continued, "*Vigi* closing ground in fourth place, followed by *BarbsHope* and two lengths back, *Scottskim*. Trailing the pack are *ChrisChat* and *Blue*."

Trailing the pack, suck it up—you've been here many times before. Races are won at the end and there's still half a race to go. And there's always next year. Next year.

He thought about Al and how he saved his ass in the fire. If it wasn't for Al, there would be no *this* year, no life, no kids, no Kitty. He missed him, the big fighting bulldog. He thought about all the schoolyard fights Al would jump into without knowing which side to take or what the issue was. He would just jump in and swing away, sometimes changing sides mid-fight. Deep down, he never forgave him for that Pinkerton thing; you do stupid things in desperate times—but never against friends. He still missed him. If he were alive, he'd probably be on his sixth wife; and that would be Paula. Ben smiled at the thought: Al and his multiple wife.

"At the three quarter pole, *TheSchneid* has the lead with *Donnyboy* gaining on the outside. *Vigi* in third, followed by *ChrisChat, Scottskim, Caron* and *Blue.*"

Fourth place, I hope I don't get knocked back to fifth or sixth. Would I settle for fourth right now? He knew the answer before he asked. He wasn't in this game to settle for anything.

He thought about Jamaica and *dutching the books*. How did he ever get away with that? A crack in the system as Caz used to say, just a crack.

Willie's bloody finger jumped into his view and he would always feel responsible for that, a finger. It must have made Willie feel so ugly—but he never said anything, just joked. He couldn't count how many times they saved each other's asses or how many cars Willie screwed up in his station. The clunker came to mind. Ben had eventually given it to Rick when he drove and it became a classic. Rick and Scooter and May, the one on the way, were great kids, *grew up to be beautiful people*.

Ben looked up to the screen with the horses packed in tight. Focusing was difficult and they were just a blur.

"At the head of the stretch, it's *Donnyboy* on top, *TheSchneid* fading and *Vigi* on the outside closing. The pack is tight and *ChrisChat, Scottskim* and *Blue* bring up the rear."

Shit, I should've checked to see who the other guys had so I would know . . . what's the difference, it's over.

The screen was hazy so he closed his eyes once more. He could hear what he had to. The horses battled around the turn as they fought for position for the final leg. Their hooves dug deep into the dirt and resonated a powerful thunder as they gained leverage and thrust the massive bodies a few feet closer to the finish line. He felt their muscles tighten with each stride, conscious of who was in front, who was behind and the gap between them and the finish line just ahead. Thirsting to win, they dug in and fought for each inch.

Kitty should be here by now—sweet Kitty, as Caz used to call her. He remembered how her face glistened as they walked in the rain on the boardwalk. And how she tricked him to stop going to the track and marry her. It was the best deal he made in his life. Sweet Kitty.

Ben felt the horses' breath as they gasped their way through the final few yards. He heard the hooves collectively slam the ground as they stretched to stay in front of their intense competitors. It would be only a few more long seconds. Sandy lit a Merit and watched the race on his monitor. The horses were in the stretch run, a few yards to go.

"It's *Vigi* taking the lead with *ChrisChat* on the outside and *Blue* on the rail. It's *Vigi, ChrisChat* . . ."

Sandy wondered whom Ben had. He glanced at the other monitor and viewed the crowd. Ben's program slipped from his hands onto the floor. He didn't move to pick it up.

"It's *Vigi* and *Blue, Vigi* and *Blue*. At the wire . . . it's *Blue! Blue* wins!"

The Sportsbook crowd showed more emotion than they had in the last few days. This was a big finish—a seventy-dollar horse won. *Did anyone have it?* Everything would change. Everyone wanted to know:

Anyone have it?

Ben sat slumped in his chair, his program still on the floor. Through the monitor, Sandy watched Ben, motionless. He knew. He checked the Tournament Standings, which had not been posted yet, then walked over to the photo and gave it a thumbs-up for today and for all the years.

Sandy didn't see the Standings Board light up:

BEN C. COLLESANO
WINNER OF THE
NATIONAL HANDICAPPERS TOURNAMENT

He didn't have to.

#

DUTCHING THE BOOK was based upon real people and events that changed the shape of horse racing and wagering. It was written by Ritch Gaiti, who has written novels, screenplays and many magazine articles and has been featured on national radio and TV, including an appearance on the Today Show. Ritch focuses on telling compelling stories and writes in several genres from humor to drama, both non-fiction and fiction. DUTCHING THE BOOK is his first venture into quasi-fiction and is a tribute to the people who really lived it.

Ritch Gaiti's other published books:
- TWEET, (Sedona Editions, 2011), humorous fiction about one average guy who changes the world because he didn't know that he couldn't. Recently, Tweet, has been optioned for a feature film.
- POINTS: WOMEN HAVE THEM, MEN NEED THEM (Running Press, 2008), a humorous non-fiction relationship book (under the pseudonym *I. Glebe)*.

You may view all of Ritch's books at http://www.SedonaEditions.com.

Ritch is also a recognized artist, exhibiting across the U.S. in several galleries and museums (including the International Museum of the Horse, The American Quarterhouse Association Museum, The Gilcrease Museum, and The Great Plains Art Museum). His artwork can be viewed on www.gaiti.com.

Ritch has also written, directed and produced short films and documentaries. Before getting involved in arts and entertainment, Ritch was a technology executive on Wall

Street. Ritch also is a private pilot, enjoys tennis and skiing. To contact Ritch directly: Ritch.Gaiti@verizon.net

Made in the USA
Charleston, SC
18 January 2012